THIS SPINNING W(

C000021081

POEMS BY JIM POTTS have appeared in *Ars Intrepres: International Journal of Poetry, Translation and Art, Acumen, Cadences, The Haiku Hundred* and the *William Barnes Society Newsletter.* And in translation in *Porphyras, Odos Panos, Endefktirio, Tomes, Ipeirotika Grammata* and *O Phileleftheros* (Greek); *Calende, Revistā de culturā* (Romanian); *Lyrikvännen* (Swedish); and *Minimanimalia, Canzoniere Animinimalista* (Italian). One of his poems was selected for BBC Radio's *Time for Verse.*

CONTRIBUTIONS BY JIM POTTS have been included in the following volumes: *Literary Links: Celebrating the Literary Relationship between Australia and Britain* (ed. R. Russell, 1997), *Literatures of War* (ed. R. Pine and E. Patten, 2008), *Greece and Britain since 1945* (ed. D. Wills, 2010), *The Ionian Islands: Aspects of their History and Culture* (ed. A. Hirst and P. Sammon, 2014), *Travel, Tourism and Identity* (ed. G. R. Ricci, 2015), *The British Council and Anglo-Greek Literary Interactions, 1945–1955* (ed. P. Mackridge and D. Ricks, 2018), and *Proceedings of the 10th International Panionian Conference, Corfu 2014,* vol. 5 (2018).

ARTICLES BY JIM POTTS have appeared in the following periodicals: *The Anglo-Hellenic Review, Dorset Life, Educational Broadcasting International, International Times, Isis, Marshwood Vale Magazine, New Directions in Prose and Poetry, Sight and Sound,* and *Wiltshire Life* (UK); *National Library of Australia News* and *Heat: Literary International* (Australia); *The Corfiot, Greece Property and Home, Icho ton Paxon* and *To Zagori mas* (Greece); and *Friendship/L'Amitié* (Czechoslovakia).

JIM POTTS OBE read English at Wadham College, Oxford. As a postgraduate he studied Education at the Institute of Education, University of London, and Film Production in the Department of Drama at the University of Bristol. He worked in the field of international cultural relations and as a media consultant for 35 years (1969–2004), and served in many countries (Ethiopia, Kenya, Greece, Czechoslovakia, Australia, Sweden and the UK). He produced educational and documentary films and television programmes in Africa, organized film-training workshops and edited the journal *Educational Broadcasting International*, as well as cultural outreach journals in Australia and Sweden.

He played a leading role in some ground-breaking cultural relations and public diplomacy campaigns such as the 1997 'New Images: Australia and Britain into the 21st Century', 'New Wales in New South Wales', 'Scotland in Sweden', 'British Design Season (Sweden)', and 'UK British Literature Focus' at the 2004 Gothenburg Book Fair, as well as helping to initiate the touring exhibition 'Literary Links: Celebrating the literary relationship between Australia and Britain' in collaboration with the National Library of Australia.

He has written and lectured on music (especially the blues, *rebetika* and Epirot music), literature (mainly Greek and English poetry) and the visual arts. Selections of his poetry have been published in literary periodicals and translated into a number of languages (Czech, Greek, Italian, Romanian and Swedish) and he is currently working on a comprehensive collection of his poetry. He also writes a regular blog, *Corfu Blues and Global Views* (corfublues.blogspot.com) and frequently contributes articles to the William Barnes Society website.

His films include *The Cross: Artform of Ethiopia* and *Sunday They'll Make Me a Saint*, about the life and work of the Greek–American writer D. K. Toteras. His YouTube channel, MrHighway49, has videos featuring his own songs, demos and performances (some in collaboration with the Italian composer, Raul Scacchi), one of his films and excerpts from others, and old or rare blues recordings by neglected artists.

Current and future projects include two volumes of his poems, one in the original English and one containing ninety poems translated into Greek by Demetris Dallas; the *Secret Journals of the Poets' Revolution* (about Czechoslovakia); *An Evening in Epirus*, a bilingual piece about threshing floors in Greek culture for performance on a threshing floor; the editing, with Colenso Books, of a hitherto unpublished novel set in Czechoslovakia by Willa Muir (best known for her translations of the works of Franz Kafka, made with her husband the poet Edwin Muir, and for her memoir, *Belonging*); and *Art and the Dorset Landscape*, originally a book project, and now largely ongoing blog posts.

He currently divides his time between the inspiring landscapes of Dorset, Epirus and Corfu, when not visiting his children and grandchildren in far-flung corners of the world.

THIS

SPINNING

WORLD

BY

JIM POTTS

FORTY-THREE STORIES
FROM FAR AND WIDE

COLENSO BOOKS
2019

First published September 2019 by
Colenso Books
68 Palatine Road, London N16 8ST, UK
colensobooks@gmail.com

ISBN 978-1-912788-02-6

Two of these stories have been published before.

"Margarita's brass beds" was first published
(as "Maria's brass beds") together with the poem
"It's a round, spinning world" quoted in the Introduction,
by Ars Interpres Publications in *Corfu Blues: Poems and Songs
inspired by Greece and the Balkans, 1967–2005*
by Jim Potts, edited by Alexander Deriev (Stockholm, 2006),
and they are republished here by permission of
Alexander Deriev of Ars Interpres.

"The Gap" was first published by Roving Press Ltd in
Dorset Voices: A Collection of New Prose, Poetry and Photographs
(Frampton, Dorset, 2012) and is republished here
by permission of Julie and Tim Musk of Roving Press Ltd.

CONTENTS

CONTENTS

ACKNOWLEDGEMENTS

I am delighted that this collection is being published by Colenso Books, which has brought out important works by Konstantinos Theotokis, Theodore Stephanides, Lawrence Durrell and Sappho, to name but a few; and I am immensely grateful to Anthony Hirst of Colenso Books for editing this collection, for being so extremely positive and supportive from the beginning, and also for making the translations of German poetry by Rilke and Heine used in the story "Stacheldraht (barbed wire) or European Unions".

For permission to include previously published material in this volume, I would like to thank Alexander Deriev of Ars Interpres Publications, who published *Corfu Blues*, and Julie and Tim Musk, of Roving Press who published *Dorset Voices* (for publication details, see the back of the title page). My thanks also to my two co-editors of *Dorset Voices*, Maria Strani-Potts and Louisa Adjoa Parker.

I should acknowledge that some of the facts and chronology underpinning the story "The dropout" are drawn from *Half the Perfect World: Writers, Dreamers and Drifters on Hydra, 1955–1964* by Paul Genoni and Tanya Dalziell (Monash University Publishing, 2018); and "Making friends for Britain? Francis King and Roger Hinks at the British Council in Athens" by David Roessel, in *The British Council and Anglo-Greek Literary Interactions, 1945–1955*, edited by Peter Mackridge and David Ricks (Routledge, 2018).

Above all I want to thank my wife, Maria Strani-Potts, for encouraging me to write short stories. As the author of a novel and a collection of stories herself, she read them with care and insight. It is appropriate that this book is going to press close to the date of our Golden Wedding Anniversary. I hope it makes a timely gift. This book is dedicated to her, to other members of my family and to the memory of my parents (see page ix).

Our Greek wedding took place in London at the Archdiocesan Chapel of the Archdiocese of Thyateira and Great Britain, at the end of August 1969. My best man, or *koumbaros*, was the Greek-American writer Demetrius Katsaros (who wrote as D. K. Toteras). My old friend John Willis, fellow film student, later award-winning documentary film director, television executive and BAFTA Chairman, kindly agreed to play the role of the father of the bride.

Jim Potts
Dorchester, Dorset
August 2019

To Maria

to Nina-Maria and David

to Alexander and Priscillia

to my brother

Roy

who has many exciting stories
from foreign parts to share — if only he
could be persuaded to write them down

and to my five grandchildren

Jack · Ella · Théo · Milo · Eva

And in memory

of

Ken and Nina

my father and mother

Introduction
(between fact and fiction)

> 'Who else do you know at Oxford? Do you know Freddy
> French-Wise?'
> 'No'.
> 'Or Tom Obblethwaite or that youngest Castleton boy?'
> 'No, I'm afraid not. I had a great friend called Potts.'
> '*Potts!*' said Lady Circumference, and left it at that.
>
> Evelyn Waugh, *Decline and Fall*

My mother once told me that she hesitated to marry my father, because she didn't like the surname *Potts*. I've always felt rather proud of the name. *Potts, James Potts*. It packs as much punch as *Bond, James Bond*. So take care what you say!

When I visited Jamestown, near colonial Williamsburg in Virginia, USA, I discovered, on a restored church, a plaque in memory of an unrelated person (not a distant ancestor) called John Pott, a doctor, who is elsewhere referred to as "Dr. Potts", originally from the hamlet of Harrop, near Rainow, Pott Shrigley and Bollington in Cheshire.

According to the Minutes of the Virginia Company of July the 16th, 1621, and in the words of Dr Theodore Gulstone, who had recommended him for the position of Physician-General to the Colony, he was "well practiced in Chirurgerie and Physique, and expert allso in distillinge of waters". George Sandys, the Colonial Treasurer, is credited with saying that Dr Pott(s) on his arrival, "showed a great fondness for company and distilled waters".

Dr Pott(s) became notorious — and not for the last time — in 1623 for allegedly preparing the poison which was served in alcohol to native Americans during a "peace ceremony" at Jamestown. Two hundred of the Indians died or became ill and fifty more were killed by the colonists. The poisoning was said to be in retaliation for the massacre by the Indians on the 22nd of March 1622 of three hundred and forty seven colonists.

In 1624, King James I, revoked the Virginia Company's charter and made Virginia a crown colony, answerable directly to the King in England. In 1625, Dr Pott(s) became a member of the Governor's Council, and in 1628 he was elected Governor of the Virginia Colony. He held that post for little more than a year and, shortly after he was replaced, he was arrested and later convicted of stealing cattle. He was, however, granted a royal pardon by Charles I in 1631, partly on the grounds of his importance to the Colony, as its only physician.

I mention the case of Dr Pott(s) because a number of my stories or sketches deal with aspects of colonialism, and he provides us with an early example of an alleged colonial atrocity (though the doctor himself was later cleared of the charge).

I have the same first and middle name as my paternal grandfather, who was born in 1872 and died in January 1922 at the age of forty-nine. He was an excellent sportsman, a fine cricketer — a bowler, according to the obituary published in *The Manchester Guardian House Journal* (no. 22, January–February 1922).

No. 22. JANUARY–FEBRUARY, 1922.]   [For Private Circulation

"J. R. P."

J. R. POTTS AS A CRICKETER.

In his younger days Potts was one of the fastest bowlers in the club cricket of this part of the country, but when he played for the "Guardian" XI. his pace hardly reached medium. He was, in fact, slow to medium, and, moreover, one of the cleverest bowlers of that pace I have ever seen in club cricket. He

He was much missed by his loyal team-mates and all his work colleagues at *The Manchester Guardian* newspaper, which he had joined at the age of fourteen and where he worked for thirty-five years. He had married in August 1907, when he was thirty-five. He was highly respected for his fourteen years' service as the honorary auditor of the Poynton Horticultural Society.

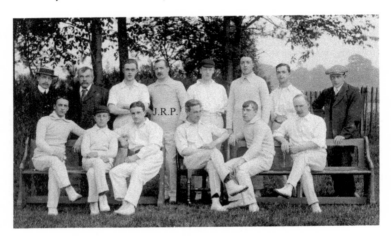

My father, born in 1911, was also a keen sportsman and cricketer. He spent five or so years with *The Manchester Guardian*, before moving down to Bristol.

Anthony Burgess (born 1917) once wrote about the difference he perceived between *The Manchester Guardian* and *The Guardian*:

> At the time of my birth, Manchester was a great city, Cottonopolis, the mother of liberalism and the cradle of the entire industrial system. It had the greatest newspaper in the world, meaning the only independent one. *The Manchester Guardian* debased itself when it grew ashamed of its city of origin: a superb liberal organ was turned into an irritable rag dedicated [...] to the wrong kind of radicalism. (*Little Wilson and Big God*, 1987)

I don't subscribe to Burgess's view; nor do I subscribe to any newspaper. I like to chop and change, to see what catches my attention every day in the newsagent or supermarket. I also read a lot online.

The Prospectus announcing the first number of *The Manchester Guardian* on the 5th of May, 1821, stated that

> It will zealously enforce the principles of civil and religious Liberty, in the most comprehensive sense of those terms; it will warmly advocate the cause of Reform; it will endeavour to assist in the diffusion of just principles of Political Economy; and support, without reference to the party from which they emanate, whatever measures may, according to the matured and unbiased judgement of its Conductors, tend to promote the moral advantage, or the political welfare, of the Community […].

These are words worth remembering, and sentiments to which I *can* subscribe, but I won't leave it at that, like Lady Circumference.

Whether they were early settlers in British colonies, American jazz or blues musicians, Irish fiddle players, farmers, soldiers and officers, journalists, doctors, inventors (of, for example, the prosthetic leg), QCs, or art historians, people called Potts carried the surname from the UK to the USA, Australia, Canada, South Africa, New Zealand and Bermuda.

Many of them "punched above their weight", as our politicians are fond of saying. It's a tiresome cliché. Journalists and political commentators keep "feeding that narrative", when talking up the global influence of the UK. "Do they all think that we live in a post-fact society?" I heard someone ask on TV, "Drill down and you will find the truth." In this book I'm not trying to punch above my weight, or to write about soft power and hard power with approval, or disapproval, but I hope my short sketches or narratives occasionally hit the mark.

These stories are fictional and the narrators and chief protagonists portrayed in them fictitious, but they are situated in real places and there are many historical characters (some of them of relatively recent date) and documented events are introduced. The stories have been inspired by their locations and often informed by political upheavals in countries where I have lived, worked, or been a visitor.

Before I left my post in Czechoslovakia, shortly before the Velvet Revolution (which began on the 17th of December 1989), some brave Czech poets and translators produced a small *samizdat* dual-language edition of sixteen of my poems.

Later Václav Havel, when he was President of the Czech Republic, signed the title page of a copy of this publication with the message *Jamesovi Pottsovi* ("To James Potts").

JAMES
POTTS

16 POEMS
BÁSNÍ

Koháček & Trnka Publishers Praha 1989

Diplomat s tajným posláním

Kdo nepronikne pod ochranné zbarvení Jamese Pottse, bude tohoto muže nejspíš považovat za vzorného úředníka Jejího Veličenstva a za nadmíru úspěšného šiřitele britské kultury po Čechách. Tím vším, a jistě rád, James Potts skutečně je, ovšem ve svém prvotním určení je přece jen někým jiným.

Maskován kravatou, limuzínou, razítkem a korektním chováním dostavuje se tento kulturní ataše už tři roky do svého pražského úřadu. Přednášky, výstavy, publikace — hle, toť jeho dílo. Kolik jen britských básníků uvedl před pražské publikum. Za to mu všechna čest, leč pohříchu žádná sláva.

A to je křivda, kterou nutno napravit.

Neboť uvítací projev není Jamesi Pottsovi nejmilovanějším žánrem, ač dělá vše pro to, aby takový dojem vzbudil.

Snaží se tak zapřít své „žhavé jádro básnické". Není však nejvyšší čas zbavit se tohoto tajemství?

Praktická kariéra učinila z Jamese Pottse Euro i Afroběžníka, leč běda; v patách praktické kariéry vždy kráčela inspirace, a tak „žhavé jádro básnické" ne a ne vyhasnout. Naštěstí.

Bluesman, filmař a lyrik Potts se ve stopách papá Hemigwaye ocitl až pod sněhy Kilimandžára. Na pobřeží Jónského moře naslouchal ozvěnám homérského zpěvu. Žádný div, že tyto inspirace významně vstoupily i do jeho básnického díla.

V oné ostré konkurenci inspirací se však neztratil ani génius loci magické Prahy. Přehlédneme-li dnes Pottsovu lyrickou produkci, jejíž ukázkou náš svazek je, zjistíme, že Hašek s Kafkou políčili na pana kulturního ataše tenata věru bytelná.

Z tohoto plodného spojení vzešla další z nesčetných lyrických facet Prahy, tentokrát v jazyce světovém. A James Potts tak dokázal, že jeho tajná pražská mise byla úspěšná.

LADISLAV VERECKÝ

The heading of the introduction to *16 Poems* was the ironically-intended "Diplomat with a Secret Mission" (*Diplomat s tajným posláním*) — my *secret mission* was apparently a love of literature, poetry and freedom of speech.

In connection with this publication, I took part in a poetry reading at the Karel Čapek Bookshop in Prague on the 24th of October 1989.

KNIHKUPECTVÍ KARLA ČAPKA

si Vás dovoluje pozvat
na večer poezie

Našim hostem bude
anglický básník

JAMES POTTS

a bude recitovat své verše

České verze přednesou překladatelé
Ivo Šmoldas, Pavel Šrut
a Ladislav Verecký

úterý 24. října 1989 v 18 hodin

The *Státní bezpečnost* (StB) or "State Security" (the Communist secret police of Czechoslovakia) were inordinately interested in me and my "secret mission" and kept extensive surveillance records. The covers of all of my now declassified StB files and unwarranted agents' reports were once stamped

$$\boxed{\text{PŘÍSNĚ TAJNÉ}}$$

From my reading of these "Top Secret" files came the fictionalised version of that experience in the story "Operation Hercules".

Many of these stories were drafted *in situ* up to fifty years before publication; only two have been published before. Most were written or rewritten during the period from December 2017 to May 2019, when I should have been working on a collection of my poems.

One of my poems, "It's a round, spinning world" prompted the title for this book — a poem which developed into a song lyric, set to music by the late Raul Scacchi. (The song can be heard at https://www.youtube.com/watch?v=ZxE0TvB0nFw&t=18s.)

> It's a round spinning world we live in,
> A round, round spinning world —
> And the legs of the tables are not of an equal length
> As we reach out for the cup
> It crashes to the floor.
>
> It's a round spinning world we live in,
> A round, round spinning world —
> And the eyes of the madmen who'll inherit the Earth
> Look down in despair through doors in the sky,
> Through door-ways in the sky.

Sometimes I do feel like a disturbed man in despair, if not yet driven mad, looking down at the earth through my spy-hole in the sky. I gaze down at the activities of spies, would-be spies and secret policemen, at revolutions and coups, at fishermen and film-makers, wealthy widows and misbehaving husbands.

WARNING
THESE STORIES
ARE SHARED WITH YOU
IN STRICTEST
CONFIDENCE

January

It was the end of January, and a blizzard during the night had covered Stockholm with a fresh fall of snow. *Vita Guld* ("white gold"), the working men of Sweden call it. When the streets were paved with snow, they could expect good overtime and extra earnings; so many hands and shovels were needed to clear the paths and the treacherous steps. White gold, high wages! *Let it fall, let it snow some more!*

That was not what Edward was thinking. Looking out of his window at five o'clock in the morning, he surveyed the bleak view without any sense of pleasure or anticipation. There had been times when he would have looked forward to a long, invigorating walk in the snow, across the bridge and around Djurgården; perhaps to some cross-country skiing as far as Blockhusudden. As a child in England he had always loved being out in the snow, downhill tobogganing being such a rare and special thrill.

This bleak January morning there was an icy wind whistling over the frozen water; the thick ice was covered with snow so that he couldn't tell the difference between the land and the sea; visibility was so limited that he could only see a hazy outline of the Nordic Museum, and the silhouettes of the bare black trees were outlined starkly against the snowy emptiness surrounding them. Edward's depression was growing deeper than ever before. There were no people to be seen, no signs of any cars moving.

He thought of his parents lying in their lonely graves in Somerset, not far from the hills where he used to go tobogganing. His mother had died three years earlier. He thought of his brother recovering slowly from a complex operation in hospital, possibly destined to a life of severe disablement and immobility.

Edward himself was losing the will to carry on. He hadn't lost interest in living but he'd really felt so nihilistic. He would have pulled himself together if he could have left his job, his apartment, and this place he found himself in without really knowing any longer why on earth he was there. He'd seldom posed the question "Why?" He'd never said "No" to a proposal to transfer him to a new country.

Edward felt oppressed, as well as depressed. After nearly sixty years, close to his contractual age of retirement, he had finally come face to face with an overpowering sense of the Absurd, although he'd never been much taxed by philosophical problems. For thirty-five years he had always half-expected to wake up one morning with that sense of existential nausea, of complete and utter pointlessness. The condition had been well diagnosed and described by writers he'd once studied, like Camus and Sartre. Edward was in no mood to rebel, as Camus had prescribed as the best course of action, provided it involved a creative and liberating act of rebellion, not one born from nihilism.

Edward had managed in the past to evade the consequences of his growing personal awareness of the absurdity of life, by changing jobs and countries every four or five years (although he had little control over where he was sent). He had discovered the stimulating variety provided by his experience of new places, new countries, people and cultures. He had kept his boundless sense of curiosity alive; he'd always been open to new adventures and challenges. Variety was the spice of life, there was no doubt about that. He'd never been like a city-worker, facing the prospect of the same journey to work on the same overcrowded tube train every day for forty years.

Nevertheless, his sense of the absurd had come early; he had now reached the point when there was no spice in life, little remaining curiosity or expectation of new inspiration, no more sense of adventure.

His horizons felt as limited as the Stockholm skyline in the snow. He'd been wrapped up in cotton wool and locked in a drawer. He could see no way of escape. He had *iron in the soul*, the feeling Camus had experienced when visiting Prague, where Edward had also lived and worked.

Edward felt trapped, without hope, like a black, leafless tree in an endless expanse of snow, standing out there in the freezing cold. He just couldn't see the point of it all. What had he achieved? Nothing. At least when Camus came to Stockholm, it was to accept the Nobel Prize for Literature. A car-crash wasn't such a bad way to die.

Nothing ever changed. Governments were given a white-wash; good men were forced to resign if they dared to speak half the truth. Politicians talked passionately about peace while their minds were set on war. War crimes went unchallenged, international courts were powerless against those with real power. What use was soft power?

Edward sat in his armchair, looking out at the frozen world. The wind was really howling now. A solitary car passed, its headlights shining weakly and ineffectually through the falling snow. The headlights looked sad and forlorn, reflecting Edward's mood. He thought of re-writing his will.

Then his eyes fell on the framed photograph of his little grandson, who would soon be one. Edward remembered what he'd written when the baby boy was just two days old:

Hello, Grandson. Don't cry, life's fun!
I hope I'm here, when you're twenty-one.

Edward thought of his daughter in the USA, of his son who'd just returned to London from a skiing holiday in Austria, to find out that he had won a scholarship abroad and was feeling excited about the future.

He heard his wife call out from the bedroom, asking him to make her usual morning cup of tea.

Rock 'n' roll Down Under

Bill's friend Mike told him a story about the coming of rock 'n' roll to Australia, and about the time he'd been out fishing with his father beside the Hunter River in Newcastle, New South Wales. Mike had caught a fish, which he'd decided to cut up to use for bait. Gutting it, he saw something shining amongst the smelly innards: it was a fabulous, flashy, diamond ring. He became convinced that it had belonged to Little Richard, one of the founding fathers of American rock 'n' roll. He was sure it was worth many thousands of pounds, but he handed it into the police and never found out what happened to it. He always wished that he had kept it.

Mike had lived in Newcastle all his life, Bill had only lived in Sydney for five years, where he worked as a music and arts journalist, having been head-hunted by *The Sydney Morning Herald*. He'd often walk across Rushcutter's Park and try to imagine exactly where the huge, tin-roofed death-trap called the Sydney Stadium had stood, how it had looked and felt, with its wooden bleachers and its revolving stage in place of the original boxing ring. He was planning to write an account of the period between January 1957 and February 1958, when the likes of Little Richard, Bill Haley, Freddie Bell, Big Joe Turner, Lavern Baker, Eddie Cochran, Gene Vincent, Jerry Lee Lewis, Buddy Holly and the Crickets had all played there. Bill tried to recall what his life had been like in conservative and provincial White Australia back in January 1957 when he'd just turned thirteen, an impressionable teenager on the look-out for some local excitement. It was the period when the stifling "cultural cringe" still made aspiring young Australians dream of going "home" to London or setting off to see Europe.

The first Aussie rock singer, Johnny O'Keefe, had come under the spell of the records of Bill Haley. Johnny and his group the Dee Jays were brought in at short notice as backing musicians — and to perform three songs — on the Little Richard package tour, which also featured Gene Vincent and Eddie Cochran. Johnny was a witness to one of the great mysteries and legendary incidents in the early history of rock 'n' roll.

Bill's friend Mike had actually been at the wild, frantic show in Newcastle, one of the stops on a three-week tour. The show was fantastic, but he'd heard from one of the backing musicians, a friend of his brother's, that Little Richard was in a strange frame of mind, very disturbed, thinking of giving up his career in show-business in order to serve the Lord, seriously contemplating dropping out of the tour and flying back to the USA. Years later Bill was to read what Johnny O'Keefe himself had to say of the events, about the bass player who'd told Little Richard that, if he really wanted to serve the Lord, he'd have to throw away all his jewellery, his diamonds and his rings.

Little Richard had immediately opened the window of the bus

and thrown his jewellery into the Hunter River. When they got to Melbourne, to play in the stadium there, disaster happened. Little Richard was obsessed by the first Sputnik which Russia had put up; it could be seen shining up in the sky on the night of the show.

His mind was truly shaken, he fell down on his knees praying, as he was afraid that the end of the world was coming; he declared that he would never sing any more, that he wanted to fly home and die in America. He was scared of flying, but he had no choice. He'd sometimes imagined that his plane had caught fire, or that God or his angels were holding it up in the sky. In fact, the plane in which he had at first been booked to fly home crashed into the Pacific.

There were many different versions of the story of Little Richard and his rings. Some people said that he'd thrown them into the Hunter River; others claimed that the location was Sydney Harbour, that he'd thrown them in from the Harbour Bridge, or from a ferry-boat.

Little Richard insisted that he wanted to find peace of mind, to dedicate his life to God, to become a preacher. A friend of his claimed that the truth was somewhat different, that this was the only way he could think of to break a binding but unprofitable contract with his record company. Bill and Mike agreed that this was a highly cynical interpretation of the myth.

Remembrance Sunday

A good friend, who was in the same year and college as me at Oxford, and who shared my love of the Blues, sent me this deeply disillusioned note in November 1964, just before he was admitted to the Warneford Hospital in Headington, to be treated for severe depression.

Today seems a significant time to fix an axis around which my future and my past might revolve. Today England remembers that it is fifty years since the outbreak of World War I and twenty-five years since the outbreak of World War II.

The people wear red poppies. The old men wear their medals. Bands play; wreaths are laid on the war memorials. Church bells peal and chime.

I wear no poppy. I remember nothing.

This week I "celebrate" my twentieth birthday — twenty years old — old enough to be called a man, but not by merit. I will win no medals. When I am really old, poppies will still be worn, but will I have ever fought for my country, or for my beliefs? I doubt it. I do not feel at home in my own country. I'm uncertain about my beliefs. I feel like an outsider. I would prefer to live under a southern sun.

This year marks the quatercentenary of the birth of William Shakespeare. In April I went to Stratford-upon-Avon on the 400th anniversary of his birth. There were wreaths of beautiful flowers on his tomb, sent from all over the world. There were many commemorative souvenirs on sale. I visited the Shakespeare Festival and his birthplace, where I learnt that Shakespeare had quite possibly never even been over that ground or under that roof. It was possibly not even his birthday. Everyone is wondering, who was W.H.?

Yesterday I wrote an essay on *Othello*. It bore no relation to what I really feel about Shakespeare, or about *Othello*. I tried to explore the meaning of "catharsis".

Last year, President Kennedy was killed in Dallas.

Last month, Nikita Krushchev was deposed in Moscow.

Last week I shook hands with one of my idols, a very old blind blues-singer from Tennessee. I could hardly understand what he said. He signed his autograph with an X. His recordings had provided me with thoughts and emotions I'd never felt myself. For me, although he was illiterate, he was as profound and powerful a poet as Shakespeare.

Who was Shakespeare? Who am I? What kind of person am I going to be? What shall I do with the next fifty years? If I go and find an island in the sun, it will be alright for six months or so, but for *fifty* years? I don't want to spend all those years living in a city, either.

Should I try to remember my first girl-friend, lament a lost love?

Should I wear a red poppy?

Who can help me find catharsis?

> The last I ever heard from my friend was an enigmatic postcard sent from Crete in 1977, carrying this quotation:
>
> *It is generally agreed that Oxford widens one's horizons, especially*

if they have been narrowed by spending one's childhood the way one must if one is to have a chance of getting in. (Eric Korn, Times Literary Supplement, 1 April 1977)

Buck Burrows

Where the remote Bermudas ride
In th'Oceans bosome unespy'd . . .

Andrew Marvell, "Bermudas"

The Bermudas are a group of beautiful islands in the North Atlantic. They are now known simply as Bermuda. When first discovered, the islands were considered dangerous and forlorn places, inhabited by wicked spirits. "The Devil's Islands", William Strachey called them.

Before very long, shipwrecked sailors and reluctant settlers realised that the islands were much more agreeable and habitable than they had appreciated at first.

"Truth is the daughter of Time," Strachey wrote, "Men ought not to deny everything which is not subject to their own sense."

Anthony Trollope was not impressed when visiting Bermuda for two weeks in 1858. At the time it was a British colony with a convict establishment of around 1500 prisoners:

That Caliban should have lived here I can imagine; that Ariel

22

would have been sick of the place is certain; and that Governor Prospero should have been willing to abandon his governorship, I conceive to have been only natural. (*Aaron Trow*)

In his book, *The West Indies and the Spanish Main,* he wrote:

If these be the veritable scenes of Prospero's incantations, I will at any rate say this — that there are now to be found stronger traces of the breed of Caliban than of Ariel.

When describing the proper treatment of hardened criminals in an establishment of penal servitude, Trollope's first thought, when suggesting what should be done with them, was

to rid ourselves of them from amongst us. This we should do were we to hang them; this we did when we sent them to Botany Bay; this we certainly do when we send them to Bermuda.

Trollope felt that there could be no other place in the world about which there could be less to say than there was about the island.

Mark Twain was far more enamoured of Bermuda than Trollope had been. For Twain, Bermuda seemed like heaven on earth, and he visited the island many times.

On 10 March, 1973, Sir Richard Sharples, the Governor of Bermuda, and his Aide-de-Camp, Captain Hugh Sayers, were assassinated by alleged associates of the Black Beret Cadre, a Bermudian Black Power movement, who had drawn up a hit list of public figures they wanted to target. Two men, Buck Burrows and Larry Tackyln, were eventually hanged for the crime. The hangman had to be brought over from England. The hangings, on the 2nd of December 1977, led to violent riots.

When John first visited the islands forty years later, he came as a tourist to enjoy the unspoiled nature and the pink sandy beaches, but he soon tired of the lazy life and spent much of his time reading about the history of the islands. After visiting the graves of the two murdered British officials, who were buried side-by-side in the graveyard of St. Peter's Church, in St. George's (founded in 1612, the oldest English town in the New World), he became determined to find out more about the shocking assassinations of the Governor and his ADC. Before returning by bus to Hamilton, he visited the walled area of the churchyard where black slaves and free men were once buried; it was now part of the UNESCO African Diaspora Heritage and Slavery Trail.

You can go to heaven if you want. I'd rather stay here in Bermuda"
- Mark Twain

Back in his hotel in Hamilton, John discovered that it was possible to access the archives of the Government of Bermuda, and to study formerly Top Secret files of the Bermuda Intelligence Committee. He was a keen amateur researcher. Going slowly through the files which he was brought by the helpful archivist, he came across the monthly reports from the 1960's and 1970's in a document entitled "Individuals and Organisations of Security Interest". That, in itself, proved very revealing about past attitudes of suspicion and the focal points of surveillance on the island.

The most interesting document of all was the original note by Buck Burrows, in Buck's own hand, written during an earlier prison sentence. It went some way towards explaining his political motivation, although it was clear that he was a hardened criminal. He'd been a gambler and armed robber, yet he'd once worked as a cleaner in Police Headquarters.

John started reading the short note. He'd never expected to come across anything so dramatic and direct.

> The White man kidnapped the black man also his sons and daughters, and forced them to leave their home-land. On the journey to the Conlonylist countries some of our brothers were brutally beaten and even killed. Some of our sisters were raped, and yet the white man felt thoroughly justified in carrying out these brutal acts. My fore-fathers before me were and felt as slaves, in these contemporary times I feel I am a slave and I will continue to feel that way until I reach the land of Africa then I truly would be a free man.

John found that Burrows had also written a confession, when he was in prison after the assassination:

> The motive for killing the Governor was to seek to make the people, black people in particular, become aware of the evilness and wickedness of the colonialist system in this island. Secondly, the motive was to show that these colonialists were just ordinary people like ourselves who eat, sleep and die just like anybody else and that we need not stand in fear and awe of them.

Ironically, John also discovered, in the *Sunday People* of the 18th of March 1973, that a British journalist, John Smith, had interviewed the Governor shortly before the assassination and warned him that he could be next on the killer's list, but

> the genial Governor just laughed and said, "Oh, come now, nothing is going to happen to me. People in Bermuda are just too friendly for that sort of thing." He cut another slice of chocolate cake as afternoon rain drummed on the windows. He sipped his tea and added, "I get on very well with them."

In past history. —

The White man, kidnapped the black man also his sons and daughters, and forced them to leave their home land. On the journey to the contemporary countries some of our brothers were brutally beaten and even killed. Some of our sisters were raped, and yet the white man felt thoughly justified in carrying out these brutal acts. My fore-fathers before me were and felt as slaves, in these contemporary times I feel I am a slave, and I will continue to feel that way until I reach the land of Africa then I truly would be a free man. Cola

BUCK BURROWS

The Governor had never believed that there were Black Power militants on the island. Perhaps the assassination was an "act of temporary madness" as his widow, Baroness Sharples, was later to suggest.

Most Bermudians were deeply shocked and shamed by what had happened. Not only were Sir Richard and his ADC shot beside the steps going down to the Residence garden, just as they had taken the Governor's Great Dane out for a walk shortly after their dinner guests had left, but the dog, Horsa, was also shot and killed by one of the gunmen.

In spite of all his discoveries, John would leave Bermuda with the strong impression that race relations had become very much better. On the day he was due to leave the island, the 14th of July, Hurricane Bertha caused the cancellation of all flights. To kill the time that evening, he drank several Rum Swizzles, followed by a Dark and Stormy. He started imagining that he might be marooned there like the captain and crew of the *Sea Venture* in 1609.

He wondered what it would be like to live on the island forever. He thought that, in spite of the past sufferings of so many unfortunate individuals, it might indeed be rather agreeable.

The ghosts of Max Gate

It was All Souls' Day.

The ghosts of Thomas Hardy and William Barnes met above Max Gate. They'd been friends and neighbours when they lived, but this wasn't some jolly annual writers' reunion. Thomas Hardy's fervourless soul was still hovering in gloomy purgatorial limbo.

His unsettled ghostly spirit could sometimes be perceived by the hyper-sensitive at Max Gate and at Stinsford churchyard. Sightings or hauntings in other parts of Wessex were rare.

On All Souls' Day, as on this day *every year* since the death of Hardy, the merciful, forgiving spirit of William Barnes, who was a saintly, true-believing parson-poet during his life on earth, was sent down from Heaven on a mission to persuade Thomas of the errors of his over-subtle thinking. The Reverend Barnes' task was to offer his old friend some rays of blessèd hope and certainty, to help him banish his doubts, to rekindle a sense of faith, to dispel his deep-seated feelings of unbelief.

Hardy always told him that, although he regretted exclusion from the joys and grace of Heaven, he remained a rationalist, an unconvinced soul with enduring doubts — but that he wasn't an absolutely atheistic phantom. He still suspected that a merciful God was the creation of Man, a self-deceiving projection of humanity's wishes. He'd never forgotten the words of William Blake: "All deities reside in the human breast."

Hardy wished he could have been more like other people; that he could have shared their simple, unquestioning faith and hopes for heavenly bliss, without ever having expected to escape from his allotted share of suffering, the endurance of life's inevitable tragic ironies and other mortal pains.

Hardy never failed to confess his eternal feelings of guilt about his treatment of his first wife, Emma. The Good Parson sent down from Heaven comforted him as best he could, but Hardy's spirit remained unsettled and in limbo. After every ghostly reunion Hardy's spirit made the same excuse for having to leave: "I must go to Stinsford, where my poor shrivelled heart is buried. My soul will *never* find peace until heart and body are reconciled."

From a Corfu diary

Friday, 15 December, 1967

Yesterday, the Greeks were ordered to take down all the pictures of King Constantine. His portraits immediately came down from the classroom walls at the school, but they've been put back up again today, following the most recent official instructions. They'll probably be taken down again on Monday. The King's not coming back from Rome.

My thoughts have been somewhat disturbed this afternoon by the rhythmic singing of bed springs next door. The neighbour is a young woman whose current boyfriend is a pleasant enough fellow in his late twenties. He's quite generous; he's the sort who fills your glass to the brim whenever it's empty. He brought me a present of a bottle of wine, so I have no complaints. He's become paranoid-possessive, though, ever since his ex-fiancé was unfaithful to him, with a man who has two wooden legs. He employed a private detective to follow her when she went to see her "sick mother" in Athens; he can't understand why she left him for such a man. What can one say?

Monday, 18 December, 1967

I went round to the school on Saturday morning. The headmistress was doing some decorating. She was spraying artificial snow patterns of angels and churches on the windows, and I offered to help her. Suddenly, down below in the street, a man collapsed in an epileptic fit, foaming at the mouth, kicking and twitching without control. A great crowd gathered round him, fascinated. He looked dead; they felt his pulse and pulled his hair, to try to make him stir. About twenty minutes later an ambulance arrived. The headmistress, meanwhile, continued spraying snow on the windows.

Later, I was invited to eat with the headmistress and her husband at their apartment. They talked politics. He told her of the news from Philiates, his home town over on the mainland opposite, in Epirus, near the border with Albania.

The townspeople needed a new cemetery, so they sent a bulldozer into a field last week. The bulldozer uncovered some Ancient Greek graves containing skeletons more than two metres long, some still with hair on their skulls. The villagers, ignorant of the importance of the finds, stole the rings, vases and other artefacts they found, and told nobody. The rest of the graves and ancient urns have been utterly destroyed by the bulldozer. Nobody has reported the find; the locals who know about it help themselves to whatever they dig up or discover.

One of the head's friends dropped round for coffee after we'd eaten. He put on a show of bravado and passionate anger against the military government, probably to impress us.

"Five stupid, stupid men; if there were more people like me, believe me, I would crush them!"

I wasn't convinced. He admitted that he wasn't personally affected. He was more concerned about his young cousin, who'd formed a close liaison with a very much younger Greek girl.

"He sees her in secret, Romeo and Juliet fashion, all blown kisses and balcony whispers. She's very young. Her father's a tailor. He found out about their relationship only yesterday, and he went hunting for my cousin at his office, brandishing a large pair of tailor's scissors. He was making wild cutting motions, madly slicing the air with this vast pair of scissors. It was clearly his intention to attack my cousin, or threaten him with castration. Luckily, he'd made a bolt for it."

"If the tailor does catch him," the headmistress commented, "I hope he knows how to stitch him up again."

I happened to meet the young man that evening. He was still going on about the tailor's giant pair of scissors. "I was facing the death!" he exclaimed.

His girlfriend had just phoned him. They were planning to go on meeting in secret, but he wouldn't be venturing anywhere near her house or her father's tailoring shop.

Fifty Years ago

It was fifty years ago that I started writing a journal in earnest. I kept it up for about six months. I began it in the autumn of 1967, when I was 22, living on the island of Corfu, where I was attempting to become a writer. I stopped writing it in the spring of 1968, when I was 23.

I only started writing a journal again when I was living in Prague about twenty years later. That was a more sustained, mature and rigorous effort, written between 1986 and 1989.

I regret that I didn't make a more consistent attempt to keep a diary or journal, as my memory isn't too good these days. I destroyed some embarrassingly intimate diary entries written whilst at university.

I have forgotten a lot of incidents from my life that might have made good or even amusing stories. I have preserved most of my poems, which enable me to recollect significant experiences, emotions and moments. I need to put them into some order, before they all end up on the rubbish tip.

I want to go back half a century, to focus on my search for peace and quiet on the island of Corfu between 1967 and 1968, which I now see as a particularly significant period in my life.

In August 1967 I drove down to Brindisi in my grey Austin A35 van, accompanied by my girlfriend. I'd been offered a post as a teacher of English at a Greek cultural institute. I'd decided to spend two months on the island, including a month camping, in advance of taking up the appointment. I needed to make contact with the director, without alerting her to the fact that I was going to stay with my girlfriend for the first month. I wasn't sure how conservative she was. I had little knowledge of morality or codes of honour on a Greek island, but I did have images in my head of the stoning of the widow and of the villager brandishing a knife

in the film *Zorba the Greek*. It was just as well that I hadn't read
Konstantinos Theotokis' *Corfiot Tales* at that time.

We'd slept on the deck of the ferry from Brindisi to Corfu;
maybe we snatched an hour or two on unoccupied aircraft-type
seats when no-one was looking. We were pretty tired when we
approached the harbour of Corfu Town, with the beautiful view
of the Old Town and its two fortresses, of Vido island and the
peaks of Pantocrator mountain.

Having made contact with the registrar of the institute, to
confirm that I had arrived, and to collect some papers, my
girlfriend and I headed for the far north of the island, as far away
from the town as we could get. The road was very rough, stony
and dusty. We camped in an olive grove next to the beach at Roda,
which was then completely undeveloped and without electricity,
with only a single simple *taverna* where one could order an
omelette floating in oil, or some fish.

We were something of a curiosity in Roda, and inquisitive
young Corfiots befriended us, took us for trips on small fishing
boats, or crowded round my Phillips cassette recorder (borrowed
from my mother), to hear the sounds of their own voices.

Great crowds of women and children gathered round to watch
my girlfriend cooking, to watch us eating or reading. They would
just stand there, a yard away, and stare, without saying a word.
Whenever we turned our backs, they'd take a quick peep into our
tent.

Tourism was developing fast in other parts of the island, and
the local economy was doing well. The people we met seemed
relatively unconcerned about the Military Junta at that stage, in
1967, and rather welcomed the stability, the clamp-down on
corruption and the disciplined new order, especially as they hoped
to obtain house- and hotel-building loans more easily.

After two weeks at Roda, we travelled to Paxos, where we
camped discreetly in another quiet, secluded olive grove, above
the sea, on the road from Gaios to the Paxos Beach Hotel. We
swam a lot in the crystal clear water, avoiding the plentiful prickly

sea-urchins.

When my girlfriend returned to England, I started to explore Corfu on my own, and found a tiny monastic cell (an empty store-room or cellar with a single bed) at the pebbly little cove of Nissaki, where I stayed for a month. It was only a few metres from the water's edge. A blissful existence, and rather more appealing than my next place to stay, an inexpensive room I rented in a noisy square opposite the main bus station, then located in San Rocco Square, Corfu Town.

Unable to stand the dust and noise, I moved to an unfurnished bungalow in Garitsa, in Odos Anapafseos — "the street of rest and eternal peace" — in the middle of October 1967. It was the no-exit road to the town's main cemetery. I imagined it would be very quiet indeed.

I didn't realise at the time that I was such a close neighbour of the deceased parents of my wife-to-be. I hope that they, at least, had found some peace and quiet, and weren't turning in their graves at the thought of their only daughter risking her reputation by planning to visit an Englishman at home.

As it turned out, though, I could hear the clamour of schoolchildren taking part in athletic contests in the sports stadium nearby, and I shouldn't forget to mention that the window of my room directly overlooked the airport . . .

In search of silence

For most of his life, in all the countries and places where he had lived, worked and travelled, Jack had been in search of perfect silence; he sought and needed silence — *at night*, that is, so that he could get to sleep.

There were, admittedly, certain sounds that he loved dearly, and which often helped to calm him:

birdsong — especially the dawn chorus, the sound of a pigeon cooing, of a nightingale or skylark singing . . .

peals of English church bells rung by hand, bells of all sizes hung round the necks of cattle, goats and sheep in Greece and variously tuned to identify and track the flocks and herds, a shepherd or goatherd playing his pipe when settling his animals down for the night . . .

the sounds of the sea, waves breaking before reaching the shore, lapping the shore, then receding from shingle, sucking and dragging back pebbles from the Chesil Beach, the murmuring, purling, burbling of streams and brooks . . .

Jack's employment had taken him far from those agreeable and healing sounds — to cities and parts of the world where silence was a very rare phenomenon:

In Corfu, during the tourist season, aeroplanes with their roaring jet engines took off and landed every ten minutes; their flight paths were such that they made their steep ascents and descents right over his apartment.

In Prague, he'd had to live in an apartment directly above a butcher's shop, a 24-hour factory operation where sausages were made, and where everything was constantly being moved about in metal carts on metal wheels. Only yards from his window, the continuous sound of trams screeching along metal tracks was added torture to his ears.

In Addis Ababa, he'd experienced an even greater shock to his system, when would-be revolutionaries, hostile to aristocratic or royalist landlords, hurled volleys of rocks and stones that hailed down clattering onto the tin roof of his rented bungalow, in the middle of the night.

In the mountains of Epirus Jack thought he had found what he had been searching for all his life, real silence — until a neighbour acquired two guard-dogs which were kept tethered at all times. Their barking and whining proved intolerable. They would go mad when they caught the scent of bears roaming in the vicinity. He'd almost forgotten the early days with the mice scuttling round the rafters and along the ceiling above his bedroom.

Near Mombasa, on the Kenyan coast, nocturnal bush-babies used to leap around in the attic space of his holiday cottage.

There were other sounds with which he had to contend, in common with most other human beings, who endure them on a regular basis — their own and others' routine fits of snoring, sneezing, coughing, farting . . .

Then there was the problem of the talkback phone-in radio programmes his partner left blaring all night long, even though she was soundly asleep.

But then he remembered the Serbian monk from Chilandari Monastery whom he'd met nearly forty years before, visiting Mount Athos in his quest for silence. The young monk, who'd spent some years in the USA, had shown him his pocket-sized cassette tape-recorder and tiny headphones, on which he would listen to the gospel blues of Blind Willie Johnson and born-again Bob Dylan songs to while away the hours when not praying or chanting during the liturgical cycle of the all-night vigil. At other times this funky monk would climb the mountain to a deserted hermit's cell, where he would sit and softly play his B-flat blues-harp, as another form of plaintive, soulful meditation. If it didn't provide the final answer, it helped him focus his mind on the important questions. It seems that his spiritual father had not raised any objections.

Recalling this, Jack resorted to wearing ear-pod headphones to block out unwelcome and intrusive noises, until he discovered that he could download his favourite forms of music onto a tiny iPod — 1950's rock 'n' roll with honking, screeching saxophones and heavy drumming, Greek music with amplified bouzoukis, Aboriginal ceremonial music with clap-sticks and the deep droning sound of the didgeridoo, American rhythm 'n' blues boogies played on electric slide guitars accompanied by wailing harmonicas.

Now he was in his element. There was silence in the room. It was bliss, lying there listening to the raucous but paradoxically soothing "lullabies" — the wild sounds of his own choice, the comfort-music of his youth and early travels which he'd been missing for so long.

Jack was fortunate if he managed just two hours sleep each night, but he was dancing, dancing inside his head.

Retirement and revenge

How often had he worn his mask, played the game, repressed his true feelings, lived a lie? How often had he put on his suit and tie, polished his black shoes and gone off to work with a heavy heart?

Every working day of his life!

The day of his retirement would be the first day of his liberation and belated revolt against convention, routine and conformity.

When the big day came, he and his wife had an almighty row.

"You take me for granted."
"*You* take *me* for granted."
"You're not on my side."
"*You're* not on *my* side."
"You never listen to me."
"*You* never listen to *me*."
"Try for once to make me happy."
"Try for once to make *me* happy."

Happy... happy... happy... happy... happy... happy... happy... happy... happy...

So sad. So very sad.

"One way or the other, they'll get you in the end," thought Paul.

He regretted that he'd ever agreed to sign up for his company's Preparing for Retirement programme, and then recommended to his wife, Elizabeth, that she should attend the special programme for spouses, run by an external consultant. Little did he know that Elizabeth's course leader would turn out to be Pamela, the woman who'd had to leave Paul's company soon after their affair had been discovered.

Stacheldraht (barbed wire)
or
European unions

Wie soll ich meine Seele halten, daß
sie nicht an deine rührt? Wie soll ich sie
hinheben über dich zu andern Dingen?
Ach gerne möchte ich sie bei irgendwas
Verlorenem im Dunkel unterbringen
an einer fremden stillen Stelle, die
nicht weiterschwingt, wenn diene Tiefen schwingen.
Doch alles, was uns anrührt, dich und mich,
nimmt uns zusammen wie ein Bogenstrich,
die aus zwei Saiten eine Stimme zieht.
Auf welches Instrument sind wir gespannt?
Und welcher Geiger hat uns in der Hand?
    O süßes Lied.

How then shall I restrain my soul,
how hold it back from touching yours?
How lift it over you to other things?
Oh, I would love to stow my soul
'mongst things forgotten in the dark
in some far-distant silent place
which echoes not when your heart's deep resounds.
Yet everything that touches you and me
grasps us together, and like a bow-stroke
draws out from our two strings a single voice.
Upon what instrument have we been stretched?
And what string-player holds us in his hand?
    Ah sweet, sweet song.

Raine Maria Rilke, *Liebesleid / Lovesong*

It was the 29th of March 2019, the day that the UK was supposed
to leave the European Union and, while Donald had scant regard
for the *modus operandi* of the institutions of the European Union,

40

he had now lost all respect for the arcane procedures and party-political shenanigans of the British Parliament; he despaired of the strident bickering and back-biting of the mutually-abusive members of parliament. He admired the writing of a small number of journalists, but had little time for the majority of media-commentators or pushy, self-promoting pundits and partisan talk-show panellists. Disappointed by the apparent lack of balance on the BBC, he often turned to LBC to hear a variety of different voices, ordinary people of all persuasions who phoned in to air their views and grievances throughout the course of the night.

Donald felt completely unrepresented by the country's governing party, by the opposition parties and by his own MP. There was so much bluster and circular talk about democracy, so little evidence of decent, democratic behaviour.

Donald was half Scottish, born in Edinburgh, but he had no sympathy for the policies or aggressive rhetoric of the independence-seeking Scottish National Party. He'd believed in devolution and the relatively modern procedures of the Scottish Parliament, but he believed even more in the integrity of the United Kingdom. He'd been known to call the more extreme nationalists of the SNP "a parcel of fools", a term that they happily applied to their English opponents.

All that Donald observed on TV when in London was an end-less display of smug, opinionated arrogance; all he ever seemed to hear on the radio was yet more evidence of hypocritical self-interest, disguised as arguments in support of the national interest.

He *cared* about Europe, the cultures of Europe, the varied landscapes of Europe as he had experienced them in a dozen countries. Not that he cared for those countries more than he did for Australia, New Zealand, Canada or the USA, countries to which many of his own people had migrated and where they had struggled to establish themselves and to make a living. As far as the UK was concerned, he was a unionist, with a small u, but he also felt that he was a citizen of the world.

The languages he could speak adequately were all European. He'd started learning French and German at school. He'd developed an early passion for the twentieth century literature of both countries. His ambition had always been to work abroad, preferably in Europe. He was to spend much of his life in European countries.

If he had reservations about the Franco-German dominance and the direction of the European Union, he was much more open-minded and enthusiastic about individual Europeans and specific European countries. He was amused to discover a thirty-second video on YouTube on the 29th of March 2019, a message of love from Scotland to Europe: "Scotland is Open, Scotland is Now: Europe, let's continue our love affair."

The kind of love-affair that Donald valued and cherished most was not so much country-to-country as person-to-person, in his case man-to-woman and *vice versa*. He was not immune to moods of nostalgia. He sometimes recalled his first experience of love, which had inspired him to write poetry and which, for a period of four years, had dominated his thoughts and diverted his attention from his studies.

Emilia von Fürstenberg, whose family had inherited the right to use the aristocratic "von" in their name (although the German nobility had been abolished in 1919), had come for the summer to West Linton, the Scottish Borders village where Donald's parents were then living, sixteen miles from Edinburgh; she was hoping to improve her English, as part of an ongoing exchange with the daughter of one of Donald's neighbours. Her family home was in Ostfriesland, Germany, not far from the border with Holland and about a hundred and forty miles from Hamburg.

It wasn't long before the two youngsters were introduced, and started to help each other with their respective languages. Both of them were very innocent teenagers; they were deeply attracted to each other, but the relationship remained shyly platonic, with suppressed undercurrents of a powerful longing and a deepening passion. They played mildly flirtatious cat-and-mouse games which held promises of closer physical contact in the future. They would listen to records and circle round each other as if on the verge of embracing, aching to touch but never quite daring to make contact; her bright eyes and lingering glances seemed to invite him to come closer, then she'd tease him by pirouetting around him, but ducking away at the last moment.

They'd go for long walks down lonely country lanes, even sit in silence on a convenient tree-trunk to watch the sunset, while Donald, in blissful anticipation, tentatively slipped his arm around her shoulder. He never felt the pain of the barbed-wire digging into his back. They were both over-protected and inexperienced teenagers. Neither of them could actually pluck up the courage to kiss. Somehow it would have spoilt the spell of pure young love, first love, true, eternal love, *ewige liebe*, this ideal attraction and romantic affinity and union of soul-mates. She would tenderly recite these words of Rilke's:

> Doch alles, was uns anrührt, dich und mich,
> nimmt uns zusammen wie ein Bogenstrich,
> der aus zwei Saiten eine Stimme zieht.

> Yet everything that touches you and me
> grasps us together, and like a bow-stroke
> draws out from our two strings a single voice.

Donald had found a poem by Goethe which seemed to express his feelings when they were apart:

> Ich denke dein, wenn mir der Sonne Schimmer
> vom Meere strahlt;
> Ich denke dein, wenn sich des Mondes Flimmer
> in Quellen malt.

> I think of you when the radiance of the sun
> shines at me from the sea.
> I think of you when the shimmer of the moon's
> reflected in the stream.

Their feelings were sublimated through these exchanges of poetry. She taught him the whole of Rilke's "Liebeslied", until he knew it by heart; she sent him notes and letters which ended with the bright red lipstick imprint of her puckered lips, which made him burn up inside; in his bed at night he would secretly kiss her photograph, the fragrant lock of her hair that she had given him, her letters and the red shape of her lip-print on the paper. He was completely obsessed with her, and the obsession continued after she returned to Germany. Twice he managed to visit her. Some of his friends thought it inappropriate for him to pursue a German girl rather than "an English rose". One or two of them taunted him with insulting talk of the War, of Nazis, of "the Hun".

On the first occasion he travelled to Ostfriesland, her parents arranged for Douglas to stay with their friends a few houses away, for the sake of propriety. When he wanted to ask her mother for permission to take her out, perhaps to the cinema or for a walk, he had to begin his request with the polite and formulaic words, *"Sehr geehrte gnädige Frau"* ("Most gracious, revered Madam"). Emilia's parents were friendly and hospitable, but watchful and formal. That certainly had the effect of putting a damper on the romance. He had to be well-dressed and on his best behaviour at all times; they never had a chance to relax. Having to present himself as the model of a proper, good-mannered young English gentleman did not make for a very sexy image.

When Donald returned to West Linton, the unfulfilled longing was still there, and it appeared to be shared by both of them, as strongly as before. The letters with the imprinted red kisses continued. She sent photographs of herself in a bikini, more food for his phantasies.

Another year, in the Easter holiday, he decided to hitch-hike to Ostfriesland, with the thought in the back of his head that, although he was now only nineteen, he would propose to her, perhaps suggest that they should get engaged. He imagined that he was willing to die for her. It didn't take many days for it to dawn upon Donald that, although she still liked him, she had found another boyfriend close to home. She would leave Donald with her parents for a few hours every other day to go on "errands" in town.

She hadn't dared to tell him the truth. She had given her mother all his passionate letters to read (but hadn't revealed what she had been responsible for provoking and unleashing in her temptingly seductive letters to Donald).

The kindly but controlling mother was taken aback by the intensity of Donald's love-letters, and advised her daughter not to tell him how things stood, because she was convinced that he might commit suicide. Donald was heart-broken when he learnt the truth; he felt he had been cruelly deceived. Before he left, he put on a brave front and pretended to the first great "love of his life" that everything he had written had been merely the expression of literary convention, embellished with well-tried phrases and hackneyed stock devices. She looked crestfallen; all she could say was, "I thought you were different from all the other boys." She didn't understand that he was trying to save face. Before everything had fully come out in the open, she'd arranged for Donald to go out with one of her best friends, who had recently broken up with her boyfriend. Donald had duly obliged but he was unenthusiastic; he had learnt his lesson.

The truth was that he too had changed, grown up, been transformed. He would no longer wear the clothes his well-meaning father had bought him, a tweed jacket and cavalry twill trousers. He'd become a bit of a rebel against social convention. From now on he would let his hair grow long, wear blue jeans and an old donkey-jacket. He regretted that they'd never run away together to Hamburg, to hang out at the Star Club.

She had embraced her role and status as the daughter of a wealthy industrialist with an aristocratic pedigree and pretensions; she hadn't needed to go to a "finishing-school", she had started to resemble a fuller, more mature young woman, a mixture of immaculate mannequin and haughty hausfrau before her time; she'd been groomed, manicured, made up and expensively coiffured for a different kind of future; in her elegant and stylish outfits she'd lost much of her former spontaneity, her pony-tailed freshness and youthful appeal. She wasn't the same girl, the soulmate for whom he'd fallen so heavily.

This painful experience hadn't put him off the desire for future relationships. Although hurt and deeply disillusioned, he now felt free. It would be a long time, though, before he would trust anyone, or lose control of his deepest emotions.

By the second year at university, Donald was coming into his own. He dated attractive young women from France and Germany (French and German being the languages he knew best), as well as from England. He fancied many more, from Norway and Sweden. He was more attracted by a foreign accent than a familiar English one. He discourteously declined some invitations to "aristocratic" summer balls, where eligible young graduands were being sized up as potential good prospects for pretty young women, who would, until the late 1950's, have been introduced to society as debutantes at coming-out balls.

Donald had lost most of his "hang-ups". He'd banished any thoughts of purely romantic or platonic relationships. The swinging sixties had begun. In London things were even hotter. The Beatles and the Rolling Stones were riding high. Donald was on the prowl at student dances, shaking his hips to the Stones' "It's all over now" and "The Last Time", or doing a slow grind to "You better move on".

He seldom went back to West Linton or to Edinburgh. Whenever he could get away, he headed for new or favourite haunts in Europe, where he had a number of brief love-affairs, before casting his roving eyes further afield to Italy and the Mediterranean. He was making up for lost time.

The French government might have vetoed the UK's applications to join the European Economic Community in 1963 and 1967 (the UK finally joined on January 1st, 1973), but as far as *European unions* were concerned, Donald felt that he had been quite a trail-blazer, if not exactly a Casanova or Don Juan.

He was to spend the following fifty years working in a number of European countries. On balance, Donald was a *remainer,* if only for emotional reasons and because he was committed to the exchange of DNA, bodily fluids and the free movement of people. It wasn't just Scottish nationalists who could proclaim, "Europe, let's continue our love affair."

In other respects, Donald was a *leaver.* "Love them and leave them" had become his cynical motto.

He had never fully recovered from that wound — and not just to his pride — which Emilia von Fürstenberg, his first great love, his long-lost love from Ostfriesland, had inflicted upon him, upon his soul, his being, his psyche.

Often he repeated to himself that immortal line of Rilke's:

> *Auf welches Instrument sind wir gespannt?*
>
> *Upon what instrument have we been stretched?*

Beside the seaside

When I was a kid on a day-trip to the seaside in school holidays, I used to love playing the penny slot machines and the coin-push machines in the Weymouth amusement arcades, trying to make all the piles of pennies and other shiny coppers cascade down into the tray, but seldom succeeding, even though so many coins seemed to be piled up precariously, layer upon layer, overhanging and just ready to fall and overflow into my lap!

Even more frustrating (and a complete waste of time) were the tantalizing claw-crane grab-and-win machines: the grabber-claws were always so loosely adjusted and ineffective that the crane, even if skillfully positioned and manipulated, could never lift a prize more than a few inches before it slipped through the three claws and fell back down again. They must have been designed by crooks and daylight robbers.

I would always drift back to whichever coin-push machine seemed to have the most coins dangling over the edge of the drop.

One day, when I'd changed my last half-a-crown into a pocket-full of copper coins, I was getting unusually agitated and I tried to shake the machine surreptitiously. But it refused to budge. It seemed to be bolted solidly to the floor. The woman behind the counter of the glassed-in money-changing booth spotted what I was doing and started screaming at me. Her assistant, a young bouncer who must have been about twenty, came up to me and shoved me hard against the wall. Then he grabbed me by the scruff of the neck and punched me in the solar plexus. I saw red and grabbed the concealed flick knife that I carried — more for show than for self-defence. I lunged at him and the blade sliced into his arm. He fell back, bleeding profusely, against the machine on which I'd been playing. As he sank to the floor, around a hundred copper coins sprayed all over him like metal confetti.

The woman called 999, of course. But I stayed long enough to scoop up most of the coins before I scarpered. Some of the pennies were covered in his blood. By the time the bobbies arrived, I was long gone, feeding a juke-box at a coffee-bar down the other end of the esplanade and having fun playing on the pin-ball machines.

I guess I'd broken even.

That was the last time I could show off my skills until I managed to escape from Borstal on Portland. Later on it became a Youth Custody Centre. Then they called it a Young Offenders' Institution. None of them could have been mistaken for an amusement arcade. Now it's an Adult and Young Offenders Establishment. I've been back a couple of times. They know me well, even though I've changed my name as often as they have.

In the nineteenth century it'd been a prison for convicts. They were the lucky ones. After all the hard graft quarrying Portland stone, most of them got free passage down under to Australia.

Now that I'm an adult, I've learnt to appreciate the sea air, but I reckon that Weymouth is just as good as Bondi Beach.

A broken ankle

Margaret, are you grieving [...]?
[...]
No matter, child, the name:
Sorrow's springs are the same.
Nor mouth had, no nor mind, expressed
what heart heard of, ghost guessed:
It is the blight man was born for,
It is Margaret you mourn for.

Gerald Manley Hopkins, "Spring and fall"

William Johnson had been a successful professional golfer in his heyday. In his late sixties he moved back to his old home in Dorset, and enjoyed playing a round or two every week on the course where he'd first taken up the sport — the Came Down Golf Club. It was there he'd often dreamt that one day he might win the Ryder Cup. It had a friendly clubhouse and bar, where he could meet his old friends and impress them with tales of his past glories.

His life had been on hold since he'd broken his ankle at Durdle Door that April. He bitterly regretted that he'd lost seven weeks of active life. If he'd been there a week later he might have disappeared over the cliff in the big landslide, so he knew he shouldn't complain.

The weather wasn't good for most of the period the ankle was healing, so he didn't miss too many sunny golfing days. He couldn't cope with crutches, and he was tired of dragging himself up two flights of stairs on his backside. He couldn't go to the cinema, unless a film was showing at the screen on the ground floor. It was a listed building, without a lift and with no facilities for the disabled.

Now he had been given the good news that the ankle bone had healed, meaning that he would no longer need to struggle with crutches whenever he wanted to go out. The blue fibreglass lower-leg-and-ankle cast was cut off with a small circular saw. The ankle was still swollen, and it would need time to regain its strength, but he felt like a man who'd been released from prison and a heavy ball-and-chain.

He told the orthopaedic nurse that he had learnt a lot from the experience, about disabilities and those with more serious, chronic conditions. He now had much more empathy. "Everyone should have a leg in plaster for a month or so, to understand what it's like," the nurse commented.

It was in William's self-centred and indifferent nature that, soon after his recovery, he forgot this exchange and the nurse's words.

Ten years earlier, his elder brother, who had always been a better sportsmen and golfer, a hero to William during their schooldays, and a giant of a man standing at six-foot-seven, had had a serious accident. He had served as a soldier, a natural leader of men and a courageous army officer, often deployed in the face of imminent danger in Borneo, the Persian Gulf and the Strait of Hormuz — a desolate, volcanic moonscape where he was based on Goat Island with a hundred Omani troops, and with orders to clear a terrorist insurgency from the Massandam peninsula, to land SAS teams along the coast around Hasab (with the support of naval gunfire), and to carry out an opposed landing at Buka. Ironically, he escaped all injury until after he'd returned to an unexciting life in Civvy Street, when he broke his thighbone and shattered the femoral head and acetabulum socket. He had recently been losing his balance and had experienced several hard falls. On one occasion he had had to crawl back to the house, dragging himself slowly along the rough ground for well over an hour. Now he had fallen again and was being urgently assessed in hospital, as William learned on the phone. Not only had his brother broken his one good leg, but his knee had also been severely damaged. He was lying there, doped with morphine.

When William heard this grim news about his brother's condition, he felt paralysed, and fell back in his chair. It wasn't a question of fraternal sympathy, of telepathy, or of a morbid imagination. It was an overwhelming and intensely physical sensation of pain, perhaps born of a selfish fear for his own future. How soon might he himself become incapacitated? Would he ever be able to play golf again?

He never recognised that it was *he*, and not his brother, who was the cripple.

The incoming tide

The road was in a terrible state, washed away and rutted by the storm. It had never been covered by asphalt.

Out of curiosity, he foolishly decided to continue down to the end, negotiating many bends and hair-pin corners in order to see the beach below.

He stopped to ask an elderly villager, who said the road became reasonably good a little further on. All of a sudden it was no longer a track of mud and stones, but of deep wet sand.

The wheels turned, the engine revved furiously, but the car wouldn't budge; it was embedded in the sand. For three hours Peter tried everything he could think of to move the car. He managed to lift it a little, enough to put planks and scrap metal under the front wheels. No success.

It grew cold and dark and he was feeling desperate. The tide was coming in and would take the car away unless he found help. He came across an old woman, who was alone, apart from her pregnant daughter. They couldn't help. They said there was nobody who could assist them within miles. The nearest village was an hour's walk away. If he went, the tide would almost certainly reach the car. Even if he got to the village, there was apparently no telephone. There seemed to be nothing that could be done.

Peter, who never usually panicked, felt frightened. He couldn't afford another car.

About an hour later, he saw a lantern; a middle-aged man approached, it was the woman's son.

He seemed more hopeful; he'd helped other people in a similar situation. He went to fetch some long metal tracks on which the car's wheels could grip. He brought them back. They worked. Peter's relief and gratitude were immense.

He gave the man all the money he had on him. They offered him some bread and cheese.

He still had to drive up the mountainside, which was also dangerous and difficult, especially after dark. The car nearly skidded over the edge several times. The engine whined in first gear, as if it was about to give up the ghost.

For almost the first time in his life, Peter started praying. He felt a truly helpless human being. When he finally reached the asphalt road, he stopped and spoke aloud his thanks to God.

The magistrates' court

"How do you plead?"

"Not guilty, Sir, I mean Madam," blurted out Barry.

"Be quiet, Barry, I'm your solicitor and I do the talking, that's what my fee is for."

The solicitor turned to the magistrate:

"He's only thirteen, bright for his age, but he's feeling very nervous. He goes to a good Prep School. He's sitting for a scholarship exam."

Barry had already sworn on the Bible that he'd tell the whole truth, nothing but the truth.

"Well, what do you have to say?" asked the magistrate.

Barry was thinking about the truth of the matter, how he would have to twist it a little, whatever the solicitor had told him to say. Barry hated having to admit that he and his friends had been playing at being firemen. But that was what his solicitor's fees were for, to tell the court why he was really a good, studious middle-class boy — the others used to call him "four-eyes" and laughed at his round, metal-rimmed National Health spectacles — led astray and influenced by two bigger, rougher boys from a London housing-estate who'd started making a bonfire in the middle of an abandoned farmyard. Hardly arson! OK, they had also thrown stones and broken a few of the ruined old farmhouse windowpanes which had already been broken several times before.

Oh vivid images, breathless, scared, running back to the caravan, ruined holiday. "Oh, mother, something terrible has happened, how can I tell you? Help me, help me, the man took my name and address, he's going to call the police and take us to court."

Something terrible, panic turning me inside out, like the time I got hold of the sledgehammer in the garage and bashed the big red fire-extinguisher, I thought it was empty, but I was curious to see what would happen, and all this endless foam kept steaming out, gushing out like the sperm I'd just managed to produce the night I dreamt about my brother's girl-friend. The fire-extinguisher's foaming agent spewing out in a great arc, covering all the bicycles and cars, eating into the metal; I was so scared I hid under the ping-pong table in the sun-parlour trying to stop breathing, my heart pounded like a drum for three hours until you found me, and now here I am in court, people looking at me, and I feel I've betrayed my two friends by having a solicitor, and they don't have one because they have poor parents, I feel so ashamed that my parents could pay for one; sitting for a scholarship doesn't make me any less innocent or guilty than them just because they go to a Secondary Mod. Having to say "playing at being firemen" makes me feel so stupid, teenagers of thirteen don't "play". But what's worse is that my parents are going all neurotic because it might ruin my career later on, a "black mark . . . keep it quiet, or you might be expelled from school, then you'll never get a job if people find out, pray it's not put on record, promise never to tell anyone, not even your brother, he might let it out if he gets drunk."'

All the family sworn to secrecy — and after all that Barry was found to be innocent. His two friends got off with an absolute discharge, though their fathers had to pay four shillings in court costs on the way out.

"It was a darn sight cheaper than that useless solicitor bloke," thought Barry, somewhat ungratefully, "and anyway, most kids I know would be jolly proud of what we did!"

Terror alert

The Terror Alert was *High* on New Year's Eve, 2003. Tom Ridge, the US Secretary for Homeland Security, was allotted more time on Fox News than the victims and survivors of the devastating earthquake in Iran. Flight restrictions had been imposed over major cities, and armed sky-marshals were being deployed on some commercial airline flights in the USA, in spite of objections from pilots.

President Bush was determined to show American voters that he was taking every precaution to ensure their security, especially in the lead-up to the Election.

If it wasn't for the massive loss of life in the Iranian earthquake, he might have been listening more carefully to the hardline hawks who had been advising him to instigate regime change in Iran and Syria. He decided that America had more to gain, on this occasion, by sending in some US aid in the form of a field hospital. That would play better in the international media and would give some hope to Colin Powell, his Secretary of State, who was eager to encourage greater dialogue with the Mullahs in Teheran.

Alistair Callander had logged on early that morning, and was reading the news on the internet. In the back of his mind was the awareness that he was about to begin his last year in Scandinavia, and that he was due to retire at the end of 2004, after thirty years with the International Peace and Friendship Foundation, better known as the IPFF.

All day long, Alistair had felt an underlying sense of deep unease and concern, on a scale he had never felt before. After he switched off his computer on New Year's Eve, he kept wondering what the year 2004 would have in store, apart from his retirement, which he had to take on his sixtieth birthday, far too soon and much too young, he had always felt. He found it hard to get to sleep, and his mind kept going back to his schooldays, when he was a member of the Combined Cadet Force.

◆

He had been obliged to spend two weeks one summer at Larkhill Camp on the Salisbury Plain, the home of the British Army's School of Artillery, and at Bovington Camp in Dorset, home to the Royal Armoured Corps, learning to calculate the range of the target, the right elevation for the guns, and to shoot with deadly accuracy at the targets with 25-pounders using live rounds, as well as experiencing the thrilling sensation of riding inside the belly of a tank up and down artificial hills and tracks which the Army had created on Salisbury Plain.

The Army spared no expense to win the hearts and minds of teenagers, in the hope of recruiting them a few years later. Alistair was no different from the other boys. He loved being around tanks and big guns, but he rebelled against any form of bullying used to ensure the installation of discipline. He wasn't easily roused to anger. He could tolerate a lot and make many allowances, but there was a borderline. He couldn't forgive anyone who crossed that borderline. He recognised that he was something of a dissident and an outsider; he was already becoming committed to the ideas of conflict prevention, mutual respect and the culture of peaceful relations. If he wasn't exactly a pacifist, it was because he accepted and supported the right of self-defence. He did not believe in pre-emptive strikes unless there was hard evidence or incontrovertible intelligence that an enemy missile was primed to be launched, but he was the first to admit that proof might be hard to find. He made the decision to become an active and responsible citizen committed to building a climate for dialogue and peace.

◆

It didn't always work. He remembered the time that he and his college friend Brian had decided to visit Dublin one Easter vacation. They'd met two Irish girls, Cathleen and Dolores, at a club. It was the year the IRA blew up Nelson's Column in Dublin. They had their own first taste of terrorism when they took Cathleen and Dolores on a day-trip to Howth. They went for a romantic walk, in pairs, and ended up on the beach, having spent an amazing Spring-like afternoon roaming and smooching in the hills. Suddenly a gang of menacing young Irish men appeared out of nowhere and, realising that they were two relatively posh-looking English students — and *Protestants* by the sound of them — entwined with two Catholic colleens, they started threatening them with clubs which had six-inch nails sticking out of the business end. Somehow Alistair and Brian managed to avert an attack, by agreeing that they weren't welcome in Howth, and by promising the gang-members that they would leave Dublin and Ireland the next day. That was in fact the truth; they already had their return tickets. The girls went with them to the station, and waved goodbye as the train gathered speed out of Dublin station. They were sad they had to part. Alistair kept in touch with Cathleen for a while, but the cards and letters stopped coming, much to his regret.

◆

He recalled some other incidents, which had happened about a decade later, after the IPFF had posted him to Addis Ababa, Ethiopia. He'd noted down the date of one incident in his diary, 29 February, 1974, and this is what he'd recorded:

> *Thousands of students marched through the centre of Addis Ababa today, carrying placards and chanting demands for land reform and freedom of expression. Their demands were specific: that the killer of Telahun (the ex-President of the Students' Union) should be brought to court and that the ex-Prime Minister should be hanged, as well as the other Ministers. They did not approve of the new Prime minister: "Hang the lot of them!" was the theme of their chant. Later, military jeeps packed with soldiers of the regular army tried to pacify them. A loud-hailer was used to convey the message that all the armed-forces were co-operating*

with the new Prime Minister and that they approved of the choice.
This is the first time that such a demonstration and protest march
has taken place in Addis Ababa. Will the army mow them
down? The situation is unpredictable.

Alistair had been doing some filming of the march, from his office
balcony, and he'd managed to make translations of quite a few of
the Amharic slogans and chants:

LET THERE BE A PUBLIC VOTING SYSTEM!

THE ETHIOPIAN PUBLIC WILL WIN!

THE POLITICAL PRISONERS MUST BE SET FREE!

BRING ENDALKACHEW DOWN FROM OFFICE!

HANG AKLILU!

THE SPARK OF FREEDOM HAS JUST BEEN SEEN!

THE ARMY IS FOR THE PEOPLE!

BRING BACK ALL THE MONEY THAT IS IN FOREIGN BANKS!

UNTIL THE PUBLIC CAN VOTE, LET THE MILITARY TAKE OVER!

LET US HAVE FREEDOM OF SPEECH!

Like most revolutions it soon turned sour. Red Terror. White
Terror. Old scores violently settled.

Alistair was playing six-a-side cricket at the General Wingate
School cricket pitch one afternoon, when the sound of multiple
gun shots rang out to signal the executions of the first sixty —
Ministers and members of the old Government.

Summary justice and the use of arbitrary firing squads were not
to Alistair's taste. Not that it was just "not cricket" to arrest and
gun down the opposition, to murder the Emperor; it would
inevitably create a cycle of violence and civil war, and would
prevent the country from dealing effectively with its own legacy
of poverty and famine.

Apart from being a keen occasional cricketer, Alistair also used
to enjoy horse-riding. When he went riding around Entoto some
days later, all the Ethiopian children chased after him, shouting
out "Ferenji! Ferenji!" and throwing stones at him. This was not

an unusual experience, he recalled.

When he woke up on New Year's Day, 2004, Alistair was feeling a lot better. He didn't have a hangover, he felt at peace with the world, and he wrote in big letters in his new diary something that really surprised him: *This is the year I retire — hooray!*

Operation Hercules

Sometimes Andrew Longman felt that his whole life had been like *Operation Hercules*, but in fact "Hercules" had only lasted three years, when he'd held a post in the Press and Information Section of the British Embassy in Prague, just before the Velvet Revolution.

Andrew only learnt about the operation several years after he'd left the employment of the Foreign and Commonwealth Office, and about eighteen years after the fall of Communism. A Czech friend had tipped him off that he could apply to read the StB (Státní bezpečnost) files of the Secret Political Security Police that were now lodged in the archives of the Ministry of the Interior. He was given a contact name and an email address, and one day he decided to make an inquiry.

He received the intriguing answer that there were indeed a considerable number of files, written in both Czech and Slovak, which could be studied in the Reading Room of the Ministry, if he could demonstrate a genuine research interest. There were apparently too many pages to be photocopied by the small staff, and the quality was not always very good. Some files were still classified as Top Secret, for reasons of national security, but all the others, consisting of 1400 pages, had been declassified. Unfortunately none of the hundreds of photographs taken by agents of the secret police could be made available.

Out of curiosity, Andrew wrote to make an appointment. Maybe he could turn the material into a book, as others had done.

It all proved to be very straightforward. Andrew flew to Prague on 28 January 2007. The Divisional Principal of the Interior Ministry's Security Forces Archives had made sweeping changes, as he had a mission to make as much accessible to historians and researchers as possible. Until that time some archivists had seen their primary role as the close guarding of files and documents, not as helping to facilitate access to citizens or former foreign diplomats.

When he arrived at the reading-room in Prague, he found the staff exceptionally helpful, welcoming and friendly. A young archivist called Anna brought him four large boxes of files and some rolls of microfilmed documents, and let him get on with it, but she was happy to answer his questions from time to time. Andrew hardly moved from his chair for a week. He made many pages of notes, but in the end, he managed to get everything photocopied.

The Security Police had been able to obtain detailed reports about most of the parties he'd given and the events he'd organised, with full copies of the guest-lists and the names of all those who'd attended. There wasn't much that they'd missed. Agents who'd reported on him had been given code-names.

An early secret police report, the source of which must have been an informer from among his own staff, was devoted to his "Personality Characteristics". He'd been perceived as seemingly very self-confident and self-reliant (*velmi sebevědomě*) in his role, but it was noted that he'd felt uneasy when first crossing the Czechoslovak frontier, and once become very agitated when he was stuck in the lift for half an hour at the weekend in a pitch-black office cellar, after the power had failed, or the fuse had blown, and the rickety old lift had dropped to the bottom of the shaft, past its ground-floor end-stop. The doors had been shut tight. Apparently he'd called out for help. That wasn't such an unnatural reaction, thought Andrew.

The informer (a source he could easily recognise from the context) claimed, in his hostile report and unflattering character sketch, made much of the fact that Andrew had repeatedly called out for help. Andrew was prepared to admit to himself that he might have said, after the power eventually came back on, that he'd thought he was going to burst in that black hole. He'd been really bursting, after all. Too much Czech beer at lunchtime! Who wouldn't call for help in such a situation?

He discovered that outside Prague he'd been followed everywhere, sometimes by as many as fourteen StB agents and, on one occasion, by 27 different cars in the course of one day. He could now find out what meals he'd eaten, what books and records he'd bought, what items he'd been carrying, what colour clothes he'd worn, what he'd been chatting about and even the hand gestures he'd made on particular occasions or days.

On the basis of his official function (and their own practices) they had wrongly assumed and actively suspected, from the beginning and almost right until the end of his posting, that he *must* naturally have been involved in developing unfriendly, anti-Czechoslovak activities and that he was bound to have been a member of, or cooperating closely with, the British Secret Services; and that therefore he was someone who had to be closely watched, followed and secretly photographed wherever he went, especially outside Prague. They'd kept him constantly shadowed and under the most vigilant full surveillance. They'd put bugs in his home while he was away and ordered devices to be put in his hotel rooms, the ZTU ANALYZA apparatus, the ZTU

DIAGRAM and the ZTU/ORION, amongst other sophisticated devices.

Andrew felt it was a pity that none of the hundreds of secret photographs were made available. Was it vanity? In Prague they had had all the agents and technology they needed, including detailed drawings of his house and office. They'd been through his briefcase and studied various documents on the one occasion that he'd left it in his hotel room. Their objectives had been to control and monitor his activity. However professional they'd been, thought Andrew, as he read the files, they could monitor but no way could they control!

One of the most fascinating but absurdly surreal documents Andrew found on his files dated to May, 1989, when mjr.JUDr. Josef Klaus of the Kriminalistický Ústav Veřejne Bezpečnosti, sent a sample of his handwriting (somehow obtained from his office) for psychological diagnosis, analysis and interpretation to the psychologist and handwriting expert Dr. L.Novotný, CSc. It consisted of several pages of Andrew's innocuous handwritten comments on a form relating to the exhibition of contemporary British art at the National Gallery from the 18th of June to the 9th of August 1987.

Dr. Novotný's report consisted of three pages; initially he'd assessed Andrew, or rather his personality and strengths, as adaptable, consistent, logical, original, inventive, intuitive, intelligent ("highly above average in general potential, intellectual ability and professional intelligence"), possessed with wide knowledge, a good memory, a talent for improvisation, problem-solving, communication and decision-making. Andrew felt gratified. Maybe there was something in all this, after all; but then he read on. He was also described as emotional, and, on the negative side, as ambiguous, difficult to pin down, impenetrable, slippery, dissembling (dissimulating/double-faced) — "one of the results of his level of intellectuality", motivated by a complex "life strategy" and more likely to be a factor with those people or associates who didn't know Andrew well.

Andrew's was supposedly a contradictory and complex personality, full of inner conflicts: on the one hand authoritative of judgement and opinion, on the other hand ambiguous and reserved. Although sociable, interested in other people and good at making contacts, he was also likely to withdraw into himself and close up. Other "examples of his inner conflicts" were apparently his strong basic urges and instincts and an essential need for emotional phantasy, which contrasted with his coldness, distance, sense of alienation and inapproachability. The handwriting assessor went on to say that Andrew's easily made relationships were likely to be superficial and to remain at the level of contacts.

"*Real* relationships the writer considers a risk and a danger and in conflict with his egoism; his instincts loom higher in his motivation than the sphere of ideals and intellect." Apparently Andrew's value-orientation included a sense of self-esteem and self-importance, but his limited social adaptability was masked or covered by "skilful and convincing dissimulation" and efforts to rationalise, by a discreet undemanding demeanour and by witty repartee, the basis of which was *intrigue and eel-like slipperiness*, that had been inferred from the way he formed the letters *s* and *g*! Andrew didn't like that word, "*uhořovitost*". In fact the more he read about his apparent life-strategy, his alleged materialism, lack of self-restraint, irritability, anxieties, attempts to be accommodating and apparent lack of composure, the less he liked or recognised the character as interpreted by the handwriting expert.

Andrew found the punch-line quite amusing: it seemed that the basis of his personality lay in his strong affective instincts, emotionality, phantasy, lack of self-control and "tempestuous sex" *(bouřlivý sex)*, which could "break down the barrier of will and intellectual resolution!"

Andrew thought it could have been worse. It was a very detailed but pseudo-scientific "horoscope". The psychologist had obviously enjoyed trying to impress his superiors. It was absurd but funny. They must have been getting very worried about his growing influence and the range of his network of contacts, dissident friends and sympathisers. The Czech and Slovak security services would certainly have been greatly disappointed that they couldn't prove their theories. There were no honey-traps or secret scenes of tempestuous extramarital sex to be filmed, recorded or observed. There was no evidence at all to indicate that he had ever worked as a spy or as an occasional undercover agent; there was nothing whatsoever with which they could attempt to blackmail him.

If the analysts and secret policemen were persistent, that might come later. They would keep trying.

Maumbury Rings

Alan had always been fascinated by the folklore of Dorset and he frequently visited the Dorset County Museum and the History Centre.

When he was made redundant, he decided to move from his house in perfect, princely Poundbury to an apartment close to the ancient amphitheatre known as Maumbury Rings.

Whenever he went to the museum, he never failed to study the archaeological finds from Maumbury Rings, and particularly the carved chalk phallus found in the filling of one of the Neolithic shafts. He'd become obsessed by it.

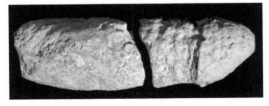

Although Alan had never married, he still hoped that one day he might father a child, and he firmly believed that the chalk phallus, although it was broken in two, might work its magic charms, as a kind of neolithic fertility totem, a Dorset mojo.

There was a police station right in front of his apartment block. This gave him a sense of security, even though the police had recently put up a sign on the entrance gate to the park, about increasing incidents of anti-social behaviour, including harassment, and about the powers they'd been granted to disperse groups of loiterers, of homeless alcoholics or intimidating young people. The sign drew attention to Section 30 of the Anti-social Behaviour Act 2003: "groups of two or more people in the relevant locality may be given directions to disperse."

It was signed by the Superintendent and the Chief Inspector of Police, and continued:

> Over the past six months there has been an escalation of incidents relating to Anti-social behaviour caused by groups of youths, young adults, rough sleepers and their associates. I consider that members of the public have been intimidated, harassed, alarmed or distressed and that anti-social behaviour is a significant and persistent problem in the locality.

The skateboard rink on the other side of the Weymouth Road, although only a hundred yards from his house, didn't really bother Alan or the police. It gave the kids something to do and it gave him something to look at when he was working in his study. Kids sometimes brought their mountain bikes across the road and rode up and down the grassy hillocks in the park. But Alan was more haunted by the past than by the present.

Only after he'd bought the apartment did he fully appreciate that this pretty park with the eerie earthworks right outside his window had, for hundreds of years, been the site of the town's gallows, of public hangings and gruesome scenes of drawing and quartering, with up to ten thousand people gathered round on the grassy banks, delighting in the final agonies of dying criminals and traitors. Eighty rebels had been executed there after the Monmouth Rebellion, sentenced to hang by ruthless Judge Jeffreys.

Alan had known about it but he'd never really been able to *imagine* such scenes of horror.

Thomas Hardy had described it as a sinister and melancholy place. He'd been fascinated by the grisly burning there on the 21st of March 1706 of eighteen-year-old Mary Channing (born in May, 1687) for allegedly poisoning her husband.

Alan had never read "The Mayor of Casterbridge" until he'd come to live in Dorchester, but the eleventh chapter of that novel had begun to fill him with dread, especially Hardy's grim account of how Mary's heart had burst and "leapt out of her body, to the terror of them all". None of the spectators, Hardy wrote with a touch of black humour, "ever cared particularly for hot roast after that".

"The historic circle was the frequent spot for appointments of a furtive kind. Intrigues were arranged there; tentative meetings were there experimented after divisions and feuds. But one kind of appointment — in itself the most common of any — seldom had place in the Amphiteatre: that of happy lovers" (*The Mayor of Casterbridge*, Chapter XI).

Alan had once witnessed the strange antics and ritualistic ceremonies of latter-day pagans, or Druids, celebrating the solstice. He was fascinated, if initially intimidated, by this motley group of strangely dressed but peacefully chanting men and women, and he plucked up courage to approach them in order to learn more about them.

Until then, his mind had gone not to these peace-loving people but to the bloody gladiatorial contests that must have taken place there in Roman times. And somewhere he'd read that, 2500 years before the Romans, Maumbury Rings had been a Late Neolithic henge. Apparently fragments of human skulls from that period had been found there. The Romans had merely adapted the henge, just as it was adapted once again — as an artillery fort — during the Civil War of the seventeenth century.

If Thomas Hardy had thought it appropriate to use the setting of Maumbury Rings for the furtive meeting of Michael Henchard and Susan, perhaps Alan himself might make a romantic connection on his evening walk at dusk, or by joining the pagan order of modern Druids and witches. He made a careful note of the dates of their rituals, especially those held on the Spring and Autumn equinox, Halloween and the Summer and Winter Solstice: Imbolc (the beginning of spring), Alban Eilir (the spring equinox), Beltane (May Day), Alban Hefin (the summer solstice), Lughnasadh (the harvest festival) Alban Elfed (the autumn equinox), Samhain (the beginning of winter) and Alban Arthan (the winter solstice).

He spoke to Arch-Druid Melkin of the local Order, and to other high-ranking Druids called Taloch and Wildfox. He joined the group and was inducted into the members' traditional rites, which celebrated the forces of nature, and he came to share their pagan beliefs, calling on the spirits in places and stone circles that they considered sacred, but he was shocked to find how they became a target for threats and abuse. A dead bird with a noose around its neck was left on the windscreen of the group's van. Onlookers shouted abuse and barracked them: "Die Witches!" and suchlike.

Alan felt drawn to a particularly attractive witch, and he soon made up his mind that she would become his partner and lover. They would meditate and chant together, but she didn't become pregnant, which was something they both wanted. They decided they would *liberate* the carved chalk Neolithic phallus from the County Museum, and re-bury it in the Maumbury Rings shaft, or approximately in the place from which it had been excavated. First they would attempt to cement the two halves together, without causing any permanent damage, to ensure the fertility magic would work.

They re-buried it in the dead of night, and then they gathered their fellow Druids around them in a ring, to celebrate in meditative silence according to an ancient ritual.

Once the baby was born, Alan returned to the museum and left the chalk phallus on top of the glass display case from which he had removed it — where it can be still be seen, once again in two pieces, but as potent as ever it was.

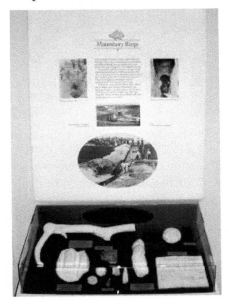

Margarita's brass beds

What sort of bed do you like to sleep in? Do you remember your first cot? Did you ever sleep in your parents' bed? Do you like to be covered by lots of heavy blankets or to dive under a feather-light duvet? Margarita likes to sleep in her comfy modern king-size bed, but when she was young she had to sleep in a big brass bed, which stood very high off the ground. She had to climb onto a chair in order to get into her bed.

Margarita still has the two big brass beds that belonged to her father; she keeps them up in the attic. Her father bought them at an auction of old palace furniture which the Greek state no longer wanted to keep. The beds were designed for a Royal palace, that you could tell, from the elaborate workmanship and artistic refinements, the little adornments on the ornate brass bedsteads such as the Royal crests and the delicately moulded screws and fancifully-sculpted bed-knobs at the head and foot of the beds and the ingenious way that all the parts of the beds fitted perfectly together.

Nowadays the beds might wobble a bit, because a few of the big, individually-made brass screws were missing, which was why the two beds were consigned to the attic bedroom; but when they were new the frames locked together as solidly as a building designed to withstand an earthquake. And when they were polished, the brass shone, how the brass shone! To keep such big brass beds shining all the time, you would need a lot of helpers, and nowadays people don't have maids and servants to spend their days polishing such enormous metal frames, with all the detailed patterns incised and engraved on the decorative parts of the bedsteads..

They'd belonged originally to Sisi or Elizabeth, the Empress of Bavaria, Empress of Austria, Queen of Hungary and to her husband, Franz Joseph I, Emperor of Austria and King of Hungary. She brought the beds to Corfu, all the way from Vienna.

Later on, they belonged to the bellicose German Emperor and King of Prussia, His Imperial Majesty the Kaiser Wilhelm II. How would you like to sleep in the bed that once belonged to a king called Kaiser Frederich Wilhelm Viktor Albert of Hohenzollern and to his wife Augusta Viktoria Fredericke Luise Feodoira von Schleswig-Holstein-Sonderburg-Augustenberg? What a mouthful! You'd soon fall asleep trying to repeat their names more than three or four times after you'd gone to bed!

Kaiser Wilhelm always liked to say that the German people needed "a place in the sun". This is what he said in a speech in 1901:

> In spite of the fact that we do not have a fleet such as we should have, we have won for ourselves a place in the sun. It will now be my job to see to it that this place in the sun will remain our undisputed possession, so that the sun's rays may fall fruitfully on our activity and trade in foreign parts, that our industry and agriculture may develop within the state and our sailing sports upon the water, for our future lies upon the water. The more Germans go out upon the waters, whether it be in races or regattas, in voyages across the ocean, or in the service of the battle flag, so much the better it will be for us.

Kaiser Wilhelm wasn't talking about Corfu, as Corfu didn't

belong to the Germans, and it was the Greek King himself who had suggested that he should buy the Achilleion Palace. Although he was a megalomaniac with a militaristic mind, Kaiser Wilhelm, the King of Prussia, didn't see Corfu as Napoleon had done, as an important strategic base in the Mediterranean Sea. He was a very nervy, aggressive man and he simply liked to spend his holidays there.

Sir Edward Grey, Britain's Foreign Secretary of the time, wrote about the Kaiser in The Daily Telegraph in November 1908, the same year that the Kaiser spent his first holiday on Corfu:

> The German Emperor is ageing me; he is like a battleship with steam up and screws going, but with no rudder, and he will run into something some day and cause a catastrophe. He has the strongest army in the world and the Germans don't like being laughed at and are looking for somebody on whom to vent their temper and use their strength. After a big war a nation doesn't want another for a generation or more. Now it is 38 years since Germany had her last war, and she is very strong and very restless, like a person whose boots are too small for him. I don't think there will be war at present, but it will be difficult to keep the peace of Europe for another five years.

Even if the Emperor's boots were too small for him, his bed was rather too big for him. Sometimes he would have it wheeled out onto the terrace of the Achilleion Palace, where he would enjoy his afternoon siesta in the shade of his favourite palm or olive tree.

Empress Elizabeth had loved Corfu from the moment she first set foot on the island. She also wanted a place in the sun, but for rather different reasons. She had drunk the water from the Kardaki Spring. The people of Corfu used to say that if you drank from the spring, you would always return to the island. Sisi was a very romantic Empress, she had been considered the most beautiful Princess in the whole of Europe. She didn't want an ordinary house. She wanted a palace which would bring back some of the glory of ancient Greece: "a Palace safe from prying eyes, a palace worthy of Achilles, who despised all mortals and did not even fear the gods."

Elizabeth was born in 1837 and was married to Franz Joseph in April 1854. In 1861 she gave orders for her palace to be built on Corfu, and she did not worry about the cost. Sculptors came to Corfu from Italy, and other workmen were brought from different parts of Europe to perfect the fairy palace, but it seems she did not like it very much once it had been built. Although a very beautiful woman, she lead a lonely, restless life, and the brass beds she had brought from Vienna did little to console her, to help her relax and calm her nerves, to have pleasant dreams of her heroes like Achilles or the poet Heinrich Heine, or even to get to sleep.

Kaiser Wilhelm bought the Achilleion Palace with most of the remaining furniture, including brass beds, in 1907. Every April, he arrived in Corfu accompanied by a large retinue. He liked to spend at least a month, sometimes much of the summer there, and he came every year from 1908 until the First World War. Perhaps he couldn't relax on the beds either, if he was so busy planning for an even bigger "place in the sun" for the German people, rattling his sabers and preparing for the First World War.

Apart from the two brass beds, Margarita's father had also bought one of Kaiser Wilhelm's sabers at the auction. Was it one of the sabers the Kaiser used to rattle so threateningly? It looked as if it had been rattled a lot.

But why did Empress Elizabeth not like her Palace, once it had been built? Well, it wasn't at all as she had imagined it. It was too large and luxurious for its beautiful natural surroundings, she felt. It was out of keeping with the countryside, the olive groves and the little houses belonging to the poor Greek farmers who lived in the area. It was really rather tasteless, she decided, more Italian than Greek, and the sculptures she had commissioned did not look at all the way she had imagined the ancient Greeks, although she liked the sculpture of Achilles, and the statue of her favourite poet, Heinrich Heine.

She never visited the island after 1896. It would have been better if she'd stayed there, with her brass beds and her sculptures of the Greek heroes and gods, because poor Sisi was assassinated in Geneva on September the 10th, 1898.

The Achilleion Palace was empty for much of the time until

1907, and the brass beds became tarnished and dull, because nobody ever came to polish them. In that year the Achilleion Palace was bought by Kaiser Wilhelm, who seemed to love Greece even more than Empress Elizabeth had done. He would come from Berlin with his wife and most of his court.

Although they changed a lot of the furniture, he and his wife liked to sleep in the two brass beds. Once they'd been polished they were as good as new, bright and shining.

So there they slept, Kaiser Frederich Wilhelm Viktor Albert of Hohenzollern and his wife Augusta Viktoria Fredericke Luise Feodora von Schleswig-Holstein-Sonderburg-Augustenberg .

Have you managed to memorise their names yet? If you like you can call him Willie or Fred.

Margarita's father just happened to be present at the auction when some of the Achilleion furniture was to be sold, and when his eyes fell on the two beautiful big brass beds, he knew he would have to make a bid for them. If they were good enough for an Emperor and an Empress, they were good enough for him. They would go very well with the beautifully-embroidered sheets, pillowcases, bed-linen and blankets that had come as part of the dowry that Margarita's mother brought with her when she married him.

Margarita herself was born in one of the big brass beds. Later on her father would sit on the side of the bed and read her stories. Sometimes he would tell her the story of the Empress Elizabeth and her fairy palace. He didn't talk so much about Kaiser Wilhelm or his saber.

Sometimes when little Margarita had to stay in bed because she was ill, she would imagine that the lumps and creases in the blankets were mountains and valleys, and that she was a traveler with a long journey ahead. At other times she would imagine that the beds could levitate above the floor or fly up in the sky.

Once she fell out of her bed, which gave her an awful shock, because the mattress was a long way from the hard planks of the wooden floor.

Margarita knew every inch of the bed, and she admired the way it had been made, with the beautifully-sculpted brass knobs, the hand-made design on the head-piece, the fascinating brass-screws, each one a little bit different.

Beds can be happy or very, very sad places. Babies are born in them, stories are read in them, dreams are dreamt in them, plans are made in them, men and women cuddle up and make love in them, but people also die in them.

Margarita's brass beds have quite a history, and I don't want to dwell on some of the sad things associated with them.

I always like to remember Margarita's children playing all over the two brass beds. Little Julian used to climb up and down, jump all over them as if the big mattresses were trampolines. Sophie used to pretend she too was traveling across the mountains and the valleys of the blankets, traveling far, far away, as far as Australia, China or America.

Sometimes they loved to hide under the beds and to pretend that all the problems of the world had vanished forever.

Margarita and her English husband slept sounder and more peacefully in those two brass beds than any Emperor or Empress had ever done!

The martyr of the people

Hugo believed in the divine right of kings and in the divine right of men, not *all* men, but in his own semi-divine rights, certainly. He didn't approve of *Droit du Seigneur*, but he had inherited some of the medieval attitudes and delusions of grandeur attributed to many men of power and influence, of the kind even to be encountered in Hollywood.

He didn't want to admit to himself that he had developed an unhealthy obsession, until he discovered some fancy, pseudo-scientific words for it: *progonoplexia* and *ancestoritis*. He'd discovered these strange and novel terms on websites devoted to family history, ancestry and heritage.

It was a Scottish–Australian who had made him take more than a casual interest in the matter of his family history. His Australian friend claimed to be able to show that Hugo was a direct descendant of Charles II and Nell Gwynn, which seemed romantic enough, if mildly embarrassing. Hugo wasn't a great researcher, historian or academic, but he had started to imagine that he could see some family likenesses in one of the portraits of Nell Gwynn and in some of the paintings of King Charles I.

He became increasingly motivated to create and draw his family tree. After he'd started out on his genealogical research, he soon became convinced that he was *indeed* a descendant of Charles II and Nell Gwynn. His great-great-grandmother, he discovered, was a direct descendant of Charles and Nell; no matter that there were hundreds of other people who could claim that they descended from Charles II or one of his numerous mistresses — and there were probably many more unacknowledged offspring.

Hugo had also become obsessed by the beheading of the father of Charles II, King Charles I, "the martyr of the people", on January the 30th, 1649. Every time he thought about the regicide, or looked at the engravings of the execution, he imagined that it was his own neck on the block. He suffered from frequent nightmares and would often wake up in a cold sweat, hearing the shocked groans of the crowd. When he read about the beheadings carried out in Syria by "Jihadi" John and his ISIS accomplices, he felt the same shivers of horror.

He preferred to think about the works of art that Charles had collected in happier times; about the restoration of the monarchy and the libertine court of Charles II. *Those were the days*, he'd tell himself, when reading the works of Samuel Pepys, John Wilmot, the Earl of Rochester, John Dryden and Aphra Behn. He'd soon bought every book he could find about the life of Nell Gwynn, and he felt proud that he could claim such an attractive and talented actress as a predecessor, whatever her reputation. She had been the King's favourite mistress, and he had chosen to recognise and ennoble their two natural children. Their first son, Charles Beauclerk, was given the title, Duke of St. Albans. And *Let not poor Nelly starve* were probably the last words the King spoke on his deathbed.

Hugo kept thinking about those last words of Charles II, his prayer that Nelly might not starve. Hugo would always go to look at portraits of Nell Gwynn and King Charles II, whenever he went to visit galleries in London. The more research Hugo did, the more excited he became. He discovered links in his family tree to famous court beauties whose portraits had been painted by important artists of the time.

He had a shock of (fanciful?) genetic recognition when he saw in a book the portrait by Nicolas de Largillière of the two young Stuarts, *Prince James and his Sister*. He was convinced that his mother, in photographs taken when she was a child, looked the spitting image of Prince James in that portrait of 1695.

There had also been a proud and strong Scottish tradition in his family, with occasional mentions of Ladies-in-Waiting to Royalty, of Earls and Countesses, of aristocrats, distinguished clansmen and landowners with extensive estates and a taste for hunting and shooting; but there was no great enthusiasm for talking about the past. His mother had certainly been brought up in the grand Edwardian style, with nannies and servants, boarding schools and wonderful holidays at the best hotels in fashionable seaside resorts. Hugo had inherited many old photographs and letters which provided extensive evidence of what *might have been* his own legacy, all things being equal.

In the absence of precise scientific DNA tests, all this was evidence enough for Hugo, who did go so far as to pay for an Ancestry kit test; the results didn't rule out a strong element of Scottish DNA. The analysis didn't tell him very much that he hadn't already guessed or imagined, except for his high proportions of Scottish *and* Scandinavian genes. Some of his ancestors must have been Vikings! His genealogical researches and speculations provided food for many phantasies, with Stuarts on one side and Vikings on the other. He decided he would buy a long Viking sword with a double-edged blade. He thought he would also try to find a Scottish claymore or a basket-hilt long sword, of the kind that might have been wielded by the Highland clansman, Rob Roy, for he felt the growing need to be able to protect himself against any future upstart Cromwells, so that he could defend his rights and his inheritance. He would keep a small armoury in his home. He didn't plan to follow his martyred ancestor to the executioner's block, to suffer the ultimate humiliation, or to feel the sharp edge of the axe.

When his great-grandfather died, the stately eighteenth-century Scottish mansion passed to the eldest son, with the entire estate of sixteen thousand acres.

Hugo was eventually left with very little, apart from some fine furniture, paintings, silverware, copies of wills, birth and death certificates, shares and leather-bound books. Although he didn't inherit much money or any land, Hugo comforted himself by thinking that he had undoubtedly inherited good genes, blue blood and aristocratic manners.

It was a tricky business, family history, but he still wanted to learn as much as he could about his illustrious ancestors, who by now had formed a significant part of his identity and his sense of reflected glory. He couldn't accept that it had become an obsession.

Luckily he never bragged about it, and he managed to bring his *progonoplexia* under control, especially after his Australian friend, the diligent researcher, suddenly announced that a number of Hugo's other ancestors, whom Hugo had largely overlooked and subconsciously discounted — ancestors from his father's side of the family — had been tenant farmers, colliers and miners.

"Ah, well," thought Hugo, who tried to look on the bright side, and who truly believed that he was a jolly good mixer, a gentleman *and* a man of the people — and that he wasn't a snob, social climber or elitist at heart — "even *that* information could come in handy if Jeremy Corbyn ever comes to power."

He wouldn't starve.

Culture shock

I still have a few letters that Philippa sent me from Ethiopia, where she had gone to work for a few years as a volunteer teacher of English for VSO (Voluntary Service Overseas). She hadn't travelled very widely, and had never ventured outside Northern Europe. She wanted to see more of the world, so when they offered her the chance to go to Addis Ababa, she jumped at it.

She left England in September, 1971. I didn't hear from her for five months. I assumed that she had forgotten all about me. In her first letter, dated the 22nd of January 1972, she wrote:

> It wasn't until the Timkat Festival, which has just finished, that I began to feel the pulse of the people. Up until then, I felt the alienated European unable to come to grips with the culture of the country. Everything started to change after I was invited to a wedding, although I still suffered from culture shock. The wedding luncheon was attended by several hundred Ethiopians and a dozen foreigners, office acquaintances of the bride. It was held inside a large marquee, a buffet banquet which must have cost much more than the families could afford. The food spread down the length of ten trestle tables. The first delicacy to catch my attention was the sheep, skinned and cooked on a spit, standing grotesquely on its own four legs, its eyeballs removed and replaced by stuffed olives. It stared reproachfully at the hungry guests, as one of the servants carved chunks of meat off its rump.
>
> Raw beef (I *assume* it was beef) was also offered in abundance. It reminded me of what James Bruce described in his travels. Animals would be kept alive for the duration of a long journey, raw steaks being cut and eaten, as required, from under a flap of skin on their backsides.
>
> Here the scene seemed almost as incongruous, bloody rough-cut steaks held in the hands and greedily devoured by

Ethiopian gentlemen dressed in Western suits, washed down with *talla* or *tej*.

The wedding was somewhat spoiled for me by a conversation with an Ethiopian colleague who was sitting beside me. The occasion prompted him to relate his own wedding experiences, which were somewhat different as he was a Moslem. His parents had chosen a suitable bride to whom he did not speak, except to get engaged, until their wedding day, a year after the choice had been made for him. He was expected, as is the custom, to prove on the wedding night that she was a virgin. He told me that his friends waited in the next room, plying him with beer, in spite of his religion, after each unsuccessful attempt (he was very tired and psychologically out of shape). Finally his best friend came to his aid, and cut his arm, putting a few drops of blood on a handkerchief. The bride's virginity and the bridegroom's virility were thus assured to the general satisfaction of the wedding guests.

Philippa's next letter was undated, but I received it shortly afterwards.

I had a relaxing day exploring the area around Entoto, learning to drive a Ministry of Education Land Rover down tracks amongst the eucalyptus trees. Just now I witnessed something quite shocking. A small crowd of children and old women were gathered in the road leading to Trinity Cathedral, behind Parliament. The Emperor was back from his visit to Nigeria and had gone to pray. This may be his normal practice, or it may have something to do with the fact that Brigadier Sandford died yesterday, aged 89 (ironically I was eating my first plums from Mulu Farm today).

I went to catch a glimpse of His Imperial Majesty as he left the cathedral. Outside the gate the police were behaving in an unnecessarily violent fashion, beating the onlookers back with their heavy wooden sticks. There seemed to be no justification for the actions of the police, as the crowd was really very small. The Emperor's limousine stopped outside the gate of the cathedral and several high-ranking army officers jumped out and joined the police in beating back this small crowd. The Emperor simply sat in his car and seemed quite unconcerned at this treatment of his loyal subjects who had been applauding and ululating enthusiastically. The officers got back in his car and it was driven on towards where I was standing. An old woman carrying a prayer-stick knelt down to try to give a letter or a petition to the Emperor as he passed. A policeman pushed her and she fell, her letter falling to the ground. The Emperor's face was grimly indifferent, even though his car nearly ran the woman down. I felt very disillusioned. I'd witnessed this quite by chance.

I received another letter from Philippa in July. She'd just been to see Eisenstein's classic film *Battleship Potemkin* at the USSR

Exhibition Centre. There was a small audience of around forty
Ethiopian university students. It was a special screening.

They'd been told that the film was about the Russian
revolution of 1905, a topic which obviously intrigued them. I
had seen the film once before in London, where some people
had laughed at the word-captions and overt propaganda. Here
in Addis the reaction was quite different. The film really *lived*
for the Ethiopians. It was topical and potently relevant. They
were glued to the screen, watching it with unusual intensity; I
could hear suppressed clapping and whispered comments
from all corners. The atmosphere was electric, they were all
deeply involved. At the end, when the lights went on, they
were calm and quiet and made no comments, but there were
many points of reference for them, the role of the armed
forces and their brutality in recent Ethiopian history (towards
the students, and at the time of the attempted coup); the
scenes of the famous stone lions at Odessa; the autocratic
figures; the legless cripple coming down the Odessa steps (like
so many cripples in Addis); the figure of the Orthodox priest
— and the overpowering sense of the *people,* the injustices
suffered by the vast peasant population under the autocratic
rule of the "big men".

Afterwards they would only comment on Eisenstein's technique, such as "the diagonal compositions were very effective" and "the cutting was unusual and interesting". I did learn one of the reasons for their reticence. 49% of the university students have been expelled. Not long ago six hundred students were taken out to Senafe to a sort of work camp, in order for the police to catch the ring-leaders who have been organising the boycotting of lectures. I forgot to mention that the Emperor has been celebrating his eightieth birthday.

Philippa's last letter was very brief, sent a few weeks before the end of her VSO assignment, when she was due to leave Addis to fly home.

I also omitted to tell you something rather more important. I am pregnant. I can feel the baby kicking inside me. I feel quite unprepared for parenthood.

In spite of that, she wrote that she'd been out on the streets, perhaps the only *ferenji* caught up in a student demonstration. She promised to write again, to describe the fast-moving situation in the capital. She never made it back to England. I learned from one of her Ethiopian friends that, only a few days later, she'd decided to take photographs of another, bigger, protest march.

She was hit by a stray bullet, perhaps a ricochet. She was taken to St. Paul's Hospital for the Poor, but shockingly it took more than an hour to get her admitted. The nurses and doctors did their best to save her, but she'd lost too much blood and she died that evening.

A year later her Ethiopian friend sent me a copy of a poster for a revolutionary play about the suppression of the students' uprising, which he said had been inspired in part by what had happened to Philippa.

He added that soon after the revolution he'd been drafted to a work-brigade to help educate the peasants in the countryside, teaching literacy and modern agricultural practices and trying to help build schools, as part of the Derg's *Zamacha* campaign, "A Drop of Sweat for Development". He admitted that he knew nothing whatsoever about agriculture or building. The peasants had tried to teach him.

I sometimes wonder if he was the father of the baby that Philippa would have had if she had lived.

Miroslav's dream

It seemed like a random check at Prague's Ruzyně Airport when a minor official asked me to open my bags. I'd just returned from an officially approved visit abroad, to give a reading at a Festival of Czechoslovak Culture.

At first he was quite polite. He took a look at my diary, my notebook, a pad on which I draft poems. He started to read and to ask questions, to press me for the names of my friends. It seemed that he wanted to vet me, my thoughts, my ideas, my beliefs. He questioned my choice of words and some that he couldn't decipher.

It was now an interrogation. He was becoming more hostile and suspicious. "Now I've been given your case, I have to be thorough and probe. Tell me whom did you meet, and why? And what do you mean by *this* scribble?" He pointed at some lines on my pad.

"They're just some ideas for a poem," I replied, "some ideas I had to jot down during the flight."

"We'll have to see about that," said the man. "Please write down the full names of your friends."

"Some of them now live abroad."

"Never mind, I'm sure we can find them. We need to know much more about you, your schooldays, your childhood, all your jobs. Come with me."

I questioned his right to detain me in a small office in a corner of the arrivals lounge. "Why pick on me?"

"Someone saw you on the aeroplane, writing for much of the flight. Whatever you bring back into this country is subject to spot checks and searches. We're charged with an onerous duty — to prevent plots and acts of subversion. Your behaviour caught our attention, the way you were writing so fast. You seemed somewhat over-excited, preoccupied and strangely intense. You aroused the steward's suspicions; we received our agent's alert. We'll have to retain your diary, your notebook and list of friends. You may go, but we'll soon come to see you, if we find that your thoughts are a threat. It's for the sake of the nation's security. That's the way that we work. It's not just the printed word that we're policing; it's the hand-written word we fear most. We will consult our hand-writing experts. We have graphologists, analysts and psychologists, and others on whom we can call. Don't worry, we have a good team. We'll find out what you think when you dream."

If I hadn't thought of myself as a dissident until that moment, the experience at Ruzyně Airport made me one. Within a short time, I was sentenced to six months in Ruzyně Prison, where I got to know another inmate, Václav Havel, who gave me hope and courage.

After I was released, I wasn't permitted to travel or to fly again until after the Velvet Revolution.

It would be twenty-three years before one of my secret dreams would come true. I had proudly signed Fero Fenič's petition of the 19th of December 2011 to change the name of the airport:

> The airport is a crossroad, a place of mingling and meeting and a symbol of the free movement of people and ideas. For Czechs, it was and is the gateway to freedom and for foreigners it's the first place through which they enter our country. Renaming it "Václav Havel Airport" shows our declaration to uphold values which we admire […] but it is also a reminder that we need to protect our freedom and democracy every day.

The Gap

David read the aluminium sign carefully before climbing over the fence to stand on a small natural platform, a rock-ledge overlooking the sheer drop into the wild ocean and the wave-beaten rocks below.

```
LIFELINE COUNSELLING  131 114

SALVO CRISIS LINE       9331 2000
```

Two choices!

For over six months he had been intensely aware that about two thousand people commit suicide each year in Australia, around twenty of them choosing to leap to their deaths from The Gap. Perhaps one or two had been pushed or thrown.

For several weeks he had been coming for walks here, contemplating the metre-high fence, with its three easily climbed timber struts, and the heavy-duty chicken wire covering the gaps between them. Apart from the fencing, it reminded him of some stretches of the Dorset Coastal Path. He still missed Dorset, the English county where he'd grown up. He'd emigrated to Australia when he was twenty-four, but only recently had he begun to regret it. He felt trapped. He couldn't afford to go home. He'd burned all his bridges.

He'd often read the small, discreet, easily missed aluminium sign tacked to the top wooden cross-bar here at The Gap. He'd heard talk of the local council plans to install closed circuit TV, free emergency telephones and a much higher fence, impossible to scale.

The Gap, Sydney's favourite suicide spot, on the way to the South Head of Port Jackson, belongs to the wealthy, well-groomed suburb of Watson's Bay. David had always loved coming here, to this ocean cliff and coastal walk with its dramatic views out over the ocean, and of the annual Sydney-to-Hobart race, as the yachts come out of the Heads and start sailing south towards Tasmania.

He loved the old colonial architecture and restored weatherboard fishermen's cottages with their tin roofs (now millionaires' homes and weekenders) at Watson's Bay, where he'd often go to have a cold beer or to eat fish and chips. He would sometimes sit under a tree and watch the firework displays in Sydney Harbour. He liked seeing them at a distance, away from the crowds.

He used to enjoy swimming at Camp Cove, which was netted, and where he felt safe from shark attacks. He didn't like taking unnecessary risks! He really loved the coastal walk to South Head, which lead past the secluded, mostly male, nudist beach of Lady Bay, to Hornby Lighthouse. He was sometimes tempted to join the Lady Bay swimmers, especially on his way back, when he got a good view of the beach, and of the naturalists sunbathing on the rocks or just standing there on the sand, exposing themselves to the curious scrutiny of all the passers-by.

David thought about writing a last text message. But then he decided he would dial the first number; he didn't fancy a crisis support conversation with a suicide-prevention volunteer from the Salvation Army. He had nothing to live for, anyway. He didn't need a lecture about Hope. "Hope saves lives," they say. David had no hope. There'd been a huge gaping gap in his own life, since his wife had walked out on him after they'd spent six years painstakingly restoring their dream house near Bowral, in the Southern Highlands of New South Wales. She'd become bored with the endless DIY and his collecting mania, his fussiness about antique furniture and interior decoration: one room per year, for six years! She'd needed another type of DIY, which he was always too tired to provide. He was more interested in watching cricket on television. He'd played himself when he was younger; although a good bowler, he'd hero-worshipped great batsmen and had always fancied himself as another Donald Bradman.

Now that the house was finished, it no longer had any meaning for him. He'd done it all for her.

He was about to dial the 24-hour Lifeline Counselling number, when he realised that his mobile phone battery was dead.

Only one solution!

He summoned up all his strength and hurled his mobile phone towards the sea. It smashed to pieces on the rocks below. He wouldn't need it anymore; but watching the impact made him shudder. It wasn't so much the flying bits of shattered plastic, so much as the loss of all the stored telephone numbers of his friends and loved ones which had hurtled into the void, into the surf to drown, without a chance to save themselves, or him.

He looked back at Macquarie Lighthouse.

He'd researched and staked out his suicide spot quite carefully. It gave him some comfort to know the local history of the place as he was soon going to become part of that history himself. It was more likely that he would become a simple statistic, one more forgotten person who contributed to The Gap's one per cent average of Australia's annual national suicide figures.

He thought of the shipwrecks that had occurred near this spot since the arrival of the First Fleet.

It suddenly occurred to him that perhaps he should have volunteered to become a part-time coastguard, even if they no longer needed lighthouse-keepers like Robert Watson!

Perhaps it was not too late for him to save some lives or to offer hope to sailors lost in storms! The sailors wouldn't be slow to express their gratitude. He could sell his house and move to the Eastern Suburbs! Could he even raise the wherewithal to return to England, to his beloved Dorset? What kind of work could he find there, even if he managed to get his act together?

He lit a cigarette, and climbed very deliberately back over the fence, feeling in his pocket out of habit, as if for the ghost presence of his mobile phone.

He found instead a tube of high-factor sunscreen, and applied some slowly to his lips and nose.

He promised himself he would come back soon, and perhaps even work up the courage to descend the stone steps to the beach at Lady Bay, to find some new mates, to celebrate Australia Day his *own* way.

Dorset could wait, like it had always waited. West Bay wasn't Watson's Bay, and the fish and chips weren't as good there, but the place held powerful childhood memories for him. It wasn't much of a harbour, even, but it was a *haven*.

He started humming the tune he knew for an old song called "Linden Lea" and recalled some of the words he'd once known so well:

> I be free to go abroad,
> Or take again my homeward road . . .

The returner

I'm *a returner* or *repeater* in the jargon, but they don't remember my name. I won't admit that on TripAdvisor, even though I've been coming here every summer for over thirty years. I never complain. I'm a loyal customer. I keep coming back. That's why they call me a returner. I always give the hotel five stars and a warm recommendation, but I don't always get a room with a view, even when I've made a special request and an early booking. There's always some good reason why my room is at the back of the hotel, overlooking the car park instead of the beach. I can understand the problems they face. There are many other repeat guests or returners who expect a room at the front. They have probably been coming for forty or fifty years. Some of them first came to stay over sixty years ago. They are obviously given the highest priority.

The proprietors always give me a smile of recognition when I check in with my suitcase and my lap-top. They give me a big hug when I depart for the airport at the end of my stay.

They make me feel part of the family. I wonder why they never remember my name. It is a shame that the Wi-Fi never seems to work, but I never mention that either. They say that the server is overloaded. Too many guests want to log in at the same time of the day or the night. If someone complains, they unplug the server, which immediately clears the system. At least everyone has the same fighting chance to get online, before the system becomes overloaded again.

I can get a good signal if I sit at a coffee table in the reception area. That's not very convenient when I'm doing research, which is one of the reasons that I keep returning to the island.

One day I hope to finish my book. I've decided to call it *The Returner*. When they see my name printed in big bold letters on the dust-jacket, maybe *then* they'll remember my name. I'll make sure

I present them with a personally inscribed copy, which I will sign very clearly. After my name I may even add, in brackets, *your happy repeat guest since 1985.*

Yemmerrawanne and John Henry

This is a story about two individuals, one who lived in the eighteenth century, the other in the twentieth, whose homelands were far from the British Isles; it is also about two Englishmen from the West Country, of different views and persuasions.

George and his cousin Jeremy would often argue about the concepts of collective guilt, inherited racial guilt related to serious wrongdoing, the gross abuse and infringement of human rights. They could become very heated about issues of potential legal liability; of the significance and advisability of politicians' formal apologies; of enduring moral responsibility for various nation's actions in the course of past centuries.

Although George had been born in Bristol, a city which had become rich as a result of the slave trade, he could never accept Jeremy's argument that he was indirectly complicit in the human trafficking that characterised the slave-trade, or that he should feel the need to atone or help to compensate for it, in whatever way he could.

Just because they were both British, did that make them indirectly responsible for the treatment and fate of the Aboriginal people of Australia?

George couldn't agree with his cousin that young German people should feel a sense of collective guilt for the fate of the Jews under Hitler. Jeremy had voted for Tony Blair in the general elections of 1997, 2001 and 2005. Did he therefore share a degree of responsibility for the invasion of Iraq, or for believing the contents of the "dodgy dossier"?

Jeremy could come up with a whole catalogue of cases. He blamed the Turks for past genocides, or alleged genocides; the Americans for their decimation of the indigenous people, the native American Indians; the Japanese for their treatment of POWs and Korean comfort women, or sex slaves; the Chinese for their killing of prisoners of conscience and of protesters in Tiananmen Square, for the vast numbers of deaths caused by the Great Famine and during Mao's Cultural Revolution; the Belgians for their atrocities in the Congo during the reign of King Leopold; the Bosnian Serbs for the massacre at Srebrenica; the Russians for the slaughter of their Royal Family, and the cruel excesses of Joseph Stalin, including the Gulags, his forced labour camps, and so on. George refused to accept that the present generations could be tarred with the same brush as their ancestors, but he did feel strongly that such events should never be forgotten, in case similar things should ever happen again.

Jeremy didn't give much credence to the idea of national character, but there was little doubt in his mind that, on occasion, drunk or arrogant British, German or Russian tourists were highly resented in some holiday destinations; that local people's memories stretched back far longer than the tourists realised, and could be reawakened by any sign of stereotypically condescending behaviour. The antagonism of the locals, he claimed, was often exacerbated by current political developments and tensions. They could certainly never forget, however often the visitors, or their politicians back home, might say "I'm sorry".

There were some martyr-villages in Greece where German tourists still had to tread carefully; villages in Cyprus or Ireland where the British had to speak circumspectly. Unaware or ignorant loud-mouths and insensitive journalists were perceived alike as bulls in china shops.

George argued forcefully that a new generation shouldn't be expected to inherit the guilt of past generations; nevertheless, he had adopted a personal and internalised sense of projected ethnic guilt concerning the fate of two very different individuals. One of these was the young Australian Aboriginal, Yemmerrawanne, who'd been brought to England by Governor Arthur Phillip when he set sail from New South Wales in 1792. Yemmerrawanne died in England only a year after his arrival.

If one could or should feel guilty simply on the basis of one's

DNA, national or ethnic origins, shared to some degree (in this story) by many white "Anglo-Saxon" peoples, he personally lamented the fate of Yemmerrawanne, and of an Afro-American blues-singer called John Henry Barbee, whose tragic ending seemed to stand for so many other deaths of blues artists, like Bessie Smith, Robert Johnson, Sonny Boy Williamson I, Blind Lemon Jefferson, and the harmonica virtuoso, Noah Lewis.

These were the kinds of stories, whether factually correct or embellished as legends, whether based on true or false rumours, which moved him most deeply. He found it much easier to focus on *individual* cases of suffering, like that of Anne Frank, whose house he had visited in Amsterdam as an impressionable teenager, rather than on large scale massacres and episodes of violent ethnic cleansing, or on acts of genocide. These were almost beyond his comprehension and the limits of his imagination.

He had been profoundly sickened and shocked by photographs of lynch mobs of grinning Southerners, some of them posing or pointing, some of them probably members of the Ku-Klux-Klan, gathered round the corpses of men who'd been strung up and hanged from the branches of a tree, or burned to death on a bonfire of blazing wooden planks. Two truly appalling photographs, one from Omaha, Nebraska, dated 1919, the other from Marion, Indiana, taken in August 1930, had been reproduced in the UK edition of *A Matter of Colour: The Struggle for Racial Equality in the USA* (1965). And then there were the war photos of Dimitri Baltermants, the Soviet photo-reporter, images of traumatised, grief-stricken relatives trying to identify the corpses of loved ones in a muddy field in recently liberated Kerch, Crimea, in 1942.

For George, men like Yemmerrawanne and John Henry Barbee were symbolic representatives of much wider social and historical ills and injustices — *that much* he could concede in his increasingly virulent arguments with Jeremy.

He'd learnt of the case of John Henry Barbee not many months after he'd been to the 1964 American Folk-Blues Festival at the Fairfield Hall in Croydon, when he was about to start his second year at university. In 1965, he bought the Storyville LP, *John Henry Barbee: Portraits in Blues*, Volume 9, recorded in Copenhagen on the 8th of October 1964. John Henry, he learnt from Paul Oliver's sleeve-notes and Horst Lippmann's concert programme notes, had first recorded in 1938, but he'd soon disappeared from view. It seems that he'd gone into hiding, believing, wrongly, that he'd killed a white man, his wife's lover ("Mr. Charlie", his boss, the field inspector who'd "thrown an eye on her"); he'd caught them in bed together and used his gun on him. The man survived the shooting (he'd only been wounded in his leg), and soon recovered — but John Henry never knew that. He made a run for it, jumped into a river and kept on running and hiding; that was the last anybody saw of him for a quarter of a century.

He was rediscovered in Chicago in the 1960's, and he was brought over to Europe as part of the influential blues package show which featured many of the blues "greats". Paul Oliver and others described how John Henry had to leave the show early because of a back problem, which was diagnosed as cancer, although the doctors didn't give him the full picture. He was sent home to die in peace, according to a report by Joe Boyd, the noted American record producer who'd come over to London in 1964 and returned to set up an office in 1965. In spite of feeling weak and ill, John Henry expressed optimism during the flight that he would recover and return to perform in Europe; sadly that was not to be. No one else expected him to live more than a few months. He started having treatment for his condition as soon as he got back to the States. With the money he'd earned on the tour, he bought a car (his very first). He was involved in an accident; he ran over a man, who was killed. John was thrown in prison. Joe Boyd wrote that "he was unable to post bond or to contact his benefactors; he died of cancer in jail" before his case came to trial.

For George, John Henry's story seemed to be the essence of the blues, at least as troubling as the widely-believed, but inaccurate account of Bessie Smith's death in Clarksdale's Afro-American Hospital, after she'd been (allegedly) refused admission to a white hospital, following a bad car crash.

Many years later, George was recruited by the Australia Council, on a five-year contract. In Sydney, he soon became fascinated by Aboriginal art. He would go to exhibitions at the

Boomalli Aboriginal Artists Co-operative and at the Art Gallery of New South Wales, and he'd see as much as he could in Canberra and Melbourne. He grew to admire the works of contemporary urban artists like Harry (H. J.) Wedge, Judy Watson and Rea; of the great Kimberley artists, Rover Thomas and Queenie McKenzie; of the Wandjina paintings of Rosie and Lily Karadada; of the Arnhem Land bark paintings by Mithinari Gurruwiwi; of Tiwi Island artists like Aileen Henry and Janice Murray. He soon built up a small, impressive collection of paintings. He spent more time with his Boomalli friends, with Hetti Perkins and Brenda Croft, who introduced him to other artists and musicians, than with his colleagues who frequented the Sydney Opera House.

As he learnt more about the variety of Aboriginal art, mythology and culture, he developed a taste for authentic field recordings of didgeridoo music, and ceremonial songs accompanied only by clap-sticks. He attended Australia Day celebrations on the 26th of January, as well as the Aboriginal Survival concerts which mourn the same date as Invasion Day and which featured performances by groups like Yothu Yindi, who'd always sing their protest anthem, "Treaty". At the same time, he read widely in Australian history; he wanted to immerse himself in the country and its past, with a view to applying for citizenship at the end of his contract.

He read a lot about William Dampier, who'd come from East Coker, near Yeovil; about Captain Cook and about Governor Arthur Phillip, the first Governor of New South Wales. When the Governor returned to England, setting sail on the 10th of December 1792, he took with him two Aboriginals from the colony, Bennelong and Yemmerrawanne, who was a great favourite. They docked in Falmouth on the 19th of May 1793. The two Aboriginals were feted in London, and provided with tutors and other forms of support, but Yemmerrawanne fell ill after four or five months, and it was arranged that they should both move to Eltham, where they could be better looked after by a doctor.

Very sadly, George was to discover, Yemmerrawanne, who was only about nineteen years old at the time, died of a chest infection on the 18th of May 1794. He was buried in Eltham, at St. John's Church.

When George was still on contract with the Australia Council, there was a growing demand amongst Aboriginal elders that all the human remains and specimens of Aboriginal people kept in British and European museums and medical collections should be returned to Australia for proper burials, according to traditional rites. This was proving to be an uphill battle, as some British scientists, even in the Royal Society, argued that the skulls and bones should be retained, as they might prove useful to medical science in the long run; they could reveal important DNA information, helpful in the treatment of unknown diseases. In any case, some argued, cynically and unscientifically, the human remains were unlikely to be reunited with any true descendants of their own "largely-extinct" nations or clans, from their own original territories, moieties, totems or skin name cycles.

George became deeply involved in this campaign to repatriate human remains from his homeland, and he was disappointed to learn that, although the headstone of Yemmerrawanne still stood in Eltham, in St. John's churchyard, it had been moved several times over the years, and no one knew *where* exactly the body had been buried. Although he was unwilling to give up, George could only suggest, finally, that a scholarship should be inaugurated, in memory of Yemmerrawanne, to honour his name. Even that proved to be controversial, and at the end of his five-year contract, he returned to England.

His scholarship proposal had nothing to do with a feeling of guilt about the settlement or 'invasion' of Australia, but the matter inevitably came up in the course of one of his arguments with his cousin Jeremy, who accused him of being a paternalistic 'bleeding-heart' conservative. He also implied that his compassion was just phoney, fashionable postcolonial romanticism, a guilt-trip, and as such was entirely misplaced.

George had not only made close friends with Aboriginal artists and musicians when in Sydney and Alice Springs, he had also read some of the rare, early anthropological books about Aboriginal customs and "secret knowledge". Many of those books were kept under lock and key in Australian libraries, out of respect to Aboriginal people who wanted that knowledge kept secret. He had also come into possession of a sacred wooden *churinga*, or *tjurunga*, incised with highly secret symbols and patterns. He had never spoken about it, shown it to anyone, or revealed how he had acquired it.

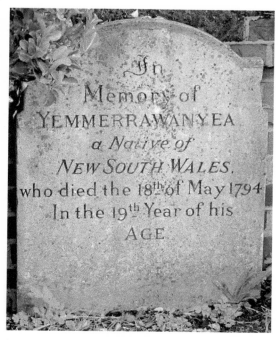

One day, George became so incensed by the cynical stance adopted by Jeremy, that he could no longer suppress his anger. He uttered words that should never have been uttered by anyone, not even by fully-initiated Aboriginal elders; he wasn't even sure if they might constitute a terrible form of curse. It wasn't more than two weeks later that Jeremy fell ill with a serious lung infection that the doctors found to be resistant to every kind of antibiotic.

George, feeling immensely guilty, even if the illness had been coincidental, visited Jeremy in hospital on a daily basis until the very end.

He mourned his death in the way he had learned in Alice Springs. He picked up his two wooden clap-sticks, squatted cross-legged on his living-room floor and started to wail a long ritual lament.

Decolonise your mind

Nick Adams had taken early retirement from the BBC, where he'd had a moderately successful career as a versatile documentary film producer. He was now making his living as a technical assistance adviser, usually on secondments to overseas television broadcasters and media organisations, helping to set up film units and to train film-makers, mainly in East and West Africa. The British Ministry of Overseas Development was responsible for his welfare and conditions of service, for recruiting him, negotiating his contract renewals and for paying his salary and allowances. This time he had struck lucky with his job description; his roving assignment was to work across four different countries, Ethiopia, Kenya, Ghana and Nigeria, but the nature of the job and the contract meant that his wife and children had to stay behind in England. His wife didn't want to leave her research and teaching job as an anthropologist at Oxford University.

Nick was a strange mixture. He'd inherited, and still held, some unwitting but unreconstructed colonial attitudes, but he was also committed to social change and development; he was unusually idealistic, a natural conservative with some almost revolutionary ideas. He wanted to help, but he didn't want anybody to feel grateful. He certainly didn't expect to be kidnapped, whatever the motive, whether for revenge or for ransom.

He saw himself as a public-service realist documentary filmmaker in the tradition of John Grierson, Basil Wright and Sean Graham (who'd gone to Accra in 1948 to establish the West African Film School, where he also made a feature film, *The Boy Kumasenu*) but Nick also admired the French anthropological films of Jean Rouch, such as *Les maîtres fous*. He secretly wished he'd been around in the pioneering days of the Crown Film Unit and the Gold Coast Film Unit.

He was also an amateur folk-singer, and he wrote his own

songs; he accompanied himself with a guitar, in the contemporary protest mould. He didn't go along with the old-fashioned and often unaccompanied *fol-derol-de-rol-de* school. For a start, he didn't cup his hand to his ear. He would occasionally be persuaded to perform at gigs, at hootenannies or "open mike" pub evenings. He was once invited to sing some Bob Dylan songs and one of his own ballads on Ethiopian Television; on another occasion he got cold feet at a Nairobi hotel hootenanny, as he didn't think his songs or bluesy style of singing would be acceptable to the stuffy audience. He didn't like the atmosphere, or the phoney-purist type of music, so he left in a hurry, before they could call him on stage.

He felt much more at home in Addis Ababa than in Nairobi, where post-colonial tensions and resentments could be felt more palpably. In Kenya he had felt little interest in safari parks or wild-life filming, but he sometimes needed to shoot some stock footage. Once he'd been chased by a charging rhinoceros. He'd got back to the safety of his car only just in time. The rhinoceros continued to charge after the car. Safely back in Ethiopia, he filmed with his trainees in the Danakil Desert, exposing the impact of the widespread famine. This hadn't met with the approval of the officials close to Emperor Haile Selassie, who wanted to suppress news of the famine. On another occasion, after filming in the old walled market town of Harar, Nick had been able to follow up his interest in the life of Arthur Rimbaud, and in the periods (around five years all told) that the former poet had lived and traded in the region. Nick tried hard to find Rimbaud's house; he filmed the one he was shown as *La Maison Rimbaud.* He also visited the Father of the Catholic Mission, the same mission which had helped Rimbaud in his time of ill-health and suffering caused by his left leg, which had to be amputated later.

Nick discovered that the current Catholic Father believed in medical diagnosis by the use of a hand-held pendulum and complicated charts. All he needed was a hair from Nick's head, or a drop of his blood, to prepare a detailed diagnosis of any ailments he might have. He drew a diagram of Nick's heart and valves, warning him of the dangerous consequences of his life-style. Nick took note and kept the diagram with him for many years; he had faith in the scientific approach and careful use of the medical pendulum. He was also conscious of his own late father's medical history and cause of death, which the priest didn't know. This wasn't just a demonstration of spurious homeopathic divination.

In Kenya, some of the other local film-makers, and even one of his own trainees, resented Nick's expatriate salary; they were envious of his living conditions, feeling that he was holding a job that could have been Kenyanised, or at least Africanised. There were other local tensions, which Nick didn't yet fully understand, between Kikuyu and Luo members of the Kenyan staff, between Amharas, Tigrayans and Eritrean colleagues in Ethiopia. Nick understood better the bitter feelings that many Kikuyu people still felt towards the British, and towards some of the aristocratic White Settler farming families, tea or coffee planters and big game hunters, as a result of the loss of ancestral Kikuyu lands and the horrendous treatment in concentration camps during the Mau Mau rebellion and Emergency in the 1950s. Later researchers would come to call it *Britain's Gulag*, and to expose and document incidents of torture, including beatings and alleged castrations. Britain would acknowledge this in time, and pay compensation to elderly survivors. Nick knew nothing about this when he was working in Kenya, and would have found it hard to believe; he'd accepted the standard colonial narratives without questioning them; they all demonised the Kikuyu rebels, who'd taken secret oaths, and blamed *them* for any violence. He did read writers like the Ugandan Okot p'Bitek (he loved *The Song of Lawino*), the Kenyan Ngũgĩ wa Thiong'o (formerly known as James Ngugi) and the Nigerian Chinua Achebe, all of whom condemned the injustices and alien customs that still persisted, and who called for further Africanisation and decolonisation. Nick didn't feel entirely at ease in expat haunts like the Norfolk Hotel. The eucalyptus trees of Addis Ababa suited his temperament better than the showy jacaranda and flame trees of Nairobi.

In Ethiopia, he found the people took things less seriously and had fewer colonial "hang-ups" or cultural cringes. The Amharas, on account of their ancient civilisation, proud history and colonial practices of their own, always felt superior to everyone else, and they could crack friendly jokes about the former British Empire, "where the sun never set". They seemed to get on well with the Italian soldiers who'd stayed on and tried to assimilate; many of them married Ethiopian women. The Abyssinians had beaten them back in 1896, at the Battle of Adwa, after all — even if they later suffered greatly, during Mussolini's invasion of 1935–1936. They wouldn't forget or forgive the use of chemical weapons and sulphur mustard air bombs. So much for treaties and the power of the League of Nations! On the personal level, relationships were good.

His Ethiopian colleagues were happy to cooperate on a project to make a documentary about Emperor Theodore (Tewodros) and Queen Victoria, General Napier and the British Military Expedition to free diplomatic and missionary hostages, the 1868 Battle of Magdala and the dramatic suicide of Tewodros. Nick composed a song, "Ballad for Kassa, Tewodros II", especially for the opening sequence:

Come gather round people, a song I will sing
Of Kassa the outlaw, who became a great King.
Raised up from the dust, violent and cruel,
They said he was mad and too reckless to rule . . .

But he was a great man, born ahead of his day,
To unify Ethiopia there was no other way
Than to fight and to conquer, to torture or kill
All who refused to submit to his will.

Some called him "The Lion", and he really could roar,
He was raised up by God to reform and restore
All that the Empire had once been before —
A land to be proud of — for rich or for poor.

He wrote asking for aid from the great English Queen,
He wanted advice to make modern machines;
But she never even bothered to send a reply,
So he locked up her envoys in a fortress so high.

The Queen sent an army to set the prisoners free,
Such cannons and soldiers, you never did see;
They captured the fortress, the battle was won,
But Kassa just stood there, and took out his gun.

He would never surrender; he was a brave man and proud,
"I am still King of Kings!" he shouted out loud.
"Have you ever seen a lion just lay down and die?"
He blew out his brains without even a sigh.

Nick enjoyed going to Mombasa and the Kenyan coast, and on one occasion he went with two of his trainees to film and record in a Mosque school, set amongst huge baobab trees. The film crew was well received, but that evening Nick stayed in a separate hotel from his trainees. It was rather more luxurious than theirs; it never occurred to him to question why he should be able to claim and enjoy a higher *per diem* subsistence rate.

That was the night he was kidnapped.

He was never to find out how a small gang had got past the night-watchmen and security guards, broken into his room in the middle of the night and grabbed him while he was fast asleep. What use were the hotel's *walinzi*? Perhaps every *askari* and *mlinzi* had been bribed. He was to discover only several years later *why* he'd been targeted.

They smothered him in his bedspread; his eyes were blind-folded with a dark blue towel, his mouth stuffed with a face-flannel and a pillowcase was pulled down over his head, for good measure. The intruders must have had some inside accomplices; they carried him out of an emergency exit and bundled him into the back of a four-wheel-drive truck, where they covered him with a smelly old tarpaulin. He could hardly breathe, but as soon as they were in open country they removed the pillowcase and the towelling gag. The tightly-wrapped rough blindfold remained. He could feel the pressure of a rifle barrel digging into his ribcage; he was scared that it might go off as they bounced along over deeply-rutted dirt roads.

For two months he was held in captivity; he was moved several times, guarded around the clock by three young armed fighters, and subjected to strange, disorienting treatments by a fearsome-looking *mganga*, a local medicine-man, healer and herbalist, who, to Nick's eyes, once his blindfold had been removed, resembled a caricature image of a witch-doctor, known in Swahili or Kikuyu as a *mchawi or m'ró-gi*. Nick imagined that the *mganga*— that is what he professed to be, according to some rough hand-painted market signs lying around his hut, which said *Mganga Yuko Hapa* ("Here is the Healer"), *Kutoa Uchawi* ("Provider of magic") — also practised exorcism, the removal of spells and prophetic acts.

This *mganga* had certainly devised "black-magic" witchcraft, *o-ró-gi* or other *uchawi* magical methods, involving the administration of herbal and ground animal-bone concoctions, potions which the guards forced him to swallow just before they joined in the frightening sessions in which he had to submit to their whims, as the *mganga* recited incantations and tried to cast spells to "decolonise his mind", and the minds of their other enemies and captives, Nick came to believe, not knowing that he'd been specially targeted. During the course of the "healing treatment", the *mganga* tormented him for several hours a day, indoctrinating Nick into the truth, as his captors perceived it, of the British mistreatment of the Mau Mau resistance fighters at the time of the anti-Colonial uprising. All Nick could do in his humble and humiliated state, was to keep thanking them for the lessons, slavishly repeating *Asante sana, asante sana*. The four men would sometimes get drunk and try to recall, or pretend to recall, ritual ceremonies which they would re-enact in front of him, interspersed with threats to his life. One day the ceremony involved the renewal of blood oaths, which some of Nick's captors insisted that their fathers had taken. They taunted him with questions. "Do you know the meaning of the *Githaka* oath, *Mũthũngũ*, or the *Batuni* oath? Are you listening, *Bwana Mzungu*? You should know that we have all retaken those oaths, we have renewed our vows before our God; may the oaths kill us if we ever break them. So try to understand what your own fate could be, if I don't exorcise your evil spirit. Beware the curse that has been put upon you! *Mzungu Aende Ulaya. Mwafrika Apate Uhuru!* ('Let the white man go back home. Let the African be free!') Remember? *Uma, uma!* ('Get out, get out!')"

Nick had feared at first that he'd been captured by Somali pirates or by an obscure jihadist group. His captors knew English, as well as Kikuyu (Agĩkũyũ) and Kiswahili. He was now sure that at least two of them were Kenyan, one a Somali *shifta*. They made no mention of a ransom, but they gave him very little food to eat, not much of it was palatable or even edible, and he lost over fifteen kilos in weight. He had no idea if he was being held in a remote part of the northern coast of Kenya or over the border in Somalia. It wasn't Nick who was able to give orders now, to ask questions or try to initiate conversation with the help of the dated little self-study book with its brief introduction to basic grammar and examples of common or once-useful Swahili phrases and words. He always had the book in his pocket: *Up-Country Swahili*, with its quaint colonial subtitle, *Swahili Simplified, for the Farmer, Merchant, Business Man, and Their Wives, and for All Who Deal with the*

Up-Country African. It had first been published in 1936, but it was never out of print. The author had retired from the British Army at the end of World War I and had decided to try his luck as a Soldier Settler in Kenya.

When Nick was finally released, thanks to the efforts of the British Embassy and Consular Section in Nairobi and the intervention of a special unit of the Kenyan Army, he was a changed man. He hadn't been tortured, at least not physically — apart from the semi-starvation diet, the force-feeding with the *mganga*'s nauseating cocktail-potions and gruel, the bites of aggressive mosquitoes, which constantly threatened him with malaria, and the disturbing noises of the bush-babies in the roof of his prison-hut — but his world view had changed radically. He'd started identifying with his captors; it was like an East African parallel to the Stockholm syndrome. When he looked at picturesque dhows, all he thought about was the fate of the African slaves transported, in days gone by, to the Mji Mkongwe or Stone Town market on Unguja, Zanzibar Island. He felt lucky that he hadn't been kidnapped by modern Somali pirates

Six months later, after he'd more or less recovered from his ordeal, he found himself on the other side of Africa, in Kano, Nigeria, researching the ancient Kofar Mata dye-pits. He'd stopped off, en route to Gombe, in Bauchi State, where his assignment was to train outreach workers in the preparation of more appropriate agricultural film-scripts aimed at illiterate farmers, for use in the fleet of ageing mobile cinema units, many of them already broken down (an aid-donor's well-intentioned gift, but without the means to obtain spare parts).

After Gombe, he went to Accra, Ghana, where he'd been asked to run a workshop on script-writing for documentary film production for development. He was no longer interested in discussing or analysing the old-style films of John Grierson or Jean Rouch. He'd been studying the works of emerging Third-World film-makers, politically-inspired documentaries designed to change people's consciousness. He'd discovered a completely different type of film language, indigenous African visual styles which, in Nick's own case, still owed a slight distant inspiration to the half-remembered works of Eisenstein and Joris Ivens. The course materials he'd prepared and this radical new approach had been deeply appreciated, even though he felt that he was learning much more than he was imparting, in terms of *ways of seeing*, culturally sensitive story-telling techniques, shot composition and editing rhythms.

One weekend, Nick visited Fort Elmina and Cape Coast Castle. He was shown the tomb of the once-famous British poet "L.E.L.", Letitia Elizabeth Landon, at Cape Coast Castle. She'd gone there as the bride of George Maclean, the long-time governor of the Castle. She died suddenly and was buried there in 1838, only a few months after her marriage and their eventual arrival, after a long, uncomfortable voyage. Nick tried to investigate some of the rumours surrounding her life and death. No one could be sure whether her death had been an accident, or suicide. Self-destruction seemed to be the enduring verdict, by hydrogen cyanide (prussic acid), but there had been no post-mortem, and there was darker speculation of a possible murder scenario involving her husband, or a jealous Gold Coast mistress.

Nick started thinking about possible alternative film treatments, how very different approaches to the scripting of the scenes leading to her death might be adopted by a British or a Ghanaian film-maker, how a radical feminist reading of events might differ from a more traditional storyline. Would an *African* feminist perspective differ significantly from that of a British feminist or indeed of a colonial male chauvinist? How would each writer treat the scandalous stories and rumours of L.E.L.'s former life in London, and her married life at the Castle? Letitia had written to her brother, "I can scarcely make even you understand how perfectly ridiculous the idea of jealousy of a native woman really is. Sentiment, affection, are never thought of — it is a temporary bargain." She complained that she never saw a living creature but the servants. Perhaps her husband had previously taken one of the servants as his mistress, and that Elizabeth was giving her bossy morning orders to the very same displaced, resentful woman.

Nick discussed these different possibilities with the participants in the margins of his workshop, but he quickly realised he was wandering well off-track; they were naturally more interested in reminding him of more mainstream historical topics, about the Atlantic slave-trade and the sinister role played by the two castles he'd been to see. The ocean's roar could never muffle the cries of the slaves once held in the dungeons. The aesthetic architectural appeal of the buildings set against the dazzling blue ocean and the wild breakers almost seemed designed to be framed through a viewfinder, to attract a cinematographer's admiring, but unthinking gaze, to distract a more superficial foreign director from the unspeakable horrors of what the buildings represented.

In spite of that temporary diversion and lapse of judgement, Nick received a letter from one of the most attentive film-students, after he'd returned to Addis Ababa:

> After the priceless seminar with you in Accra, I now view documentary films with a very critical mind. Your approach to the subject was revolutionary and challenging, which third-world film makers need most.

Nick read it aloud to Tigist, his latest Ethiopian girl-friend, while they were enjoying a spicy Ethiopian meal of *injera*, flat leavened bread made from teff, and *doro wat*, a spicy chicken stew cooked with hot red *berbere* pepper, home-brewed *talla* beer and *tej*, a delicious honey wine. He was eating with his fingers from the *mesob*, a colourful communal basket, gratefully accepting choice *gurshas* of *doro wat* she'd wrapped by hand and put delicately in his mouth, tasty morsels of peppery chicken. He was glad that he wasn't expected to eat any raw meat, on this occasion.

His wife and children back home in England knew nothing of his secret plan to start a second family in Addis — at least that's what he thought.

When Nick did go back to Nairobi, he decided to drop in at the hotel hootenanny, and this time he stayed to sing three of his own songs, one about the fate of the shackled slaves waiting for months for a ship in the dank dungeons of the Gold Coast slave-fort of Elmina Castle; another, mocking the behaviour of the old Happy Valley white settlers in Kenya, which he called "*The Expat Blues*", and, finally, his most recent composition, as critical of the current Kenyan government as much as of the British colonials. It was called *Mau Mau Blues*:

Going back to the forest, can't live in this town no more,
Going back to the forest, can't live in this town no more,
I wonder now, *wananchi,* what I was fighting for.

We've got our independence, but still life's just the same,
We've got our independence, but still life's just the same,
The men with the Mercedes, the *Wabenzi* are to blame.

Look at all the politicians, they wear the white man's shoes,
Look at all the politicians, they wear the white man's shoes,
But we're still walking barefoot with the independence blues.

When I came out of the forest, back in nineteen sixty-three,
When I came out of the forest, back in nineteen sixty-three,
They said, "Lay down your weapons, you don't need them
        now we're free."

Some called us freedom fighters, some shouted out "Mau Mau"!
Some called us freedom fighters, some shouted out "Mau Mau"!
Don't matter what they called us, they don't want to know us now.

Going back to the forest, people, can't live in this town no more,
Going back to the forest, people, can't live in this town no more,
I wonder now, *wananchi,* what I'll be fighting for.

Nobody applauded. Nick heard several people booing; someone jeered at him, calling out that he was a traitor who'd *gone native,* telling him to get out, go to hell, go back to his bloody forest, where he'd soon be "hunted down like Dedan Kimathi".

It was several more years before Nick realised that he himself was the story, the duplicitous expat, and that it was his abandoned wife back in England who'd instigated his kidnapping, paid for the hit-men, the bewitching and potions, and for her curse to be carried out. They'd had a different agenda. She'd wanted him killed, not merely converted or exorcised. She certainly didn't want him back. This time she'd structure the narrative and edit the film-script.

The other side of the wall

Living in a semi-detached house, Rupert often wondered about life on the other side of the wall.

He wasn't a snooping type of person, and he'd never been disturbed by his current next-door neighbour, Idir, who was very quiet and considerate; in fact they'd become good friends.

The English woman who'd once lived in the other half of the building had kept herself very much to herself; she'd complain if Rupert had to park even briefly in what she considered to be her own exclusive spot. That didn't bother him, as he could become touchy himself about inconsiderate parking, but he could get very annoyed by her grossly overweight and evil-looking Siamese cat, that would sit on the wooden garden fence between the two properties, trying to catch or terrorise birds in the bushes on his side of the fence. If he tried to scare the cat away, it would return his gaze with an intense glare of pure malice. It would always climb over into his garden to defecate, often scratching around in his flowerbed, damaging the plants and flowers. He was very glad when that neighbour sold her house, and moved out, taking her ugly, fat cat with her.

He was relieved when the house was bought by Idir, a friendly young Algerian man, an Amazigh (Berber) who spoke perfect and fluent English and French. He was in his mid-thirties at the time, an IT expert, who'd become a British citizen. Rupert knew relatively little about Algeria or the Berbers. Idir told him that his uncle had fought for the FLN (Front de Libération Nationale), in the guerrilla war waged against the French in the Algerian War of Independence. He'd been captured, tortured and killed. According to different estimates, between half a million and one and a half million Algerians were killed during that brutal war, which the Berbers call *Tagrawla Tadzayrit.*

Rupert had read books about the Maghreb, but his knowledge

of Algeria was limited. He'd been in Paris at the end of August, 1961, staying for a few weeks in the northern suburb of Saint-Denis, about six miles from the centre of the city. That was during the Algerian anti-colonial war. He'd been alarmed by the nearby terrorist bombings and explosions caused by aggrieved and repressed Algerians, who'd become increasingly militant. French policemen were being killed or injured. He felt a little safer when a curfew was imposed. Trying to find out more about the causes of the violence, he read a Parisian press report about a TV speech addressed by de Gaulle to his army at the end of January the year before:

> Je dis à tous nos soldats: votre mission ne comporte ni équivoque, ni interprétation. Vous avez à liquider la force rebelle qui veut chasser la France de l'Algérie et faire régner sur ce pays sa dictature de misère et de stérilité.

> I say to all our soldiers: your mission comprises neither equivocation, nor interpretation. You have to liquidate the rebel forces, which want to banish France from Algeria and impose on this country its dictatorship of misery and sterility.

Years later, he saw Gillo Pontecorvo's violent film *The Battle of Algiers*. When he was staying in Saint-Denis it had seemed as if that battle had been transferred to the streets of Paris, even before the police massacre of Algerian demonstrators, which happened on the 17th of October 1961.

Most of Rupert's knowledge of colonial Algeria had come from the novels and essays of Albert Camus; lyrical evocations of the Mediterranean, such as the essay "The Wind at Djemila", from the collections *Noces* and *L'Été*. He'd studied Camus' novel *L'Étranger* at school, for A-level French, and it had been an immensely influential book. He had little awareness at the time about how the Algerians perceived Camus, or his anti-hero Meursault, although he knew about their attitudes towards the French colonial settlers, the *Pied-Noirs*.

Because he'd been to one Maghreb country, he'd always hoped he might spend a year or so in North Africa; every year the Maghreb countries appeared high up on his list of countries he wanted to visit and explore. That was not to be. But now there was an Algerian Berber living on the other side of the wall!

When he was staying in Brussels, Rupert had discovered a CD of the thrilling nomadic Berber music of the Touareg, further south, with the songs led by the great oud-player Choyly, from the Djanet Oasis, in the Saharan region of South-East Algeria. It was exciting dancing music, but Rupert wasn't much of a dancer or a joiner.

He recalled what he'd once witnessed and written in his diary, when living in the borough of Haringey, in North London:

"*Our ethnic neighbours!* snarl the Volvo-owning English couple, who live opposite the Cypriot Turks, in London N11. There's a wedding party in the garden; the discordant oriental scales of the heavily amplified oud and tabla, climb all the way to Muswell Hill on this hot Sunday in July. Poll-tax payers clap and dance. With windows wide open, I lie on my bed and listen, restless — wishing I could join in too."

Unfortunately, where he now lived, in a town near the Somerset-Dorset border, it was anything but multicultural. There were very few foreigners to be seen at all.

His new Berber-British neighbour occasionally welcomed old friends from Algeria; late in the evening they would play rhythmic Berber music, let their hair down and start to dance.

One night, Idir and his friends had invited Rupert round for a special Algerian meal. For dessert they were treated to Algerian *tamina*, a toasted semolina and honey sweet, served to celebrate the birth of a baby, as Idir was now the proud father of a beautiful baby boy.

Rupert couldn't wait to join in with their celebrations; there was always such a happy, joyful atmosphere. They brought a welcome breath of fresh air to the staid, mono-cultural English town of committed conservatives and self-defining, *soi-disant* liberals

This had been his induction into Berber culture. He didn't have to travel far to appreciate that — he lived no more than a metre away from the Barbary Coast!

Life was definitely more fun on the other side of the wall.

The battle of the two clarinets

Amongst the hundreds of great folk-clarinet players who lived and performed in the northwest of Greece, there lived two truly outstandingly talented *klarino* players.

One was a handsome young Roma man, proud to call himself a gypsy, from Parakalamos in Pogoni, not far from the Albanian border. The other was a very elderly and highly-respected clarinet maestro, a player who'd entertained many generations of people at festivals (*paniyiria*) around Ioannina and up in the Zagori villages, for more than sixty years. He'd made many recordings, and everybody knew him; his was a revered household name.

The young Roma man had learned to play some jazz and blues, as well as the traditional music of his region, mostly music for dancing, but also "table music", slower tunes like the *skaros*, a shepherd's flock-gathering melody, and the *miroloyi*, a sad lament which always evoked a profound response amongst listeners of all ages.

Their styles of playing differed in many subtle ways.

The Cultural Committee of one of the mountain villages had the bright idea, one year, to organise a clarinet competition to take place two days before the August festival started. The plan was to have a *clarinet-battle* to see who could play the most exciting traditional dance tune, and the most moving lament. Whoever won the battle would be sure of many bookings in the future and would be invited to play at the following year's three-day festival, for a very good fee. They were allowed to use their normal backing groups for accompaniment — *laouto* (a type of lute), violin and *dephi* (a type of tambourine) — but unamplified.

The outcome of the competition would be judged on two criteria: who could get the most people, young and old, dancing under the plane tree during an hour-long set, and, later the same evening, who could make the villagers weep the most profoundly when they took turns to play a single slow, sad lament, an improvised dirge on an ancient theme, not lasting more than ten minutes.

On the evening of this highly competitive instrumental battle, the young Roma agreed to play first. His imaginative improvisations were dazzling, and all the younger villagers danced uninhibitedly to his jazz-influenced tones. His style was still grounded in tradition; it wasn't a form of fusion. He really understood younger Epirots' tastes and their psychology, but most of the older villagers sat, unmoved, at their tables, nursing a beer or a glass of *tsipouro*. Some wandered off to buy a charcoal-grilled *souvlaki*.

The younger player may have had a lot of soul and charisma, as well as an enviable technique; as a player he was becoming known for his distinctive breathing, intonation and feeling, but what he played wasn't the preferred dance music of the village, where the older people held tightly to their local customs and could be suspicious of outsiders. Up in the stony Zagori villages, the taste was for harder music. Down in the plains, audiences liked a sweeter sound; he was well aware of the regional variations, and he could usually adapt his style and repertoire to his different audiences and age-groups.

The local eighty-year old clarinet maestro was the next to battle it out, to try to give them all that they really wanted to hear.

This time, most of the sprightly older villagers leapt up to dance. It was the turn of the younger people (who'd come back to their native Zagori villages for a few weeks in the summer, from towns like Ioannina, Thessaloniki and Athens) to sit out the dance and to catch up with childhood friends, over a glass or two of pure, home-distilled *tsipouro*. Some preferred whisky or wine.

The young Roma player from Parakalamos, feeling pleased with his performance, started chatting to a beautiful young Zagorisian woman with bright eyes and long black hair. She'd already had a few glasses of *tsipouro*, and before long they were sharing a romantic tête-à-tête, somewhat removed from the rest of the crowd. She'd been dancing ecstatically, in an unusually abandoned way, while he'd been playing. He had even started playing his clarinet intimately close to her ear, as she bent forward to let the sounds stir the depths of her soul. What he didn't realise, while they sat there openly flirting with each other, was that she was the niece of his rival player, who could see out of the corner of his eye exactly what was going on. This was having a devastating effect on his concentration, on the tone and feeling of his playing. He had Roma blood himself, though he seldom admitted it in interviews, had largely distanced himself from the old culture and no longer identified with the customs of the extended clan. He had struggled all his life to win general acceptance and to overcome prejudice; he'd achieved a place of eminence and respect as an important citizen in society, and he didn't want any member of his family to threaten it.

Some of the younger, less respectful people from Athens had started to think of the grand old man, rather unkindly, as a caricature embodiment of *Charos*.

One of them, perhaps originally from Parakalamos, he suspected wrongly, even went so far as to stick a twenty-Euro note on his forehead while he was playing, saying "Bravo, *Charos*, you still play pretty well for an old fellow."

This made him doubly mad; he took it as an insult, not as an appreciative tip. It was completely inappropriate on such an occasion. He really saw red. At the end of his set, he told the head of the organising committee that he wasn't in the mood to play a deep lament that night, as he was feeling unwell.

It was agreed that the second stage of the competition would be postponed, until the following evening.

The old man strode over to the quiet corner where his niece was sitting, still flirting with the dashing young musician from Pogoni.

"We're not playing our laments tonight, I'm not feeling well. It's going to take place tomorrow night, but why don't you and I meet down by the threshing-floor tomorrow morning, the old threshing-floor past the second little church, just off the stone steps leading down to the gorge? You'll see a big church bell hanging in a tree. There's a short path off the main cobbled mule-track, which leads to a perfectly secluded spot overlooking the gorge. It has excellent natural acoustics, just a slight echo.

"One of your friends, he continued, "insulted me this evening, called me 'Charos', and 'old man', as if I was already well past it, like some kind of grim reaper, a modern reincarnation of Charon! So let's see who is really the stronger, better player — just you and I, away from the crowds, all the noise and distractions. We'll each play an improvised lament, with nobody else watching and listening, except for the hermit-monk who has his cell near the threshing-floor where we'll meet. It'll be like a private rehearsal for the evening's competition. Do you agree?"

"Why not? But the man who you say insulted you wasn't a friend of mine. The Roma people would never be so arrogant; that's against our code of honour. I thought you would know that. We respect all our fellow-musicians, even if we fall out from time to time. But I'll meet you at the threshing-floor, if that's what you want; let's say ten o'clock. You can ask the monk to act as the judge, to decide who's the morning's winner."

The next morning the two men set out separately for the agreed meeting-place, half-an-hour's walk, far enough away from the village that it was unlikely that their playing would be heard, even though sound travelled a long way around the gorge.

They met the hermit-monk down at the threshing-floor. It was beginning to take on the intense feeling of a dual to the death. They entered the circular threshing-floor together, and decided they would improvise solos in turn, playing one of the saddest laments known in that part of Greece. The young gypsy was on form again, old *Charos* soon lost his breath, he just couldn't sustain his notes and modulations as in previous years. He became angry with himself, angry with his opponent. He stopped playing and threatened to attack his younger rival with his raised clarinet. The monk tried to intervene. Both men put down their precious clarinets, and started sparring with each other, circling around the threshing-floor, with old *Charos* looking for an opportunity to strike a knock-out blow. It became almost like a ritual dance, a form of folk-ballet, as the young Roma didn't want to harm the much older man; he was light on his feet, so he kept himself just out of reach of any blows.

A shot rang out from the woods, from the direction of the spot where the hunters usually hid themselves in the season, well-camouflaged, on the look-out for brown bears and wild boar. It was illegal to shoot at bears at any time of the year, as they were, in theory, a protected species. There were still some hunters who ignored the regulations, and one or two who risked a large fine by hunting for the larger species of wild animals outside the season. Even the bird-hunting season was not due to begin until after the 20th of August. The hunter might have been aiming at a ferret, a much-loathed pest which often killed chickens in their wire coops at the edge of the village.

The young Roma had been accidentally hit, but not fatally wounded; he staggered back, dangerously close to the edge of the gorge and the sheer drop below the overhanging rock platform. He collapsed heavily onto the unstable rocky outcrop, which immediately gave way beneath him.

The camouflaged hunter emerged from the woods, carrying

his rifle, unaware of the accident.

Old *Charos* was standing there stiffly, frozen in a state of shock. He wasn't sure if he was looking at an apparition or at his alter-ego.

He greeted the man warily, as if he was an old army friend who'd just done him a favour; but his feelings were in turmoil, a strange combination of gratitude, relief and profound guilt.

He solemnly surrendered his clarinet, and said, as he handed it to the hunter: "Take it, or break it. I'll never play it again."

The monk was still standing at the end of the path, trying to peer down into the gorge, to see where the wounded Roma had fallen.

One day, perhaps at the end of the *paniyiri*, this year or next, some other *klarino* player from Parakalamos would lead the weeping and mourning, and improvise a new *miroloyi*.

The winter before the Summer of Love

The function of education has never been to free
the mind and spirit of man, but to bind them.
Jules Henry, *Culture Against Man*, 1963

He who can, does. He who cannot, teaches.
George Bernard Shaw, Maxims for
Revolutionaries 36, *Man and Superman*
(1903)

I struck the board, and cried, "No more;
I will abroad!"
What? shall I ever sigh and pine?
My lines and life are free, free as the road,
Loose as the wind, as large as store.
Shall I be still in suit?
Have I no harvest but a thorn…?
George Herbert, "The Collar"

Robert and Malcolm behaved like two hopeless male-chauvinist
hippies. They were both young, single men, twenty-two years old;
they'd recently graduated from university, where they'd read
English Literature, and had decided to extend their student days
(and thus postpone the search for employment), by going to
London to do a one-year postgraduate teacher-training course.
Robert had no intention of becoming a teacher, but Malcolm had
persuaded him that the certificate might prove a good fall-back
insurance policy if all else failed. They were both somewhat
inadequate in terms of dealing with practical realities, and they
were comically incapable of looking after themselves or their
"flat", more of a bed-sit, in a convenient and accessible district of
London, amongst the expat Australians in Barons Court. They
were always arguing, in a tone of cutting but humorous sarcasm,
occasionally cruel but basically friendly. They knew each other

well; they could say whatever they liked, and they did.

Robert was a tall, stubborn idealist who tried to disguise the fact by resorting to an attitude of rebellious cynicism. He was less fashion-conscious than Malcolm, who had longer hair and favoured extrovert "mod" fashions. Robert tended to wear jeans, a white seaman's knitted polo-neck woollen pullover and desert boots. He'd always felt that it had been the bulky white pullover that had first attracted Janet at a college dance, even though it was far too hot and uncomfortable to wear indoors on such an occasion. Maybe she'd liked the cuddly polar bear look.

Robert's relationship with Janet, his girlfriend of several years, was becoming strained. She felt that he took her for granted; she resented this with all her will. Malcolm's girlfriend, Debbie, was a nervous girl, never without a problem. They often came to stay, but seldom on the same night.

The bed-sit was a large room, with two single beds on the left. On the right, separated by a thin partition, was the kitchen-cum-bathroom. The room was always in a chaotic state of untidiness, with clothes, books and records lying everywhere. Robert's guitar was usually left on one of the armchairs; Malcolm's record-player produced a good sound but hadn't been dusted for weeks. A pile of uncorrected exercise books, a loaf of stale bread and a carving knife were on the table in the middle of the room; they hadn't bothered to brush up the crumbs from the carpet. Bright, psychedelic posters were taped to the wall, alongside blown-up photographs of Laurel and Hardy and Buster Keaton, and the covers of some of their favourite LPs. The sideboard was always stacked high with dirty dishes; there wasn't enough space for more crockery on the small draining-board by the sink in the kitchen area.

◆

The main room is in darkness. Only the kitchen has a light. It's six a.m. Malcolm is attempting to shave in cold water. He's listening to the transistor radio which is wedged between two unwashed coffee mugs. The radio is playing some wailing electric guitar music. Every time Malcolm hears a particularly high bent note, he doubles up in a sort of jack-knife dance, as if he has been hit in the belly. He has lather all over his face. He pretends to play an imaginary guitar to the music, until he nicks a bit of skin with his blunt razor-blade, and curses; he searches for some cotton wool to staunch the bleeding.

The music stops, and the quick-talking Pirate Radio disc-jockey carries on with his surrealistic, joking patter: "It's ten past six, people, and all the world's at love, and me, I'm out here on my lonely ship, with the waves rocking the boat, about to be invaded by a rival pirate or boarded by the police: they're trying to close us down; never mind, the show must go on . . . One day Harold Wilson will honour me with an OBE for services to the nation. Like him, *I'm Backing Britain . . .*"

Malcolm switches off the transistor, listens to the water gurgling down the kitchen sink, and dries his face tenderly with the towel. He can now hear the sounds of heavy-breathing, grunts and moans, coming from the main room

He goes into the dark room and shouts sarcastically:

"Christ, haven't you finished yet, son? It ain't good for your health. You'll get a stomach-ache again. If only your pupils could see you now, puffing away like a pot-bellied businessman! Ha! Thank God Debbie wasn't here tonight. I tell you, mate, it's marvellous having a bed to yourself!"

He switches on the main light.

The light takes Robert and Janet by surprise, cuddling closely but awkwardly in their narrow bed. Janet pulls the sheets hurriedly over her. Robert sits up and shouts at Malcolm:

"Do you have to come in just at the wrong moment? How the hell can I whisper tender words of love with you standing by the bed making a bloody running commentary; go back to bed, and belt up!"

Janet is wriggling about under the sheets: "How are you, *my dearest love* — get off my leg, you're nearly breaking my bones.

That's better. Why are you so heavy? I'm going on strike unless you invest in a bigger bed. There's not room for Twiggy in this one, let alone two of us."

Robert shrugs wearily. "Yes, my love, you've told me many times. Would you prefer me to sleep on the floor? I can use my sleeping-bag, you know."

"All I ask is that you don't cover me with bruises. The trouble with you two is that you're too damn selfish. I come here every weekend, and you expect me to clear up your mess for you, to make love and to cook food. You never raise a finger to help. I'm not going to wash another plate unless you let me get some sleep."

They rearrange themselves in the small bed, getting tangled up and fighting for the blankets.

Malcolm is impatient. "Stop arguing, can't you? You can work out your differences when I'm not around. Remember I live here too, and pay half the rent. I've got to teach a full timetable today, and I could have used some sleep too. At least you don't have to get up to catch the tube at seven o'clock, Janet. Damn it, I nearly forgot. I haven't prepared one of the lessons. That's what comes of having you two in the room making love all the time. I never get a chance to think."

"There's a time and a bloody place for preparing lessons, Malcolm. Turn that fucking light out!"

"Watch your language, remember you're going to be a teacher."

"If you seriously think I intend to spend the rest of my days in a classroom trying to inspire fifteen-year-olds to write poems about the moods of the sea, you're mistaken, mate."

"*Very* funny, Robert. As for being a teacher, well, I'd prefer to sell melons in Mexico, but the fact is I can't go onto the classroom with nothing prepared, so be serious, man. Have you got any ideas?"

"Take them out into the fields and meadows, give them flowers for their hair. Read them some Ginsberg and William Blake, liberate all the little lambs, cleanse the doors of perception!

Remember this?

> But to go to school in a summer morn,
> O! It drives all joy away;
> Under a cruel eye outworn,
> The little ones spend the day
> In sighing and dismay."

"It's nearly December, if you haven't forgotten, and we're in London, not the bloody Lake District or California!"

"Blake wrote that in London. Take his advice. Make use of the environment. Take them to Piccadilly Circus to analyse and decode the advertisements. 'The traditional classroom . . . is a feudal dungeon'! Haven't you read your McLuhan? They'll learn more about life riding on the underground train for five stops than they will in a whole week at school. If all else fails, read them Book One of Milton's *Paradise Lost* or, even better, some extracts from R. D. Laing's *The Divided Self.*"

Janet looks over the sheet, shielding her eyes from the light, "When you two have quite finished . . . I'm serious, Robert, if you don't let me get some sleep, I'll pack my things right now and go to a hotel. I can't stand it anymore Every week it's the same."

"I'm sorry babe, but Malcolm's in a fix."

Someone bangs on the ceiling of the flat below and an angry voice calls out: "What's the meaning of all this noise? If you don't keep quiet, I'll call the police!"

◆

The next evening, before Malcolm returns to the flat, the room is a lot tidier. Robert is reading a book in an armchair near the electric fire. Janet is washing up the last of the plates in the kitchen. There is a click, and the electric fire goes off.

"Damn, the meter's run out. Have you got another shilling, love?"

"No I haven't. I've spent a small fortune keeping you in electricity. Why don't you make Malcolm put some money in as well?"

"He never has any shillings. You must admit we do use more than him."

The key turns in the lock, Malcolm enters, looking cold and tired, carrying a bag full of exercise books.

"There's just been another suicide at Earl's Court Underground. The train was delayed for half an hour. People might choose a better time to jump off the platform than during the rush hour; it's bloody inconsiderate. Christ, it's cold in here, turn the fire on. What's for supper, Janet? I forgot to tell you, Debbie's coming round later. Is there enough food for her, too?"

Janet is angry. "What do you think I am — a bloody slave? It's taken me four hours to clean up this pigsty. We'll wait till Debbie gets here, and she can do the cooking for a change, unless you'd care to do it?"

"That's fine by me, if you don't mind eating boiled eggs. They don't teach you to cook at university."

"No, and you never try to learn, do you? How was school, anyway? Did they massacre you, or did you think up any lessons on the train?"

"I got by. Luckily there was no teaching inspection today. At times I really hate London. I've been thinking about that suicide. Most people in the tube, including me, couldn't care, just wanted to get home. To others it was a moderately sensational event, slightly more interesting than the headlines in the *Evening News*."

"You always say you love London."

"I do, really. The other day, something else happened which made me really sick and angry. I was waiting for the tube, it was quite a crowded platform, but not rush-hour. There was an old tramp, obviously out of his mind on meths, sitting on the edge of the bench. Suddenly he slipped off and lay on the platform amongst all the rubbish, like a tortoise on its back. I was at the other end of the platform, and for a minute I watched him as he tried to pull himself back onto the seat. Three or four times he tried to lift himself up, but each time he sank back down again.

All the people nearby just stood there, watching him, fascinated but disgusted. I couldn't stand it."

"What did *you* do?

"I wasn't trying to act as the Good Samaritan, but I walked up to him, gave him my hands and pulled him back onto the bench. The people stared at me as if I was contaminated, like a leper. I could see in their faces that they really hated me for doing something that they should have done; they felt so guilty. And I hated them for their puny little pangs of guilt. Everywhere you go you see these pitiless pale faces. 'The mind-forg'd manacles . . . marks of weakness, marks of woe'."

"Don't get so worked up about it, son. You wanted to come and live here. You can leave anytime you want to. You keep quoting D. H. Lawrence at me. His ideas are all very well in theory, all that chasing naked around the haystacks, very healthy and picturesque. I'm a sucker for fresh air and the rustic life, but every time Janet and I have made love in the great outdoors, either we've sat on ant-hills, been covered in mud, pestered by flies, stung by wasps or watched by cows. Not a great turn-on. No sooner do we take our clothes off but the forces of Nature come to attack our sweaty bodies, and all the time you've got to be on the lookout for inquisitive kids or farmers ready to pepper your flashing buttocks full of pellets. So there's a lot to be said for the locked door and the bed-sit, if you ask me."

The door-bell rings. Malcolm jumps up to let in Debbie, who looks very worried.

"Hello, babe, it's good to see you," says Malcolm.

"Sorry I'm late, the trains were delayed for some reason," replies Debbie.

"There was another suicide at Earl's Court. They were probably scraping up the pieces."

Debbie whispers in his ear, "They'll probably be scraping me up next week. I'm bloody depressed. My period's already six days late. I hope to God I'm not pregnant."

"Don't worry love, you're always late, you know you are. If it doesn't come soon, you can go along to a clinic for a test."

"But what shall we do if I *am* pregnant?"

"We've discussed all this before, haven't we? You know I don't like *the idea* of an abortion, but it's the only thing we can do. We'll talk about it tomorrow. Have you got a shilling for the meter? There'll be no heating or music otherwise."

Robert has overheard part of the conversation. "To breed or abort – that is the question."

He picks up his guitar and improvises a little rhyme:

> Anxiously awaiting the monthly report,
> I question my conscience, to breed or abort.
> I want to be free to wander the Earth.
> I will not be a slave in this city.

Debbie glares at him. She reluctantly puts in a coin, and Malcolm puts on "Play with Fire", a favourite Rolling Stones record, in order to shut him up.

Robert fetches a half-empty bottle of whisky. They start drinking, and dance around the room. Debbie is very half-hearted at first, but she gradually relaxes.

"By the way, Robert, have you forgotten we have to write an essay over the weekend?"

"Nobody told me about that."

"It's got to be ready for Monday's tutorial. The title is 'Recollections of Adolescence'. It's supposed to make us mature old adults try and understand the problems that our pupils have, by making us remember *our own* problems. They think that too many teachers forget what it's like being adolescent."

"They've got no right to make us do something like that. Why should I have to reveal what I've been through? It amounts to an unethical intrusion — or a sinister form of character vetting. If that's what they want, I'm inclined to chuck in the course right now. I mean it. I'll pack it all in. They can keep their teaching certificate. I'll be on my way. It's as simple as that. Do you remember that poem 'To You', by Adrian Mitchell, the one he read at that fantastic event a few months ago, with that line about being 'fed to the educational system limited'? He was spot-on, wasn't he, Janet? 'My love, they are trying to drive us mad.' A great poem!"

"Aren't you over-reacting? Have you got something to hide? Where would you go to? What would you do? And what about Janet?"

"I'm a free agent, Malcolm. I don't owe anybody anything. I'm very fond of you, Janet, you know that, but . . . maybe it's all been a post-adolescent fantasy, a naïve delusion? I'm hardly your Heathcliff, am I? We've shared some great times, but I've never been one to make compromises. Nor have you. I'm sorry, Janet. We both need to search some more. I know I'm selfish, cynical and ungrateful."

"You *are*. You're a *bastard*, Robert."

"So be it. Most people are afraid of freedom. They try to stake claims in you, to corner you, to use you as a crutch. There's always some organisation man dragging you into the circle for no particular reason. They want to know what's going on inside your head, to invade your privacy. They want you to reveal your innermost secrets, to plumb the depths of your soul. Sometimes I feel it's all over before it really started, that I've been the victim of a huge con trick. Life has become so one-dimensional. That's why I've been thinking of leaving the city. I couldn't find a way to tell you before. Maybe I'll go abroad. I'll find an island somewhere."

"You can't be serious, Robert! You've never even hinted at anything like this. I thought I knew you."

"To be brutally frank, Malcolm, I never really wanted to apply for this teaching course. I was tempted by the thought of spending a year in London. I was influenced by you after finals, because I still wasn't sure what I wanted to do with my life. You can stay here where you're happy, Malcolm. I'm not, that's why I'm thinking of cutting out. I don't feel at home here. You do. You like London; maybe not all the time. I can't live any longer in this schizophrenic city. It's worming its way inside me, Malcolm, it's spreading out its tentacles, it has got to be demolished before it demolishes me. I don't *need* a teaching certificate to fall back on. I'm sick to death of thinking in terms of security and further qualifications. I've lost count of the number of examinations I've taken, of the hours I've spent locked away in a library. I don't want a life insurance policy."

"You're the one who has the schizoid tendencies, Robert. That's all bullshit, muddled thinking, a pathetic kind of word-salad. Read R. D. Laing. It's not the city. London is a bloody good place to live. Where else in the world have young people got so much freedom to do and be what they want? This is my world now. It's my kind of scene. And I've just decided something very important. I'm going to ask Debbie to marry me, if she'll have me."

"Is that a proposal? You might address it to me." Debbie seems flabbergasted.

"There's no point in paying rent for two flats when you can live more cheaply and comfortably in one. To tell the truth, I can't stand this hippy way of life, sharing a bed-sit with Robert. He mocks everything. He even jokes about abortions. That's not on."

"Are you all forgetting that I'm still here?" asks Janet, in tears. "Let's all go to the pub to have another drink."

Robert makes an excuse. He says that he wants to lie down and to be left alone because he has a bad migraine coming on. The others leave. They're puzzled by his sudden mood-swing and uncharacteristic behaviour. They've no idea what's got into him or why he's been pontificating about freedom.

◆

An hour later, Robert is standing on his own on an underground train platform, his hastily-packed suitcase and his guitar by his side. Inside his head, a crescendo of city-noises is increasing all the time in volume, the noises of crowds, elevators, tube-trains grinding to a halt, of doors opening and closing, cries of "Stand clear of the gates", ugly metallic sounds, all at an unbearable pitch, like the worst attacks of tinnitus such as he'd experienced frequently during his troubled adolescence. He sees Janet running towards him. A train is approaching. The high-pitched ringing in his ears overpowers him. It's excruciating. The words keep going round and round, *He who can, does . . . He who can, TEACHES . . . HE WHO CAN, DOES . . . THOSE who can, do . . . THOSE WHO CAN'T, WON'T . . .* He's dizzy. He is starting to lose his sense of balance. Everything is pulsating wildly, uncontrollably, buzzing, *buzzing,* BUZZING. He feels as if his head is about to explode.

He jumps before Janet gets to him.

Not-so-sunny Goodge Street

When Jonathan was invited to rent a room in an old, run-down house in Goodge Place, the area was already due for demolition. He moved there from an inconvenient and relatively expensive shared bed-sitting room in Baron's Court. He needed more privacy to write, and to entertain his girlfriend(s).

He was now one of seven young people, mostly postgraduate students, who jointly rented the narrow Central London house, very close to his place of study, an institute of the University of London. The house was owned by a woman who would eventually turn them out and keep their deposits, claiming they'd broken or removed some of her furniture, although they'd never signed or seen the inventory that she produced when she evicted them. None of the original tenants still lived there, and no paperwork, such as a copy of the lease or inventory, had been handed down to others who moved in to take over their rooms.

While they lived there, the dilapidated, ramshackle house in Goodge Place was the scene of many lively communal late-night arguments and some highly enjoyable guitar and singing sessions. There was lanky Luuk from Holland, who worked at Foyles Bookshop; Toby, a medical student and skilled guitarist; and Don, a biochemist, guitarist and an excellent cook. They could play both sophisticated classical *and* Rolling Stones duets. Then there was Jonathan himself, a basic blues guitarist and useless cook, who was quick to praise Don's nourishing meat and potato stews. Jonathan would offer to do the washing-up. If no-one felt like cooking, they would grab a take-away *souvlaki* or kebab in pita bread from one of the Greek restaurants in Charlotte Street, or they'd have a spaghetti dish at the local Spaghetti House in Goodge Street. Once a week, a fishmonger parked his cart right outside their house, so they didn't starve. Opposite the front door, there was an advertising hoarding featuring Friar Tuck. Jonathan could never resist the idea of making an animated film in which the first letters of the name *Friar Tuck* would be swapped round. That was as far his storyboard went, and it didn't say very much for his wit, maturity or potential teaching competence and suitability.

He had been allocated the small remaining box-like room at the top of the creaky staircase. More than once, he had to use his umbrella to battle with the mice in the middle of the night.

He used to read the underground newspaper IT (International Times). He even wrote a couple of anonymous articles for it, one on the subject of "Beat Teachers", in which he discussed the teaching of Ginsberg's poem "Howl".

BEAT TEACHERS

The generation of Beat-Teachers has finally emerged from the universities. Underground education has invaded respectable schools. Text-books feature Corso, Carlos-Williams and Kerouac alongside Lawrence and Whitman. The Beat-Teacher armed with film-camera, tape-recorder, guitar and L.P.'s of Mingus, Bird and the Blues as stimuli for creative writing. Fourteen-year-olds discussing Blake and R.D. Laing, and writing about schizophrenia. This is no underground utopian halluncination. Happenings are in the classrooms right now.

How many can imagine walking down a deserted school corridor, to be attracted by the apocalyptic sermon-riffs of the recorded voice of Ginsberg in full flight:

"Moloch who entered my soul early! Moloch whom I abandon!"
— to see in the attentive faces of thirty schoolboys and girls the first fierce glints of madness and illumination as their ears are blasted by the "eli eli lamma lamma sabacthani saxophone cry that shivered the cities ..."?

Was it in International Times that he'd read that you could turn on and get high by smoking "hallucinogenic" dried banana skins, or by cutting a ping-pong ball in half, placing the two halves over your eyes, and lying down to wait until you experienced psychedelic visions as a result of sensory deprivation? Neither experiment worked for him, but both had seemed worth a try. He thought that he might have misunderstood the instructions. He would never take a risk with substances like LSD or hard drugs.

He could be easily taken in by fake news items and other hoaxes. He was influenced by modish radicals and social critics, as well as by foreign anti-establishment "gurus". He read the books and essays of Marshall McLuhan, Ivan Illich, Paolo Freire, R. D. Laing and Jules Henry (author of *Culture Against Man*). Jonathan, an admirer of the works of William Blake, was talking about the need to "de-school" society about four years before Illich published his controversial book on the subject.

He was still going steady with Catherine, who'd come up from Oxford to stay most weekends, when he met Jenny, a tall, slinky trainee teacher at the comprehensive school where they were both doing their teaching practice. He couldn't take his eyes off her in the staff room. It wasn't long before he found out that she was hot, hungry, innovative and very demanding in bed. She knew exactly what she wanted, and how often, and anticipated his every desire, initiating him into novel forms of fore-play, helping him to reach new heights of pleasure by inducting him to give and take previously unimagined sensual delights. She was a very foxy lady, as Jimi Hendrix would have called her. It was a wild time, but in spite of his penchant for adventure (sexual and otherwise), he couldn't keep up for many months with two alternating and equally needy, regular sexual partners, one mid-week and the other at weekends.

He relaxed by going with friends to the nearby UFO Club in Tottenham Court Road to listen to experimental rock music by bands like Pink Floyd, to watch mesmerising light shows, projected liquid psychedelic slides which formed magical, constantly changing multi-coloured abstract patterns. Jonathan never smoked pot himself; in some respects he was quite conservative, health-conscious and rational. The music was enough in itself to make him feel good.

He caught Jimi Hendrix's first amazing, mind-blowing gig at the packed Marquee Club in Wardour Street, in January 1967.

He felt right in the centre of the "underground" counter-culture in the autumn and winter of 1966, and the spring and summer of 1967, the appropriately named *Summer of Love*. At the same time he was becoming exhausted and suffocated by life in the city and by commuting on overcrowded underground trains, and he started to think about ways of escape. He'd grown up as a country boy, with a love of the countryside and sea.

There was something of a contrast between the staid lectures on the philosophy and ethics of education and the hippy, "drop-out" lifestyle to which he enthusiastically subscribed during that period — and what a great contrast he found between events like the *14 Hour Technicolour Dream* up at Alexandra Palace, and the strictly-invigilated examinations he had to sit in those same cavernous halls a few months later.

If he found the ethics of education a dry and largely irrelevant topic, he embraced many of the views and theories of progressive sociologists and of liberal-left tutors committed to the teaching of the English language, literature and creative writing at inner-city comprehensive schools. Jonathan would try some unorthodox things in his classes, even when his lessons were being observed and assessed. He would get his groups of usually bored and inattentive fifteen-year-olds writing about topics like *going mad* after they'd discussed schizophrenia; he once took a cage of rats into class, and read them extracts from Camus and Sillitoe to inspire their own writing. He took in recordings of the sound of the sea and of Debussy's *La Mer* to stimulate their imaginations to write about the ocean. They produced some marvellous and impressive original writing. No one was too concerned about the teaching of grammar or spelling in those days. Discipline was always a problem.

He started taking an 8mm movie camera into the class for a group project about teenage rebellion. He invited the unruly pupils (who expected to leave school at the end of the summer) to throw paper missiles towards the camera-lens and directly at him, so that he could obtain some good action shots. They cooperated with a vengeance, not just with compacted balls of paper: "To Sir, *Without* Love". He was lucky to escape relatively unharmed. Still, the footage looked convincingly authentic. He became a little more cautious in his approach after that experience, however popular it made him. Kids would always take advantage, if they could, Jonathan decided. It didn't pay to be too friendly, even if such unusual materials and methods seemed to grab their attention and to motivate them.

Jonathan duly received his postgraduate certificate in education and a letter confirming his status as a qualified teacher; a few weeks later, he disappeared. He dropped out in earnest. He didn't tell his friends or girl-friends where he was going. He lost contact with them all. He became a globe-trotter. He was last heard of in Djibouti, where he was rumoured to be active as an arms-dealer — a gun-runner supplying weapons indiscriminately to groups of Afars, Somalis and Eritreans; to make matters worse, some said he was also a drugs dealer.

His cover job was as a teacher of English. He'd taken a Somali mistress. It was said that she was very jealous, and one day she became suspicious that he'd taken another lover. She promptly poisoned him, so his adventures came to an early and unedifying end. It was not forgotten in London that he still owed a month's rent to his fellow house-mates from their days at Goodge Place. Jonathan himself had never forgotten that they hadn't returned his LP record of Debussy's *La Mer*.

He died with a clear conscience. They were more or less quits.

The dropout

Today we bought the house by the well . . . The Cyprus issue is becoming more venomous every day and they are making bonfires of Union Jacks in Athens and everything English is hated with an intensity that is in directly inverse ratio to the love the English used to command in Greece: everything, that is, except the golden sovereign.

Charmian Clift writing on Hydra
in 1956, in *Peel Me a Lotus* (1959)

While we await the clearing of the mail we study the passengers landing from the longboats which are rowed out beyond the harbour entrance to meet the trim white steamer . . . we are an established and recognized "foreign colony" now, bohemians to them, and artists and existentialists, outlandish oddities, rejectionists, dropouts from their own social systems, mavericks, even decadents . . .

George Johnston, "Greece, 1959"
in *Clean straw for nothing* (1969)

Geoff Dixon was employed as a teacher of English at the British Council Institute in Kolonaki Square in Athens. He'd always felt something of an outsider in his country of birth. Born in 1934, he was appointed in 1955, when he was just twenty-one. It couldn't have been at a worse time, from a political point of view. The last issue of the *Anglo-Greek Review* was published in the spring of 1955. The British Council's Corfu branch closed that year. Its director, Maria Aspioti, resigned from her post in protest against British policies in Cyprus and returned her MBE. The British Institute and Library on Cyprus were burned down on 12 September, 1955.

The post-war "Golden Years" of the British Council in Greece were over, at least for the time being.

Geoff worked in Athens until the teaching staff was greatly

reduced and the Institute closed down as a result of the deteriorating Cyprus situation of 1956–57 and the bomb that exploded over the Christmas holidays in December 1957. That same year, Lawrence Durrell moved to France, after leaving his controversial and compromising post as Director of Information Services for the British colonial government in Cyprus (his book, *Bitter Lemons*, was published in 1957); and Francis King was transferred from the British Council in Athens to a post in Finland. Geoff kept up with the gossip. He had his networks. Geoff's father was English, his mother American. They were divorced and his mother had returned to live in San Francisco. Geoff made a point of telling Greek friends and acquaintances that he was American. It was lucky that he possessed an American passport, which he'd started using instead of the British one, as the Aliens' Police had it in for English residents, and on some islands the few who still lived there were being forced to leave.

Sometimes he claimed that he was Australian, as his brother had emigrated and lived in Melbourne, where he had made a lot of Greek friends. Geoff was tired of reading about the Suez Crisis and the Kenyan Emergency or Mau Mau Uprising, of hearing Greek schoolchildren chanting pro-EOKA anti-British songs, some aimed at Sir John Harding, Governor of Cyprus from October 1955 to October 1957. One taunting verse, often heard from school playgrounds, went something like this:

> *Koróido pou íse Harding*
> *pou ólo míyes káphteis.*
> *Esí ke i patrída sou i Anglía i yelia*
> *apó ti charti chathí.*

> You're just a bad joke, Harding,
> always gobbling flies.
> You and your silly country England
> will be wiped right off the map.

Both the Council's Representative, Roger Hinks (once linked to the controversial cleaning of some of the "Elgin" Parthenon marbles at The British Museum, in the period 1938–39), and the director of the Institute, had thought of him as a well-educated young man, a thoroughly respectable Oxford graduate, a promising teacher, popular with the more advanced Cambridge Certificate of Proficiency students — although, in truth, Geoff had little classroom experience and, beyond his Oxford degree in English Language and Literature, no other qualification to teach English as a foreign language. Geoff had received a very positive reference from Maurice Bowra (the classical scholar and Warden of Geoff's Oxford college, Wadham), who'd been in Greece the previous year, the last year of his tenure as Vice-Chancellor; Bowra had close links with British Council headquarters in London and chaired one of its advisory committees.

Hinks was secretly relieved that Geoff was heterosexual and didn't share the same proclivities or inclinations as Francis King, or indeed of Maurice Bowra, but there was another side to Geoff's character, beneath his mask of polite, conservative respectability. They wouldn't have recognised him at weekends or during the Institute's holiday periods, when he would catch the steamboat from Piraeus to the island of Hydra, to mix with barefoot bohemian writers, artists, folk-singers and musicians, some of whom had taken up temporary or semi-permanent residence there, in spite of the lack of electric power and motorised transportation. They relied on mules and donkeys to get around the steep, cobbled paths and through the maze of narrow, white-washed lanes, to climb the hundreds of steps up to fortified stone houses perched on rocky headlands dotted with windmills.

This was all part of the attraction of the island, which had become better known as the result of Michael Cacoyannis' black and white film, *A Girl in Black*, which was first shown at the ninth Cannes International Film Festival in 1956. Geoff saw the film when it came out in Athens and immediately fell for the striking female actress, Ellie Lambetti, who starred as "Marina". He was even more impressed by the cinematography of Walter Lassally, the way he and Cacoyannis handled the tragic scenes of the children's drowning and the funeral that followed. Geoff was more ambivalent about the voluptuous and glamorous Sophia Loren, who played the part of "Phaedra" in the 20th Century Fox Hollywood colour movie, *Boy on a Dolphin*, a year later.

Geoff's mother saw that movie in San Francisco in April 1957, and wrote to tell him all about it. Geoff had no illusions about rubbing shoulders with film-stars — his ambition was to become one of the first British "Beat poets", writing by the light of a paraffin lamp in an old stone house high up above the port, with a glimpse of the sea and the harbour. New York and San Francisco didn't seem so far away, as Americans (as well as Australians and Canadians), would turn up from time to time, along with Scandinavian and other European blow-ins and drop-ins (who came to Hydra to *drop out*, at least for a while).

Geoff had been very excited by Jack Kerouac's novel, *On the Road*. His mother had sent him an advance copy of the first US edition, published by Viking, New York, in 1957. His favourite book about Greece remained Henry Miller's *The Colossus of Maroussi*.

After the British Institute started laying off its teaching staff, Geoff decided to try his luck as a writer; he had saved enough money to rent a small place on Hydra, at least for the first winter. If it proved necessary, he would give private English lessons, for which there was a growing demand, in spite of the Cyprus situation. The Brits in Greece had to be especially careful what they said in public, especially after the hanging of Michalis Karaolis in May 1956.

On the steamboat to Hydra, and on the longboat that took them ashore to the harbour-side, he'd got chatting with an American folk-singer and guitar-player, who was travelling with his wife on the same ferry. It turned out to be Ramblin' Jack Elliott, who was three years his senior. When he was on leave in London in 1956, Geoff had bought a 78rpm record by Ramblin' Jack, on the Topic label. It had been recorded at the end of 1955. It was a talking blues. Geoff had even seen him perform in a small folk-club. Ramblin' Jack was singing his way round the world. Geoff had often improvised his own witty talking blues about the characters he met.

He was well up with American folk, blues and jazz music. He liked listening to Charlie Parker and to Charles Mingus (*Pithecanthropus Erectus* being his favourite), to the songs of Leadbelly and Woodie Guthrie, to skiffle, rock 'n' roll and rhythm 'n' blues records. He had eclectic tastes; he wasn't a "mouldy-fig" purist.

He'd decided to buy a second-hand Austin A35 van when on leave in England and to take it back with him to Athens. He had enough room to take a trunk of his favourite books with him, novels by Camus, Kazantzakis and Kafka, as well as some works by Henry Miller, Lawrence Durrell's *Justine* and some volumes of his poetry. Geoff identified more with the American Beats than with the British "Angry Young Men"; he'd sympathised, but only to a limited extent, with the outbursts of Jimmy Porter, the main character in John Osborne's *Look Back in Anger*.

He also took with him a very rare first, limited, City Lights edition of Lawrence Ferlinghetti's *Pictures of the Gone World* and a first edition of Allen Ginsberg's *Howl and Other Poems*, and a lot of books about Greece, from Ancient Drama to recent anthropological studies. His car wouldn't be of any use to him on Hydra, of course, but he lent it to a grateful Athenian friend; Geoff could use it to explore Greece when he was back on the mainland.

On Hydra, Geoff kept a low profile, in the sense that he avoided being photographed with his bohemian friends. He preferred to be "invisible". He didn't want his bosses or referees, past, present or future, to discover the company he kept or how he chose to lead his life outside the classroom. If he was going to have affairs with women, whether married or single, that was strictly his own business. Geoff was nothing if not discrete. It became more difficult as Hydra became more fashionable and the expatriate "colony" grew in size. It wasn't such a problem in 1957, although the resident Australian writers George Johnston and

Charmian Clift would sometimes take photos of people they met. They were waiting at the harbour when Geoff arrived, still deep in conversation with Jack Elliott. They joined them for a drink at the Katsikas store and drinking-hole. George was obviously intrigued by Jack's hat and his guitar (he showed less interest in Geoff's guitar). Jack and his pretty wife were soon invited to stay at their house. Geoff preferred to find his own accommodation, but one evening he joined them for an informal sing-song at their house. He even accompanied Ramblin' Jack on the harmonica in a couple of Woodie Guthrie songs. On other occasions they would get together at Douskos taverna and end the evening by singing in the courtyard outside the taverna.

There was a well in another small square, in front of the Johnston-Clift house, which was to play a part in this story some years later.

Geoff, now resident on Hydra himself, was present on the evening in September 1960 that the photo-journalist James Burke photographed a group, which included Leonard Cohen, enjoying themselves outside Douskos' taverna. Geoff kept himself in the background, and managed to keep out of frame whenever he saw James Burke appear with his camera, as his photos were intended for publication in *Life* magazine. Geoff would have loved to accompany Jack with his own battered guitar, but he had to restrain the impulse to join in; he was more of a blues guitarist in any case. He knew that he was being absurdly paranoid, but he didn't know when or if he might try to secure another post with the British Council, or even with the Foreign Office. He wasn't having much success with his poetry, and he had two unfinished novels in a drawer. He had lost interest in them. He kept a diary, or a journal rather, in which he recorded with great care the development of his relationships, attractions and affairs. He never wrote down the names of the women, not even their initials, so it was hard for later researchers interested in the period to be sure to whom he was referring. Just as Geoff never appeared in any photographs, he was never to get a mention in any of the memoirs which were published many years later. He really was the invisible drop-out

There came a time when one of his less discrete affairs threatened to get him into very deep water. He decided he would have to leave the island in a hurry, as he was being threatened with violence and retribution by a jealous husband. It was just his luck that an extraordinarily fierce storm, more of a hurricane, was approaching, and all boats and ferries were ordered to stay in port. Everyone on the island was cut off. The stormy conditions continued for almost a week. Geoff was more desperate than most at finding himself stranded on the island, even though supplies of food soon began to run short, for all the residents. The winds kept blowing at around 9–10 Beaufort. Yachts and *kaikia* which had not been adequately moored were driven against the harbour wall. He thought of hiring a mule or donkey to take him up the cobbled lanes to the higher parts of the island, to lie low in a monastery, but he realised that he couldn't be invisible, or avoid being seen. There was no escape. He would have to face the music. This was no subject for a talking blues.

The man he'd cuckolded after a drunken night down at Katsikas' had been befriended, like many other new arrivals, by George Johnston and Charmian Clift; they'd helped him and his wife to find a house to rent very close to their own, before they left for a six month break in England.

Geoff decided he would try to make amends with the irate husband. He came across him drawing water from the well in front of the Johnson-Clift house. The man's wife came out of their own house, looking hostile rather than sheepish, as if she too was set on vengeance, if only to save face — and her marriage. Geoff hoped that she was just acting.

He didn't get a chance to explain. He stood beside the wronged husband, as if to help him draw up the heavy bucket of water as a symbolic act of guilty atonement.

"Have you ever seen a painting by Elisabetta Serani of what happened to one of Alexander's captains?" asked the man's straying wife.

"No, I can't say I have," replied Geoff, cautiously, nervously.

The offended couple suddenly grabbed him by the legs and threatened to tip him over and to drop him headlong down into the well-shaft.

"It was of a scene something like this!"

"Now you'll know what it's really like to be a sponge-diver," hissed the man, sadistically.

At the last minute, his wife decided to keep a tight hold on Geoff's ankles. She wouldn't let go. The strength of her grip prevented him from falling into the icy water. It was a very close call. It seemed that she didn't want to end her days in prison; nor did she want her husband to be charged with murder.

There was nobody else around. Most of their expatriate friends were still drinking at Douskos' taverna. George and Charmian had taken their children to England for a few months. No living being witnessed what had happened, except for some of the island's cat population.

The next day the winds dropped. The ferry-boat arrived even though the seas were still high and very rough, the white horses unrelenting. The boat was rolling, dipping and bobbing in and out of the troughs, swells and spray. Geoff managed to leave the island, glad to be alive; he had come close to being drowned at the bottom of a well or to having his dead body carted and wheeled away in a long-handled wooden barrow, to be tipped down a ravine or rock-chute, perhaps, dumped with the rest of the island's rubbish. He tried not to look back at the harbour, which he had once found so beautiful, which now only filled him with dread.

Years later, he still felt relieved to think that there was no photograph to attest to his time or behaviour on Hydra; no published memoirs had so far mentioned him by name. Not even the most thorough researchers were likely to dig anything up.

Geoff often thought about those days, after he'd resumed his career with the British Council, thanks to yet another good reference from the Warden of Wadham, who approved of any college alumni who had spent time on Hydra, or elsewhere in Greece.

Geoffrey (no longer Geoff, even to his friends) was relatively successful, on his own terms. He was appointed Representative on Cyprus. One evening he was giving a lecture about the Aegean Islands. During the questions at the end, a member of the audience, whose face seemed vaguely familiar, asked him if he'd ever spent any time on Hydra.

Geoff paused. "I believe I made one or two day-trip excursions there."

"That's strange," said the questioner. "I have a number of interesting photographs in my albums. I am sure I recognised your face amongst the photos I once took of a group of expatriates and philanderers drinking and behaving rather wildly outside one of the *tavernas*. My wife thinks that it was certainly you. Would you like to join us for dinner one evening? We now live here on Cyprus. I'm sure we have a great deal to talk about. It's high time I settled down to do a bit of writing and reminiscing. Perhaps you could help to jog my memory? You may recall that my somewhat feminist wife liked to be known as Timoclea. I'm sure you're familiar with the painting by Serani."

Beneath the gibbet

Most of the time, life in Castle Cary was peaceful and uneventful. Alex was preparing to go to university, and his friend Ken was set on a career in the armed forces. The year was 1962. Somerset didn't seem a very exciting place to hang around when the world had so much else to offer.

Both of them had a period of some months free to set out on more adventurous travels than either had experienced in the past. They decided they would hitch-hike down to Spain, and then to Gibraltar, before crossing over to Tangier from Algeciras.

In Barcelona they met Phil, an American beat, who introduced them to the local night-life and to the availability of amphetamines, which could be bought over the counter, at any Spanish pharmacy, without prescription; the instructions on the tube recommended them for use by athletes or by students taking exams. Alex couldn't remember all the ingredients of *Centramina,* but it was mostly Benzedrine. The little tablets had a powerful effect for just 22 pesetas a tube.

When they took the ferry to the island of Mallorca, they set out on foot for the other side of the island, a walk of about forty kilometres. They had brought very heavy army-surplus backpacks, as well as old-fashioned tents and sleeping bags, and other less essential kit for camping.

They both took some *Centramina* tablets, and the instant energy boost made the walk a doddle, and the path turned into a trampoline.

They set up their tents in an olive grove near a beautiful bay, but that night there was a terrible thunderstorm; the heavy rain became a torrent on the ground and ran like a raging river straight through their tents. The next morning, the shared experience brought all the campers together, and they befriended a French family; two of the daughters seemed to like them a lot, so they stayed for a week.

Shortly after they arrived in Gibraltar, they both fell ill; they'd slept the first night in a smelly disused gun-bunker. After they'd seen the Rock's Barbary Macaque monkeys (or were they apes?), they decided to move on. They didn't like the cold British stares. Everything was too similar to Somerset.

As they walked down the ferry-boat gangplank in Tangier with their heavyweight rucksacks, they pushed past the porters and hurried through customs, not stopping to change their remaining currency at the bureau of the Bank of Morocco, which only gave 13 *dirham* to the pound, whereas Phil had told them you could get 16 from the black market moneychangers who roamed the dark narrow streets of the Medina and Kasbah.

Tangier came as a culture-shock after Gibraltar, but the bartering in the bazaars of the Kasbah fascinated them. It took them over an hour of haggling just to buy a leather belt. In the evening, they crossed the railway track to reach the beach, that mammoth golden smile of the Tangier beach, where they sank into the sand for a troubled but visionless sleep.

After a few days in Tangier, they couldn't face the thought of the long hitch-hike home, so they made their way by bus to the port at Casablanca, to try to find a way to work their passages home on a ship. They trudged round the cargo companies in town. They had no luck, as they weren't members of the seamen's union. An English captain threw them out on their ears; Dutch, French and Moroccan captains laughed in their faces. Feeling depressed, they went to the youth-hostel, which lacked both water and electricity. They were accompanied to their bunks by a candle and cockroaches. It was better than a gun-bunker or a river running through their tents. They left the next morning.

Back in Spain they had very little luck with lifts; they had just enough money to buy some tickets for the *correo* trains, which trundled slowly along, stopping at every village.

To pass the time, Alex took some more *Centramina* tablets, and spent the night sprawled against his rucksack on the floor of a corridor, where he wrote an almost endless beat narrative the length of a whole toilet roll, on which he scribbled wild and muddled poems and philosophical thoughts which he was convinced, while he was still high, were full of deeply profound perceptions. Unfortunately he had cause to make proper use of the paper the next morning. A masterpiece flushed down the toilet.

Finally they made it, completely washed-out and exhausted, back to Dover. At some point they had to separate, in the hope that it would be easier to get lifts; they looked less threatening on their own.

Alex was the last to reach Somerset; he was dropped off at night at the cross-roads known as Jack White's Gibbet, on the road between Wincanton and Castle Cary. There was no traffic at all, and Alex decided that, if he was going to spend most of the night on the grass verge at the side of the road, opposite some dark woodland, he might as well finish off his remaining *Centramina* tablets.

He'd once read some accounts of Jack White, who'd murdered a stranger called Bob Sutton for his money, bludgeoned him to death, back in 1730; he was caught, and sentenced to be hanged in chains, and his corpse was left to dangle in a gibbet-cage, on the very spot where Alex had collapsed. He had never been afraid of the dark or of ghosts, but he hadn't counted on the hallucinatory effects of the pills, taken in a much larger dose than was prescribed on the tube.

Alex could hear the owls hooting, the ravens croaking and bats were flying all around him. He could see the gibbet cage swinging right above his head, and every so often he could hear the corpse crying and moaning "Jack's cold, so cold". Alex felt drops of blood oozing out of the carcase dangling above him. The corpse of Jack White spoke one last time, before Alex panicked, leapt up and fled down the road, "Have mercy on my soul! There are hellhounds in pursuit of me; it was the Devil told me what to do."

◆

Alex went to work overseas, but for more than fifty-five years, whenever he was on home leave in Somerset, he would avoid driving past Jack White's Gibbet or anywhere near the spot. When he retired and finally returned to England, he decided to settle in Dorset.

He determined to research the historical facts surrounding Jack White, and the various versions of the legend which he could find in the archives of the Castle Cary Museum and in the pages of *The Castle Cary Visitor*. He was reminded of the spooky dialect poems and ballads by William and Douglas Macmillan, influential local figures in both the Somerset folklore and the temperance movements. Their poems and tales had scared him out of his wits as a child.

The Museum was opposite the George Hotel, the old coaching inn which also played a part, in some accounts, as the place where Jack may have met the stranger with whom he started drinking, the man he later followed and killed. Other versions gave the fateful meeting place as Yarlington Fair.

One winter's day, when he couldn't decide whether to have lunch at the George Hotel or at the Stag's Arms in Yarlington, he picked up all his courage to return to the spot where he was sure the gibbet had once stood. He took many photographs, half-expecting that grim, shadowy shapes, unseen to the naked eye, would be captured by some form of supernatural digital magic. He didn't stay there long as he was starting to shiver; the dark patch of woodland opposite unnerved him, and it was getting cold, *very cold.*

He drove as fast as he could back to Dorchester, as if he was being pursued by the hounds of hell.

That night he tried to remember his happy childhood days in Somerset, when Jack White's Gibbet was just a signpost and a place-name on the map.

He had to admit that there were many good things to be said for Somerset.

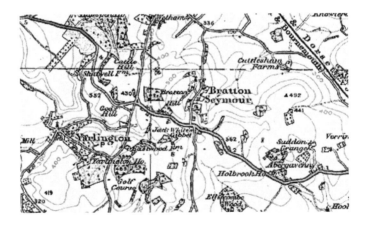

A librarian in Addis Ababa

> For books are not absolutely dead things, but do
> contain a potency of life in them to be as active as that
> soul whose progeny they are [...] A good book is the
> precious life-blood of a master spirit, embalmed and
> treasured up on purpose to a life beyond life.
>
> John Milton, *Areopagitica* (1644)

The English-language library was located in the Artistic Building,
on a busy thoroughfare in the centre of town, above a well-known
stationery store.

Wayziro AlemNesh valued her own precious life-blood less
than the books on the library shelves. No one really knew her, this
quiet, seemingly friendless young married woman. She stamped
the books and filed the cards, smiled shyly, exchanged just a few
words, seldom stopping to pass the time of day. She was hard-
working, a diligent assistant, who performed her duties to
perfection. She saw herself as a guardian of the books; very few
ever went missing, but they were all very well used in the spacious,
busy, brightly lit library, which had lots of desks at which people
could sit and study. Her behaviour gave nothing away, but she was
determined to die.

Some days before her death, as her colleagues clearly recalled,
she asked for her library key; yes, some of them had seen her with
some rope, but they never suspected its purpose or sensed her
utter loss of hope. They thought she was going to tie up a parcel.

On the eve of a public holiday, when the library was deserted
and dark, AlemNesh left her house and husband, wearing her best
silver neck-cross and her white cotton *shema* dress with its beautiful coloured embroidery, and a shawl round her shoulders, to step
out for a breath of fresh air and to visit a neighbour. Instead of
that, she crept furtively back to the library, and bolted the front
door behind her. She must have known that no one would be able

to save her.

She was a conscientious woman. In my mind I can see her clearly, rearranging books as she tip-toed past the shelves. Did she read a few last words of her beloved Shakespeare or Milton? Could cold books have helped her then? Perhaps she gave a final dust to the spine of her favourite volume, *Paradise Lost*. The master-spirits were silent; she could not be dissuaded from death.

She locked herself in the lavatory, and secured her length of rope. She left no farewell note. It seems the rope broke twice, but she was resourceful and determined; she'd managed to repair it each time, by looping and knotting it together. They found her two days later. She put an end not only to her life, but also to that of the baby she was carrying.

It is not her death so much which disturbed us, tragic as it was, for that was a personal thing, but all the months and years before it, when we didn't say or notice anything.

◆

A few years later the library was in the news again. Angry, marching students had started throwing rocks at the office and tried to set fire to the library, but the solid building wouldn't burn. The younger schoolboys and schoolgirls who were studying there, reading for hours in their rags, many of them bare-footed, tried to save the precious books. They called on the master-spirits, but what could the books or authors do? Could they throw back rocks, could they put out flames? The children had learnt the value of knowledge and they didn't want to lose their library; but reluctantly they left by a back door for their own safety, taking out of harm's way as many books as they could carry.

Then, miraculously, the students' siege suddenly stopped. No more stones or flaming torches were thrown. The ringleaders had seen AlemNesh's face, framed in a first-floor window. She was standing there, a figure of defiance, resolutely defending her life's companions.

Going down slow (with a clear conscience)

When Henry was old enough to start speculating about the source of his family's modest wealth, and more specifically about his grandmother's frequent impulsive acts of generosity to friends as well as family, he'd already gone up to Oxford to read History.

He'd always taken it for granted that money was not a problem; he hadn't appreciated that the substantial extension to the house in which they all lived had been mostly paid for by his grandmother's money, thanks to her ample means, the regular dividends from her still considerable inherited portfolio of shares and her bank account at Coutts. Now he'd also come to understand that his private schooling and university education had been made more feasible thanks to her discrete support, though his father carried most of the burden. Henry hadn't qualified for a state grant, but in his day there were no tuition fees to pay at university.

What was the ultimate source of her wealth, now considerably diminished as a result of her generosity? He didn't find out until after she'd died and he'd started to help his mother with the paperwork, going through his grandmother's tin box and the drawers of her antique writing bureau, sorting out her old correspondence, family papers and share certificates.

He was able to follow a paper trail which led back to a wealthy Lowland Scots expatriate, a retired "nabob", who, from the late

1750's, had risen up in the ranks of the East India Company from writer to senior merchant, who'd served for nearly thirty years in the Bombay Presidency, been appointed in the mid-1780's to its governing body, the Bombay Council, and made a fortune large enough to instruct his commissioners to buy an estate of many thousands of acres in Midlothian and to rebuild the stately home there. The huge estate included farms and all their buildings, several mining villages and a number of profitable pits. On his return to Scotland he was elected as an MP, but he had only a few years left after his retirement from the East India Company to enjoy the shooting and weekend house parties on his estate.

After his death, the house, the farms, the mining villages, pits and estate passed down through several generations of the family until they were inherited by Henry's great-grandfather, who was then serving as an officer in the Black Watch, but *he* didn't do much to consolidate the wealth he'd inherited.

He spent his life in London as an absentee landlord, living it up in the inner circle of King Edward VII, from the 1890's (when Edward was still Prince of Wales) until the outbreak of the First

World War. Henry's great-grandfather had a handsome apartment near the palace of St. James. He didn't exactly squander his fortune, but the aristocratic playboy-courtier lifestyle caused his health to suffer and before the end of the war, he'd resolved to settle down, to move out of London to live with his daughter, who'd worked in the War Office and who'd lost her husband in the early stages of trench-fighting. His young granddaughter (Henry's mother) lived with them and they all enjoyed a comfortable lifestyle, but most of the servants had to be dismissed after his illness and death. Henry's grandmother and his mother inherited much of his moveable wealth when he died, in his sixties, although the Scottish estate and all the hereditable, immoveable property went, according to Scottish law, to the eldest son from an earlier union.

As a student of history, Henry took pride and interest in the achievements of the British Empire. He was relieved to discover that he had no ancestors who might have been involved in the slave trade. But the more he learned about the activities of the East India Company, the more troubled was his conscience. His forebear had not only been a successful merchant, he'd also supplied clothing and equipment to the army officers in Bombay. Were the profits from this eighteenth century entrepreneurial activity the ultimate source of the invested capital which still supported young Henry's education and lifestyle?

In his third year at Oxford, Henry made the momentous decision to sell all his shares. He told his friends that he was going to have a new will drawn up by his solicitor, with the intention of leaving half his inherited money to the Mumbai Street Children's Charity in aid of the 250,000 street children of that city; the other half he said he would split between a Scottish Mining Museum and a Charitable Welfare Fund for the Children of Miners.

Henry disappeared. He never took his degree, but he left a note pinned to the desk in his college rooms in which he'd written, "At least I'm going down from Oxford with a clear conscience."

None of us, his friends at the time, took the trouble to investigate whether the museum and the charities that Henry said he'd chosen ever received those unprecedentedly large intended donations from an anonymous source.

It's possible that Henry did have in mind to change the terms of his will, but never actually put the changes in writing, and that he kept for himself all the money he'd realised by selling his shares.

Had he gone away hoping to enjoy the good life, not in the style of his great-grandfather, but on some remote Caribbean or Pacific island?

He'd always admired the exotic paintings of Gauguin, and the sensual lifestyle of Gauguin the man, in spite of the suspicion that syphilis might have been the cause of the painter's death. Perhaps the blues-singer St. Louis Jimmy had someone like Gauguin in mind when he wrote the song, "Going Down Slow".

Anything's possible, even for idealistic aid-workers of supposed integrity employed by charities in disaster zones, for renowned artists and bawdy-house blues-singers, or for a man going down from Oxford claiming a clear conscience.

North and south: four generations

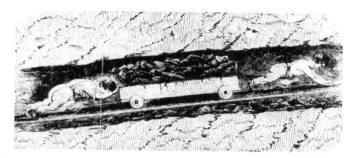

Thomas was already working in the Poynton coal mines by the age of ten. He started as a surface loader in 1850, but it wasn't long before the bosses sent him down the pit — to join about one-hundred-and-fifty other small boys slaving underground for up to seventy-two hours a week — like his father before him and his grandfather before *him*.

Thomas married in 1866. He wouldn't live to celebrate his fiftieth birthday. The hours he'd worked as a getter at the coal-face had been reduced to fifty-four a week when he was thirty-two, but by then any improvements in working conditions were much too late for him.

His widow had worked as a domestic, as a handloom silk

weaver and finally as a small-time grocer, a "purveyor of provisions". The shop was on the ground floor of their modest terraced house. She was a capable woman who brought up their four children conscientiously and correctly. They went to school and acquired the skills of literacy and numeracy, which stood them in good stead. They didn't have to work in the pits. She had saved enough money to buy a plot in the church graveyard and to erect a fine headstone for her husband when he died in the summer of 1890.

Elizabeth missed Thomas and never stopped grieving for him. He had survived disastrous accidents in the pit in which some of his relatives and colleagues had been killed (one of them was crushed between the top of the cage and headgear), but the doctors couldn't cure his chronic pulmonary problems, "black lung" or pneumoconiosis, the miners' coal-dust lung disease. Twenty-five years in the coalmines had reduced him to a shadow of a man. When he was laid off, it wasn't because of his failing health but because of the falling price of coal. One of Lord Vernon's pit foremen informed Thomas that he was superfluous.

Their eldest son, who had eventually achieved a high level of numeracy and literacy, and acquired some impressive letter-writing skills and a fine copper-plate hand, was offered a good job as a clerk in a large solicitors' office. Sadly, he was also destined to die before his fiftieth birthday. He was forty-nine.

His son, an only child, attended a grammar school. Later he moved south and married well. He became a successful, hard-working businessman after he'd returned from the War. In the late twenties and early thirties he'd had elocution lessons to eliminate his Cheshire accent, but he never lost touch with his cousins in the Poynton area. He lived more than ten years longer than his predecessors, succumbing to a heart attack at the age of sixty two.

And one of *his* sons won a place at university (the first in the family), where he became a folk-singer, singing angry protest songs about the harsh treatment of coal-miners, about child-labour, pit disasters and greedy pit-masters. He supported miners' strikes. The strange thing is that he had known nothing about his grandfather's or great-grandfather's working lives in the coal-mines. His father had never talked about them or their experiences. Not even once.

When, quite late in life, he discovered an interest in genealogy, and found the time to do some research into family history, he came to the conclusion that the mining tradition must have been in his blood. In his voice you could hear harsh gravelly overtones, strangled, rasping sounds, like coal-dust in the lungs.

The last three slices

Mr Zoiros was perched on the proprietor's stool behind the till, just to the left of the front door inside his famous *kapheneio* and cake shop, which also served ouzo with tasty *mezedes*. His customers were mostly regulars who had been coming there towards midday every morning for many decades. They saw it as their social club beneath the arches of the Liston; many of them, the older pensioners and those who wanted to be seen in their faded finery, or to meet their friends, preferred the tables under the elegant Rue-de-Rivoli-style arches to the shade of the trees and umbrellas on the other side of the road, at the edge of the *plateia*.

Mr Zoiros had nodded off, as was his wont, and he could sometimes be heard snoring rather loudly. He would wake up to put money in the till, to issue a receipt or to acknowledge local people who would simply dash in (sometimes rather furtively) to make use of his convenient and well-appointed lavatories. He had long wanted to close the *kapheneio*, but he didn't want to let down the loyal pensioners who frequented his establishment. The problem was that they didn't spend much money; they preferred to nurse a small Greek coffee and a glass of water for a few hours rather than to make room for others under the arches. Those who drank ouzos often ordered a second. It was quite an art, making a couple of drinks last for most of the morning, but it wasn't really thirsty work making small talk with other pensioners of their own vintage.

Young people seldom came to Zoiros, they preferred the trendier *kapheneia* at the noisier, crowded Pendephanero end of the Liston, rather than the more sedate cafes at the Royal Palace end.

The smarter set of Corfu Town pensioners avoided Zoiros on Sundays, Sunday being the day when villagers came to town to take a stroll along the Liston and to indulge in a coffee and a sticky cake, a beer or an ouzo.

A more important factor in Mr Zoiros' delay in shutting up his shop was his sense of responsibility towards his long-serving waiters — far more experienced and professional than most of the others in the less prestigious establishments. Mr Zoiros had decided not to close down until the last of his waiters reached retirement age and became entitled to receive his pension.

As that auspicious day approached, Mr Zoiros started cancelling his orders from the cake suppliers, the pastry cooks (the *zacharoplastes*) and stopped replenishing his stock of little sausages and frozen shrimps for the *mezedes*.

The time came when there were no more *mezedes* (apart from a few chips) to accompany a glass of ouzo, and when there were just three slices of chocolate gateau left in the cooled glass display case.

As these were in danger of going dry, Mr Zoiros tried to come to a decision — to make an existential choice.

Should he give them to the hungry stray dogs which wandered the street from time to time, or should he offer them to some of the more down-and-out foreign tourists, who reminded him of the unkempt hippies from the 1960s?

Before he could make up his mind, he fell asleep again and was snoring regularly; the last waiter to receive his pension shook his head sadly, tipping the three remaining slices of cake into the bin.

The end of the chocolate gateau, the end of an era . . .

The pensioners of Corfu Town now had nowhere to go, except perhaps to visit a priest or a psychiatrist.

Even more than a favoured meeting place for gossiping with friends, even more than the ouzo and *mezedes,* the coffee and cakes, they would miss the ease of access to suitably sanitary conveniences in the best part of town, where they could confidently drop in to "powder their noses" or "wash their hands". To an elderly pensioner, that is a matter of the greatest concern.

The school ski trip

It's never been my habit to participate in Old Boys' School Reunions (even though the school had a big celebration this year, the five-hundredth anniversary of its first foundation), or to pay much attention to the activities of Alumni Associations. I have kept up with only two or three class-mates, who have remained amongst my closest friends. When one of them decided to write a novel about his adolescent years, he asked me if I would be willing to read it, chapter by chapter, and to act as his initial editor before he submitted it to a publisher. I agreed, because I remembered most of his adventures and stories, but there were some events and anecdotes he had never shared with me. What follows is the draft of part of one of the chapters that he sent to me for my comments. I reproduce it here with his permission, as he hasn't yet found a publisher who wants to publish the whole novel.

Watching the Salt Lake Winter Olympics on television in February 2002 reminded me of my school skiing trip, to Sölden and Hochsölden, Upper Ötztal, in the Austrian Tirol. The trip took place in December 1960, when I had just turned 16.

I recently pulled my box of old picture postcards out of the cupboard, and found quite a few that I'd sent home from the Tirol.

It was my first overseas trip (unless I count Guernsey and the Channel Islands, where I'd been taken on holiday in August 1958; I was thirteen, and it was there that I first heard the name of Victor Hugo and began to understand the meaning of *exile*, when I visited Hauteville House, where Hugo had spent fifteen years in exile on the island). Austria was my first trip without either of my parents.

Mr Robertson, the school's history and drama teacher and leader of the expedition, was more tolerant about the boys' behaviour than most of the staff. I got on well with him until he gave me the unfortunate nickname "Lax". Some of the other boys

THE SCHOOL SKI TRIP

had discovered that my ever-cautious mother had secretly packed, in a plastic bag in my suitcase, a variety of brands of laxative, including the chocolate-flavoured Ex-Lax, just in case I should get bunged up from eating unfamiliar or dodgy foreign food.

On the cross-channel ferry from Dover to Calais, I bought and started drinking half a bottle of duty-free rum, which cost me seven shillings. From Calais, the school party proceeded by train, down through France and Switzerland to Austria. Like most of the boys, I was feeling alternately sick, dizzy, drunk or hung-over the whole way, completely *out of it*. The motion of the train didn't help. My legs extended vertically, at right angles from the rest of my body, so that my feet were propped on the headrest above me; there wasn't enough room in the carriage to stretch out properly, but at least I could lay my head flat on the seat. I felt too ill to get up to stagger down the corridor to visit the lavatory.

Once we'd arrived at the hotel, settled in and slept it off, we were taken to be fitted and equipped with boots and skis. We were given the necessary introductory lessons on the nursery slopes, but I had terrible problems trying to get the knack of being pulled up the ski-slope by a T-Bar ski lift; I kept falling over, I just couldn't keep my balance. I more or less mastered it, eventually, and looked forward to my first long ski-run back down from the top.

I wrote my first postcard to my parents on the 30th of December: "Arrived. It's bloody cold. It was a hell of a journey. I felt awful. You can guess why — cheap booze on the boat. We're getting skis today. Austria is the most beautiful place you ever saw — green mountain rivers, fir trees, snowcapped mountains piercing the clouds, *everything* covered with snow. The Pension Pitze, at 1362 metres, is outside Sölden, a two-mile walk, six times a day. In the hotel we have gherkins, raw cabbage and olive oil, and 'tape worm' soup for every meal."

To my older brother, working unhappily as a trainee manager in a textile garment factory in Shrewsbury, I wrote, "Skiing is smashing fun. You have to fall over to stop yourself. Some lovely birds, mmm, and my German comes in ruddy useful. Just bought 20 'Johnny' fags. Real shit." There was no *après-ski* for me; I didn't want to touch another drop of alcohol.

I was impressed by the strange iron graveyard markers and crosses in the mountain cemetery. The church had an elaborate Baroque altar. It was all very different from home. For the first time in my life, I was acquiring a limited perception of cultural differences and a growing sense of curiosity about the world outside England.

Bergfriedhof SÖLDEN
mit Nederkogel 3166 m

At the end of the trip, I went looking for souvenirs in Sölden. For my mother and father I bought a hand-carved wooden eagle attached to an ashtray, which contained dried Edelweiss flowers pressed under glass inside the wooden bowl. I'd thought of buying a cuckoo clock, but it was too bulky for my suitcase.

Nearly sixty years later, I still don't know what to do with the carved wooden eagle, which has become unstuck and detached from the ashtray. None of the charity shops show the slightest interest in the skilled craftsmanship.

I've lost contact with all the boys who were with me on the

same trip. I can't even remember most of their names or any of *their* nicknames.

I'm thinking of returning to the Tirol to mark the sixtieth anniversary of my first real overseas trip. I plan to go by ferry and train, to relive that formative school trip, which I would have almost forgotten if it weren't for the postcards, the backs of which I now find embarrassingly painful to read, on account of the naivety and immaturity of my comments.

This time I won't be taking any laxative products in my luggage (one thing I've never forgotten is the sense of shame associated with the nickname they gave me for the duration of the trip), nor will I be buying a bottle of rum. I know that it tastes much better in Cuba and Jamaica; but, in truth, I still can't stand the smell of it anywhere I travel. It only makes me want to throw up.

My old friend also told me that he's never been skiing again, although he still loves the mountains, if not as much as the sea. He tries to think of the real origins of his travel bug, well before he entered his teens. He tells me that he sometimes goes back to Southampton and recalls his summer holidays there.

Maybe it was the matchbox labels, he says, the exotic boxes washed up on the shore from all over the world, with the flotsam and jetsam from trawlers and transatlantic liners...

Everything has changed a lot, but in his mind he still walks the beach beside the Solent, as the ocean liners come and go. He remembers their names: *Queen Mary*, *Queen Elizabeth*! He knows their flags, their draft and displacement.

He collects the jetsam thrown overboard, flotsam from the ends of the earth, matchbox after matchbox; the labels depict exotic places, strange languages and signs. Once he found some old brass kit — a navigator's aid.

He's still there with his beloved dog beside him, walking the beach to Warsash, combing the tide-line, restless, curious.

Maybe it *was* those matchbox labels, or the boats forever leaving, the ships all setting out to sea on voyages, *mind-voyages*. Beside the Solent something lit inside — the burning need to travel. He gets out his old collection of matchbox labels, which he's never had the heart to throw away. He shows me some of his favourites.

Then he remembers some lines from an old blues song, which we both once used to sing in the school's skiffle group. I join in.

> I ain't got no matches
> But I got so far to go —
> Would a matchbox hold my clothes?

The landscape painter

Even on a wet and misty day, Oliver was not deterred from venturing out to look at some aspect of the Dorset countryside. He would tramp for miles down muddy lanes without a second thought. He loved to explore and experience the contrasting moods of rural landscapes in all lights and weather conditions, including the wildest of storms and squalls. He never grew tired as there were so many geological features and formations within an hour from his home, spread out across downs, vales and heathlands. Weymouth Bay was only eight miles away; the Chesil Beach and the Jurassic Coast seascapes inspired him as did the harbours and cliffs, the ruined castles, the stone barns and bridges, the hill forts, barrows and stone circles. Oliver understood why Dorset had appealed to some Utopian and eccentric Bohemian communities in the past, as well as to individuals trying to rediscover a vanished rural Arcadia. He himself was possessed only of an innate landscape instinct and a modest talent for sketching, as well as for oil and watercolour painting.

He could climb to the top of Maiden Castle within twenty minutes, and he would often sit on the remains of the foundation wall of the Romano-British temple, watching the sheep and listening to the singing of skylarks. Although the landscape of Dorset was undoubtedly picturesque, it could seldom qualify as *sublime.*

He had studied most of the work of noted artists who had lived and worked in Dorset over several centuries, and others who had only visited the county for short periods.

He loved the paintings and sketches that J. M. W. Turner had produced in Lyme Regis, Weymouth, Bridport and Lulworth Cove, and the views that John Constable had captured near Weymouth Bay, Jordan Hill, Bowleaze Cove and Osmington — and in other paintings of the watermill in Gillingham. Oliver admired the Dorset paintings and drawings (not all landscapes) of Charles Conder and J. A. M. Whistler, of Lucien Pissarro and Augustus John, of Paul Nash, Frances Hodgkins, Stanley Spencer, Henry Lamb and Peter Lanyon — the list was endless. He felt proud to be part of a great tradition, but it was also a heavy weight around his shoulders. He could never hope to compete.

Sometimes he wondered whether he should have become an art historian and lecturer rather than an artist, but he was certainly no John Ruskin, Kenneth Clark or Simon Schama either.

He shared with Paul Nash that neo-romantic obsession with the *genius loci*, the distinctive atmosphere and pervading spirit of significant sites to which he felt almost spiritually attuned; he kept returning to haunted, enchanted places like Maiden Castle and Badbury Rings. Unlike Nash, he was neither influenced nor attracted by surrealism; but, like Nash, he used his camera to record and interpret what he saw. He appreciated the photographs of Bill Brandt — especially those of Maiden Castle and Pulpit Rock, Portland — and works by John Pouncy, Fay Godwin and Paul Nash himself.

He had very mixed feelings about the endless photographs of eroded rocks with holes or arches, specifically about over-familiar and clichéd beauty spots like Durdle Door and Corfe Castle.

Digital photography, photo-shop effects and social media had undermined the value of photography, he felt.

He often perceived unfamiliar aspects of the landscape when out walking, and he tried hard to represent what he saw and felt — the *inscape*, as the poet Hopkins would call it. Photographs helped, but pencils and paints were necessary to capture the essence of what he was trying to share and communicate. He wasn't looking for a dramatic and terror-inspiring vision of the Sublime, but for the mysterious semiotic detail which compelled the viewer to look even more closely at the picture in front of him.

He half-remembered seeing a film called *Blow-Up*, by the Italian film-director Antonioni, about a fashion photographer who takes a photograph outdoors, with a sinister, shadowy and ambiguous detail in a corner of the picture which becomes more and more suspicious when enlarged — blown up — several times in the dark room.

He harboured the fear that one day he himself might photograph or stumble across a dead body on one of his lonely walks through the woods, or beneath the cliffs. The skull of a badger and the skeleton of a sheep were the closest he had come to finding a corpse. He'd photographed them for his portfolio.

He usually managed to put thoughts of mortality out of his mind. His real preoccupation was with ancient trees, or rather sacred trees in sacred groves. These were often to be found in cemeteries, but some could also be found in places where other, similar trees had once been venerated, in pre-Christian times.

One ancient oak tree that he discovered had a hollow trunk. He climbed inside it in order to feel closer to the centre of its being, to imagine himself as the *genius loci* and to take some photographs.

Suddenly another solitary walker, an elderly man in his eighties, appeared from nowhere and stopped to relieve himself beside the tree. Oliver didn't know what to do, as the man hadn't seen him. Oliver decided to announce his presence and said, from within the hollow trunk, "Good-day to you, my friend!"

The old man suffered a heart-attack, of course, falling to the ground before he'd even had time to button up his flies.

Luckily Oliver had his mobile phone. He called 999, tried to explain where he was, and then waited a very long time for the paramedics to arrive. The old man was pronounced dead, but his flies were still open.

Oliver had a lot of explaining to do.

Bears

While the human population of the villages declined, the bear population increased. Fewer people walked up and down the old cobbled paths through the woods or down the steps to the river at the bottom of the deep gorge. They seldom used the old paths to visit other villages on the other side of the gorge.

The last remaining villagers no longer kept livestock such as cattle, sheep or goats in large numbers; they no longer tended their orchards and fruit trees, which had been left to grow wild, the fruit uncollected.

Kyria Maria was one of the few villagers who still tried to harvest the fruit, mainly plums, apples, cherries, cornel fruit and quinces, to make jams and preserves. But she couldn't gather or use more than a fraction of what the trees produced. Much of the fruit just fell from the trees and lay rotting on the ground. Sometimes Maria would find some "bear's business" in the orchard, droppings full of berry or plum stones, but she never really worried or thought twice about it.

Every summer and early autumn Maria had a comfortable hammock slung between two plum trees, where she would sometimes enjoy a siesta in her orchard in the shade of the trees.

One night Maria woke up with a start. She'd heard a noise. It was about three o'clock in the morning. She looked out of her window and saw a large brown bear in the back yard, boldly approaching her kitchen door. Had she remembered to close it and lock it? She couldn't remember. The brown bear must have heard her moving in the upstairs bedroom, and ran off down the steps to the lower level of the steeply terraced garden.

The next morning Maria found a number of broken branches where the bear had been reaching for the ripest fruit.

The next night Maria decided to watch and to keep very quiet. After a while she heard a noise. She could just see the fruit trees where she had slung the hammock. And there was the big brown male bear, lying on his back on the hammock, as happy as Larry, shaking the branches of the plum tree, and letting the ripe plums drop into his mouth. The bear must have weighed as much as 200 kilos, and the stretched hammock sank down almost to touch the ground.

Maria decided to stay well clear of the hammock and the orchard for the next few days, but one evening she went to join some of the elderly ladies in the village at "the little parliament", which is what they called the long stone ledge or bench next to the communal cistern in the village square. In the summer the women would gather there in the evening to sit outside for a few hours to chat and "chew the fat" about local issues, including the problem of the bears. None of them knew what to do about it.

Some said they should cut down all the fruit trees, others suggested the installation of electric fences around the orchards and places where they kept bee hives, chickens or goats. The shepherd's mother suggested they should leave a radio playing in the orchard all night. The goatherd's auntie suggested hanging bells in the tree which would ring if the bear starting picking the fruit or shaking the trees. One lady thought the bears should be shot by hunters, but the others said that killing bears was illegal, as the bears were protected by law, and they were not dangerous unless a mother bear felt that her young cub was threatened. The lady replied that they could give the dead bear to a Natural History Museum, to be stuffed and put on display for educational purposes.

The oldest lady in the little parliament suggested that they should try to capture the bear and sell it to a zoo or even to be trained as a dancing bear like the ones that they used to see in the old days. Or else it could be taken to a Bear Sanctuary, on condition that it was never returned to the wild. Then she thought about seeking advice from Aristakis, the "Lord of the Gorge", a wise old goatherd from the neighbouring village, who kept his flocks on the steep, almost vertical, slopes of the Vikos Gorge and Mount Gamila. Aristakis was probably over ninety years old, but no one knew for certain. He was still very sure-footed. In his spare moments he read nothing but Homer; he still thought of himself as an Ancient Greek hero.

So they sent for Aristakis, who announced that he would go down to Dodoni, to consult the famous oracle about what to do.

He told them he would listen to the rustling of the leaves from the sacred oak tree, and try to interpret the oracle himself, without the help of any priestesses or cauldrons.

> The leaves are not rustling,
> The pigeons don't fly —
> But the wild flowers are saying
> "You'll live till you die."

The members of the little parliament were very doubtful about him making the journey to Dodoni, let alone getting an answer from the Ancient Oracle. They thought it was a silly pagan idea, anyway; they preferred to pay the local priest to hold a special service at the little stone chapel of Saint Nicholas, on the path down to the gorge, one of the deserted paths which the bears probably used to come up to the village. They would light candles and their prayers would be more effective than any electric fence. Saint Nicholas would protect them. If he failed, there was still the old chapel of the Archangels or Taxiarches — Gabriel, and Michael with his sword — but it was higher up the path, and as a last defence it was a bit too close to their homes for comfort. Still, the Taxiarches were very powerful and the Archangel Michael's sword was more than a match for any bear's claws!

Later that night Maria walked down the lonely cobbled path to her house all alone, and she started to feel quite nervous, as the path led past her house straight down to the thick woods in the gorge.

She could hear all the village dogs barking loudly, and one of the dogs, called Heracles, ran past her at speed, to investigate a scent he'd picked up in the air. Maria peered down the lane, as far as she could see, but it was badly lit and there was no moon. Could that be a bear standing up on its hindlegs, looking directly at her?

Maria fumbled with her key and the latch, and quickly closed the old wooden outer door behind her, securing it firmly with an iron bar.

She hurried through the courtyard, disturbing the swallows and house martins that had made their nests in the eaves and even round the flex of the naked electric light bulb hanging above the cistern. She opened the kitchen door and switched on the lights. She was safe. All the windows were barred. The houses in the village were built of stone, like small fortresses. In the eighteenth and nineteenth centuries the villagers were scared of being attacked by bandits, so the houses were designed to be easy to defend.

The dogs were still barking wildly, so they must have sensed something. There was certainly a bear out there, looking for food. Maybe there was a whole family of bears. The next day Maria learned that two of Antigone's and Phrosso's goats had been attacked and eaten by a bear that had broken in, and several beehives had been destroyed up in the area of the Ancient Settlement, on the outskirts of the village. The honey inside the hives had been devoured. The Ancient Settlement had been inhabited from as long ago as the 9th century BC, but after many centuries of continuous habitation it had been abandoned. Was that because of the bears?

The next night Maria was awoken by a loud bang. Someone had fired a shotgun at around three o'clock in the morning. Could it have been a hunter? More likely it was someone firing a shot in the air in order to protect his chickens, to frighten off a hungry bear. Maybe he had heard the dogs tugging on their chains and barking.

Maria thought that she might soon have to abandon her own house and move to the city. She could cope with the occasional scorpion or snake, but bears were a different matter. There were so few villagers left and the winters could be hard and lonely. The rains were constant and heavy and a lot of snow usually fell in February. It was difficult to heat the stone house. What a pity that she couldn't go into hibernation like a bear, she thought, or fly away to Africa like a swallow, once it had built its nest and raised its young.

She didn't want to live in Athens or in Ioannina. She would miss the clear mountain air, the singing of the nightingales and even the monotonous sound of the Scops owl. She loved listening to the sound of the sheep-bells and goat-bells when the shepherds and goatherds drove their flocks and herds across the mountains to graze. But there were far fewer bells than before. She couldn't even be sure that Mr and Mrs Swallow would return this year to build their nest in her courtyard. The swallows always returned from Africa to have their young in the same spot.

Some months later, Maria's grandson, who was studying English, happened to read a poem about animal cruelty — "Bother Bruin" by Christina Rossetti. He told her about it when he was staying in the village at the time of the *paniyiri* in August. Kyria Maria remembered having been very upset by the sight of dancing bears in her youth. Her grandson translated these moving lines from the poem into Greek, and Maria managed to memorise them. She would often recite them to the children in the village.

> A Dancing Bear grotesque and funny
> Earned for his master heaps of money,
> Gruff yet good-natured, fond of honey,
> And cheerful if the day was sunny . . .
>
> Still, year on year, and wear and tear,
> Age even the gruffest bluffest bear.
> A day came when he scarce could prance,
> And when his master looked askance
> On dancing bear who would not dance.
>
> To looks succeeded blows: hard blows
> Battered his ears and poor old nose . . .
>
> One dark day when the snow was snowing
> His cup was brimmed to overflowing:
> He tottered, toppled on one side,
> Growled once, and shook his head, and died.

Kyria Maria decided she would try to do something about cruelty to animals, especially brown bears. She didn't have the means to start a bear sanctuary on her own, but her grandson encouraged her to persevere.

Now Kyria Maria considers herself as a guardian of bears. It may sound strange, but it's true, that nowadays the village is never bothered by hungry bears in search of food. They seem to find plenty enough in the forests, and people have finally learnt to leave them in peace.

Kyria Maria doesn't tell her neighbours that she takes all the freshly-fallen fruit, especially the plums, apples and cornel fruit from her own orchard and from abandoned trees and branches that overhang the path, piled up high in a big basket she ordered from a Roma basket-weaver, to a special place on the way down to the gorge, where nobody else ever walks, except for the grateful bears.

She often picks ripe fruit that is nearly ready to fall. She has more than enough left over to make jams and *glika tou koutaliou* ("spoon sweets" — preserved fruits in syrup) for all her visitors. Everyone is happy! It is no surprise that the villagers sometimes whisper to each other, "Here comes Mother Bear."

Reward!

Tom Richards was coming to the end of his posting as Second Secretary (Science and Culture) at the British Embassy in Prague. It was October 1989, only a month before the fall of the Berlin Wall and the outbreak of the Velvet Revolution in Czechoslovakia, although he did not know that at the time. Everyone was still talking of Czechoslovakia as a hard-line country, a museum of Communism, frozen and unthawing since the suppression of the Prague Spring (although the Soviet-led Warsaw Pact invasion had taken place in the *summer* of 1968, in August, as he recalled). Some observers considered the country as belonging in the same political category as Albania, although not as isolated or extreme. The best writers were either censored or banned, their writings circulated in typed *samizdat* copies amongst friends, students and fellow dissidents. *Glasnost* was bound to come sooner or later. Since the end of August that year thousands of young people had been fleeing from the German Democratic Republic, a growing flood of refugees, abandoning their little Trabant cars and camping in overcrowded tents in the muddy garden of the West German Embassy, before they were finally allowed to leave by train.

Tom was dreading a home posting, because he knew he would lose all his overseas allowances and other perks. He would have to live in his own semi-detached house in one of the less fashionable parts of North London, instead of renting it to a series of wealthy Japanese businessmen and bankers who tolerated the area because it was near the Japanese school. He would lose his surprisingly luxurious rent-paid house in Prague, which was owned by a taxi-driver, not a member of the ruling elite; it even had an indoor swimming-pool in the basement, with a machine to make artificial waves, as well as a sauna. He always wondered how a taxi-driver in such an ideologically-rigid Communist country could have afforded to build such a property. Maybe he had a relative in a high place in the Party. Even if there was something fishy about it, it had been an extraordinarily lucky find for someone in Tom's grade; the house was well within his rent ceiling, so the Embassy's Administration Officer could not object.

He'd failed to save any money while in Prague, since he had been scrupulous about changing his money at the poor official local bank rate. He never made use of the black market money-changers, partly because he'd been warned that by doing so he could open himself up to blackmail and expulsion. He'd refrained from the temptation, more out of fear than of principle. As a result, he was almost broke, although he would have the proceeds from the sale of his car and some personal effects to tide him over for the first few months of culture shock back in London, with all the potential worries about the cost of season tickets, poll tax payments, TV licences, heating bills and similar half-forgotten obligations which were the lot of ordinary mortals, the great majority of British citizens unfortunate enough never to have escaped overseas.

He had been asked to undertake a stop-gap survey of opportunities for the book-trade between Britain and the countries of Eastern and Central Europe. This was to be his next assignment, before taking up his new post in the Eastern Europe and Soviet Department in King Charles Street. He thought that the most useful thing he could do by way of preparation was to call on the various Embassies in Prague to seek some statistics and information.

It just so happened that he was invited to a diplomatic cocktail party when he was beginning to prepare his checklist, and this promised to save him a lot of effort phoning around, because he knew that most of the diplomatic community would be there, including the commercial and cultural attachés. The party was to be hosted by the Czech Ministry of Culture, at the Wallenstein Palace, to announce plans for the reorganisation of the Prague Spring International Music Festival.

He arrived rather late, but everybody welcomed him warmly. Tom was quite popular in Prague, he'd been there a relatively long time, longer than almost all the other diplomats, so at least they recognised him and felt relaxed and somewhat unguarded when talking to him. Having secured a whisky-and-soda and several ham rolls, he started chatting to the Italian Commercial Attaché.

Alberto had been in Prague almost as long as Tom had, and the two men enjoyed swapping gossip on such occasions. Alberto was joined by another man whom Tom had never met before.

"Allow me to introduce the new First Secretary of the Albanian Embassy," said Alberto. "Fikri Kupi, Tom Richards from the British Embassy. Tom's been here even longer than I have." Fikri and Tom shook hands. "I'm very pleased to meet you, Mr Richards," said Fikri.

"Isn't it about time the British resumed diplomatic relations with Albania?" asked Alberto. "We have good relations with Tirana, so have the Germans. Even the Goethe Institute is active there."

"It's not up to me, I regret," said Tom. "There are a few small matters that still have to cleared up, as I understand it, such as compensation for the loss of British ships, Royal Navy destroyers, and of so many sailors' lives, as a result of the mining of the Corfu channel in 1946."

"My dear Mr Richards, you are treading on very dangerous ground. If the British insist with their absurd allegations, when it is your government that is illegally and unjustly holding so much Albanian gold, we shall never start talking to each other. In fact, I wonder if there is much point in us exchanging words here and now."

"I don't know the details, but I do recall that the International Court in The Hague supported the British position. I hold the personal view that it would be sensible to try to normalise relations between our two countries."

"I *do* know the details. I have studied the case very carefully, Mr Richards, and I can assure you that we are not impressed by the machinations of international power politics and gunboat diplomacy."

"Well, I suggest we change the subject, Mr Kupi. I wonder if you could be of help with another matter. I've been asked to do a study of the book trade in East and Central Europe, especially concerning exports of British books and translation rights. You don't by any chance have any figures or other information at the Embassy, do you?"

"I hardly think that the volume of trade is very great, Mr Richards, but no doubt the figures are available. We have excellent statistics for our agricultural and industrial output, so why not for books? Have you read any books by Albanian writers, Mr Richards?"

Tom scratched his head. "As a matter of fact, I have read some novels by Ismail Kadare."

"*One* author, and one who is out of favour! Are you aware of any other writers?"

"I can't say that I am."

"Would that not indicate that there is an imbalance of trade in this sector? Can you not obtain some figures from your London departments?"

"You have a point. But I'm interested in talking about the future, as well as the past. I want to discuss opportunities for new trade arrangements. Perhaps you could be of help?"

"Why don't you telephone tomorrow at around ten in the morning? I'll see what I can do."

"Thank you, I would appreciate it. Are you going to the D-Club this weekend, Alberto?" asked Tom. He hadn't noticed that Alberto had already moved off in the direction of a glamorous Czech singer.

"The Italians don't change, do they?" said Fikri with a wry smile.

"Don't worry, he means no harm. He can't help being charming," said Tom, as he helped himself to another drink, excusing himself at the same time ("I really should circulate") to wander off in the direction of the equally attractive new Desk Officer from the Czech Ministry of Culture, to whom he'd been introduced by a colleague at a reception the previous week.

◆

Tom was invited to half a dozen parties in his last few weeks. It surprised him how often he seemed to bump into Fikri, who'd been most helpful when he'd called at the Albanian Embassy. Tom managed to collect reams of useful data and background information about trade legislation from almost all the Embassies, and they promised to send him more when he was back in London. He readily gave his North London home address to anyone who asked for it. He still didn't know which geographical desk he would occupy back in the Eastern Europe and Soviet Department in King Charles Street, but he suspected it might include Yugoslavia, because the book trade was quite well-developed with the northern republics of Slovenia and Croatia, thanks to the efforts of the Publishers' Association. He'd quite overlooked the fact that he might be made theoretically responsible for Albania as well as for Yugoslavia, even though Albania barely counted in terms of bilateral activity, since there was no real movement in the country, and only vague talk of restoring diplomatic relations. There was much more concern about the Albanians of Kosovo.

He received his postings letter only a week before he was due to leave Prague. It came as a surprise to see it in writing that he was indeed to be given the Yugoslavian and Albanian desk. He'd secretly hoped to be given Poland or Hungary, where the action was. He mentioned the posting when he next sat next to Fikri at a farewell-dinner given in Tom's honour by Alberto.

"What a coincidence, Mr Richards! Perhaps you'll be able to do something towards normalising and restoring relations, and to seeing that justice is finally done. Have you by any chance read the book by Lord Bethell? It's called *The Great Betrayal*. It's very objective. Lord Bethell is a member of The European Parliament.

He's a Conservative and he sits in the House of Lords. If I manage to find my own copy, I will happily lend it to you. I hope you'll read it carefully. You'll note that your British officers always referred to Albanians as 'the pixies', a charming phrase, don't you think? 'The Pixies.' I hope you won't continue this tradition of referring to us as *pixies*, Mr Richards?"

"Certainly not; I'm sure it was a friendly, even affectionate term, or a code-word, perhaps. I wonder what they called the Brits."

"I wonder; but hearty congratulations, Mr Richards. Perhaps we shall meet again. Maybe I myself will be posted to London, once diplomatic relations are restored. Or perhaps I may receive an informal invitation to visit your country through our good friends at the Albanian Bookshop in Covent Garden."

"What's that? I didn't know you had a cultural centre in London."

"We don't, but the owner of the bookshop had established valuable contacts with our country. He imports all sorts of goods, books, records, souvenirs and even foodstuffs. He performs a useful service; I will give you the address, in fact I happen to have the card."

"The Albanian Bookshop and Gramophone Exchange, 16 Betterton Street. Not too far from my club; perhaps they stock some useful material," thought Tom, tucking the card carefully inside his wallet. His thoughts turned to his Pall Mall club, the United Oxford and Cambridge Club. Although he wasn't a very "clubbable" type, it wasn't a very clubbable club, particularly with regard to its female members, who had restricted rights about which rooms and facilities they were allowed to use. Tom enjoyed going for a quiet meal in pleasant surroundings. He liked reading the papers and he appreciated a stress-free cup of coffee in the comfort of a soft armchair, although he'd often forgotten to put the requested forty pence in the wooden money-box, even if he hadn't had a meal. He wasn't sure if he would be able to afford the annual subscription once he had to start paying the full

London rate again, as opposed to the discounted overseas member's rate. He intended to keep his membership up, even if it meant calling on a temporary overdraft facility until his next overseas posting, hopefully on promotion. The club would be the most convenient place to host official visitors from his region, and he could claim back the expenses for official entertainment.

"If you're ever in London, Fikri, do feel free to contact me at my club. I go there two or three times a week. You can always leave a message for me there."

Tom scribbled the address on the back of one of his own, now useless, Prague visiting cards.

"Here's a toast to restored Diplomatic Relations!"

They both lifted their glasses and drank.

The next day, he received a brown paper parcel with two books inside. One was a used copy of *The Great Betrayal*. The other book bore the more ominous title of *The Anglo-American Threat to Albania*. It was by Enver Hoxha.

Inside, Fikri had written, "To Tom, on the successful completion of his duties in Czechoslovakia." It was signed, "From your friend, the Pixie."

It was essential for Tom to visit some neighbouring countries, in connection with his book-trade report, before finally returning to the UK. When he was visiting the universities in the German Democratic Republic, he stayed in a hotel close to the Berlin Wall. On November 9th, it was announced on the radio that the Wall would be opened, and that all GDR citizens could henceforth leave the country and travel freely to West Berlin. Thousands crossed to West Berlin through Checkpoint Charlie. West Berliners called, "Come Over! Come over!" East Berliners headed for the Kurfurstendam. Tom would never forget what he witnessed on the following day, watching East Berliners pouring over to West Berlin and returning in the evening with their plastic bags from Herties, with oranges, cassette radios and budget-priced Johnny Cash LPs, all bought with their 100 DM *Begrussungsgeld*. Just five days earlier, an elderly professor in

Rostock had told him of his deep concerns and worries about "a return to capitalism", as he seemed sure would happen in Hungary. He expressed his sadness at the sight of young people leaving the GDR in such numbers. "There are other things than material goods to live for. Have I been living a lie for forty years? Will Socialism turn out to be just an intellectual's utopia, never realisable by human beings? Were all my ideals based on false foundations?" He seemed a sad and broken man, overcome by a sense of tragedy.

◆

A month later, after Tom had completed his travels in Poland, Hungary and Yugoslavia, he found himself back in London just a few days before Christmas, almost ready to start writing up his extensive report on the book-trade, which he had to hand in before starting his new job at the Office in the New Year. There had been a revolution in Prague in the meantime.

He'd been back in Prague briefly on November the 20th. He'd arrived at Muzeum Metro-Station at 8.30 a.m., and emerged by the Statue of St Wenceslas. The base of the equestrian statue had been transformed into an altar for freedom. Solidified candle-wax covered the stone. Hundreds of candles were burning, national flags adorned the statue and there was a banner demanding Free Elections. At 4.00 p.m. he arrived at Muzeum again, on his way to meet his colleagues. It was almost impossible to climb the station's stairs because of the pushing, excited crowds. It seemed potentially dangerous, but this was an occasion not to be missed, a turning-point in the nation's history. It seemed as if half-a-million people filled the square. Students were standing all over the statue; flags were draped over the King and his horse, candles were burning and the main banner now read "Free Elections and Pluralistic Democracy". Elsewhere people were carrying home-made banners such as "Down with Tyranny". Tom forced his way with great difficulty through the joyful revolutionary crowd, amazed at the spirit of brave solidarity, the waves of roars and the rattling of keys.

On the 25th of December, 1989, a military tribunal tried and sentenced Nicolae and Elena Ceaușescu to death, in Bucharest, Romania. They were both shot by firing squad on Christmas Day. *No Velvet Revolution there*, thought Tom. Was he too fixated on one small country, when such dramatic changes were coming and opening up opportunities throughout the region?

Back in London, it took Tom some time to settle into to his new job. The pace of change was almost unbelievable, and he often had to cover for his new colleagues. He really needed a computer and a deputy to keep up with all the work. Although developments in Yugoslavia, Bulgaria and Romania were being closely monitored, Albania was scarcely on the map at all.

It wasn't long before he began to feel frustrated. His colleagues were in the thick of it, developing the Know-How Fund for Poland, sending trade delegations to Hungary and arranging programmes for Civic Forum intellectual heroes from Czecho-slovakia. Ministers weren't showing too much interest in his countries. His boss, preoccupied with the larger countries and the ongoing revolutionary changes in the region, once said to him in a haughty, dismissive tone, "Albania? What use is that country to man or beast?" The fact was, their resources were stretched far too thinly, and there was no spare funding or capacity to respond to yet another country's needs and expectations.

On top of all that, Tom was broke and he was feeling the pinch. He had what seemed to him a huge mortgage, although he shouldn't really have complained, as he'd bought his house when properties in London were still affordable; he'd always reckoned that he'd waited too long and acted when the market appeared to be approaching its peak. What was even more galling was that he didn't much like the house or the area where he lived, but he had no prospect of selling it. He needed somewhere to live. The house had probably dropped in value because of a widening crack which had appeared in the living room, as well as ominous patches of dampness in the ceiling; he feared it might be a subsidence problem, as the house was built on clay soil, but it was more likely that it had been caused after the last tenants had moved out and someone had irresponsibly left the water running in the bath, or there had been a leak from a pipe in the upstairs bathroom. He had submitted a claim to his insurance company but the loss-adjusters had yet to come to inspect the property and investigate its multitude of issues.

All his colleagues made Tom feel shabby. He hadn't bought a new suit or smart pair of shoes since he'd been posted to Prague. The other geographical desk officers seemed to have the ears of ministers on a daily basis. They projected the confidence and authority of real "power-dressers" with their expensive double-breasted suits, red polka-dot braces and up-to-date expertise about the changes in their countries. Tom felt he was being left behind. He resolved to do some serious research about his countries. Information was power. Perhaps he would be noticed if his briefs were better than anyone else's. He resolved to bone up as much as he could on Albania. His time would surely come. He could even be instrumental in helping to restore diplomatic relations. That would earn him a few brownie-points and a promotion. He began to imagine himself as the first post-Hoxha British Ambassador resident in Tirana.

One afternoon, after a particularly good lunch at his club, he strolled up towards Covent Garden to Betterton Street. The Albanian Bookshop and Gramophone Exchange was much smaller than he had imagined. The window was full of books by Enver Hoxha, the tiny shop's interior was crammed with second-hand records and old wind-up gramophones. It was almost impossible to move inside without knocking over antique horns and piles of 78 rpm records. He didn't find anything of interest, apart from a few old blues records and some postcards of Albania, but he did have a long chat with the shop-minder, and, just as he was leaving, he caught sight of a little booklet called *Miscarriage of Justice: The Corfu Channel Case*, which had been published by the Albanian Society in Ilford, a society seemingly supporting a

Committee for the Restoration of Diplomatic Relations with Albania. He bought a copy; he wasn't planning to join any society of fellow-travellers, but he thought he might get some ideas which would help him look at the problems from another perspective.

As he left the shop, he decided to have a last look in the window. He noticed a little card stuck to the inside of the dirty window, which read, "REWARD! For a copy of the complete Naval Orders XCU (Exercise Corfu), as referred to in British evidence at the International Court of The Hague."

A strange notice, he thought, memorising it carefully before he walked away, wondering whether the British Security Services had a video camera surveying all the visitors to the bookshop. At least he had a good excuse for being there; he was still working on the appendices to his report on the book-trade with Eastern European countries.

◆

After the excitement of Prague, he found it increasingly hard to settle down to life in London, amongst the hordes of commuters. It was a twelve-hour day every day, from the time he left the house in the morning until the time he left the office at night. Bureaucracy, not Democracy, had triumphed, he decided; the amount of paper hitting his desk, most of it marked *urgent*, had become absurd. He knew he shouldn't complain. If he got out at Covent Garden in the morning, he had to walk past five or six homeless individuals sleeping in shop-doorways. If he went home in the evening from Leicester Square station, he had to run the gauntlet of aggressive beggars demanding his loose change. He felt sorry for the fact that they were homeless and hungry; he wasn't amused by the way they used their dogs to block his path. Even the buskers had lost any of the appeal they had held for him a decade earlier. East Europe wasn't so bad after all! He feared that, once countries embraced the open market, they would come to suffer similar social problems. On the whole, the people seemed to be a lot more civilised there, regardless of the authoritarian secret police and the depressing lack of freedom and consumer goods. He hadn't been to the worst places with the most repressive regimes, he had to admit. However hard-line Czechoslovakia was held to be, life certainly wasn't as bad there as it was in Albania, although he was aware that in not-so-distant past, Czech dissidents had been punished by being sent to work in the uranium mines, or risked being executed after being forced to make false confessions in show-trials. Those trials had been in the nineteen-fifties, Tom recalled. For a disillusioned diplomat who was suffering from culture shock on his first return to squalid London-town, even Tirana had its attractions. The metro in Prague and Moscow was paradise compared to the London underground in the rush-hour. A vision of the Mediterranean, even in a workers' state, seemed to him much more seductive than a duck-pond in St James' Park.

Back at the Office, he started reading up all the old files on the Corfu Channel case, and on the other obstacles to diplomatic relations. He spent some of his lunch-hours in the Research Department. It wasn't long before he came across references to the Naval Orders CXU on a confidential file. It wasn't marked Top Secret, but it carried a note to the effect that although many of the papers had been declassified, they had not yet been deposited with the Public Record Office under the normal terms of the thirty-year rule, for reasons of national security.

He tried to think of the possible reasons. Why was a reward being offered for the Naval Orders, for papers relating to the events of October the 22nd, 1946, and referred to in a court case which had taken place as long ago as April 1949? Was the offer of a reward an open invitation to someone to get involved with some low-level espionage, or was it just an appeal for information from a *bona fide* academic historian? It seemed conceivable that the Albanian Foreign Ministry was still trying, so far in vain, to produce evidence that the British warships had themselves been on a spying mission in the Corfu Channel. Was that why someone wanted to see the Naval Orders issued to Rear-Admiral Richard

Kinahan? Maybe the British actions had just been a show of force, which had led to the loss of one officer and forty-three ratings, with another forty-four men injured — or had Britain merely been making use of its right to sail through international waters without notifying the Albanians?

He had read the pamphlet produced by the Albanian Society with interest, and decided to compare that version with the facts as recorded on the FCO files. He would dig out the original Naval Orders, purely for his own satisfaction. He entertained no thought of the reward apparently being offered on the shop-window card he'd seen. It would be reward enough if he could help solve this bureaucratic muddle and impasse, if he could tidy up the loose ends and pave the way for the restoration of good relations. He had in his mind an early Ambassadorship, holidays in Butrint and Saranda, and on the nearby Greek island of Corfu. Not a bad number, he felt, when all was said and done. He was really finding life in London increasingly difficult. He could certainly use some overseas allowances again, reward or no reward.

A few days later, as he was leaving his Pall Mall club after a game of squash, he happened to notice an envelope addressed to him. He usually didn't bother to look at the message-board. He took it and opened it hurriedly. It contained a short note from Fikri in Prague, in which he proposed a date and time for a meeting in London, either for coffee, perhaps at his club, or preferably for a stroll in St James' Park, which he assumed would be convenient for both of them, and would allow Tom to get a breath of fresh air away from his office. It seemed that Fikri would be visiting London for a few days, before travelling on to Rome. He had been assigned to a negotiating team with the responsibility to explore the resumption of diplomatic and trade relations with a number of Western countries.

Life was full of such coincidences, but it was hardly surprising. Nothing surprised him any longer, after the momentous changes in East Germany and Czechoslovakia. Every month there seemed to be a new revolution. If one could contemplate the possibility of a Václav Havel being transformed from prisoner to President, from Enemy of the State to Popular Hero, then one could certainly imagine that Fikri, his old cocktail-round acquaintance, would somehow manage to obtain a visa to visit Britain, probably through Budapest, and that he was destined to become involved in high level international negotiations. Tirana couldn't remain isolated forever. People could watch Italian and Yugoslav TV and see what was happening in the countries of Central and Eastern Europe.

Tom resolved to meet him; perhaps he would even give him a little helping hand. He didn't want to see yet another round of negotiations come to nothing. He dreaded the prospect of three further years of misery in London. Facilitate their negotiating position, give them a steer, an informal brief, and everybody would thank him. Both sides would be happy if he could help to oil the wheels, engineer the restoration of normal and mutually beneficial relations.

◆

It was a crisp sunny day in January 1990. St James' Park was relatively empty at eleven o'clock in the morning. As he'd agreed with Fikri, Tom sat on a park bench, less than five hundred yards from his own office, smoking a cigarette. In his attaché case he had a newspaper, a book and a copy of the pamphlet he'd been annotating over the last few weeks, with little bits of declassified information he'd dug up in the old confidential files — nothing secret, as far as he could tell, but there was quite enough to be going on with in the archival dossiers. He hadn't made any photocopies or taken any photographs, and nobody could accuse him of spying or of breaking the Official Secrets Act. He'd just made a few notes, in the course of his routine research, but his notes in the margins and in small, neat handwriting on the last two blank pages of the pamphlet would give the Albanians all the ammunition they would need to make their case fairly persuasively. They would be so grateful that, if they ever recovered any of King Zog's gold which was being held in the Bank of England, they should give him an ingot or two, Tom liked joking to himself.

"Exercise Corfu", or XCU as it had been called since October 1946, was a pretty straightforward affair, no great mystery. The key question was whether or not the Albanians were truly responsible and thus whether or not they should pay compensation to the British government as a result of the events. The International Court had decided in 1949 that they should. From the files that he'd seen, Tom was prepared to give them the benefit of the doubt. To his unprofessional legal mind, the case was unproven, there was not enough solid evidence to uphold the judgement of the International Court. Tom's note would give them a steer, would help them finesse their arguments, give them a new angle which would lead the case to a form of closure and mutually acceptable compromise. Wasn't this the very essence of good diplomacy? Thus did he rationalise his planned actions and intervention. He wasn't leaking any hard information, breaking any oath of confidentiality or the Official Secrets Act. Not quite. The power-dressing know-alls with personal control of fifty million quid of Know-How Funds at their disposal — much of it, in his estimation, little more than slush funds disbursed without much know-how or hands-on practical knowledge of how to facilitate the transition to a market economy — those know-alls sitting so smugly in their well-staffed offices along the corridor would soon sit up and take notice. *Diplomatic yuppies!*

Fikri was delighted to see him again, of course. He'd even brought Tom a present of a bottle of Czech Becherovka, strongly alcoholic digestive herbal bitters, and three LPs of Albanian folk songs.

They shook hands and hugged each other as warmly as if they were long-lost school-chums.

"Hello, my old Pixie! I'm afraid my gift doesn't look like very much," said Tom, almost apologetically, "but I'm sure you'll find it interesting. Thank you for the Becherovka, it was my favourite drink in Prague; and the beer of course."

"I thought you always drank whisky?"

"That's true, but I used to drink Becherovka on the rocks as an aperitif. Thank you for the records, too. I'm sure Albanian folk-music must be much more authentic and unspoilt than the folksy *schmalz* you come across at festivals in Czechoslovakia. Spare me from those thigh-slapping Slovak dancers with their phoney peasant costumes, leaping around with squeals of mock delight! Did you ever read that wonderful novel by Milan Kundera, called *The Joke*? He has some fascinating observations about Moravian folk music and dancing, and how it was appropriated and exploited by the Party. Fake folk-songs were written in praise of Stalin and Julius Fučík — socialist content in national form!"

Without waiting for Fikri's answer, he looked more closely at the LPs. He was a little embarrassed to read that most of the tracks had been recorded live at the Gjirokastër National Folklore Festival, which took place every five years. Glancing at the sleeve-notes and some of the lyrics printed there, Tom noticed that many of the so-called folk-songs were contemporary, but still relatively old, polyphonic performances of compositions in sycophantic praise of Enver Hoxha, who'd died in 1985. From the slight discolouration of the sleeves, it seemed like they might have been old stock from The Albanian Bookshop in Betterton Street. He received them gratefully, and graciously, saying how pleased he was to see that one of the LPs contained authentic village music recorded back in the 1930s, with improvised traditional *Kaba* music led by the folk-clarinet, a sound he'd really learned to love.

"We have been relatively isolated in Albania. We'll probably catch up with Elvis Presley and The Beatles before long. The Bulgarians are way ahead of us in that respect; even the Russians. But you'll find our folk-singers have a lot of *kephi*, like the Greeks. They enjoy what they're singing. It's in their blood.

"I'd love to visit Tirana and Gjirokastër. The absence of traffic and tourism makes it most appealing to me."

"Why don't you come? We'd make you most welcome. Would

you like to visit Albania?"

"I would, if I'm posted there. I can't come as a tourist. My colleagues might suspect me of being what we call a 'fellow-traveller'."

"Is there any chance of you being posted to Tirana?"

"Who knows? Let me know after you've had a chance to look at my little present. We may meet again, sooner than you think, at opposite sides of the negotiating table. Oh, and by the way, I must return your book, the one by Nicholas Bethell, which you so kindly lent me in Prague."

Fikri took the book, which was indeed by the same Lord Bethell, but it didn't have the same cover; the title had mysteriously changed. It was not *The Great Betrayal*, but simply *Betrayed*.

"This isn't the copy I lent you in Prague."

"You're absolutely right. I bought a second copy, as I'm afraid I made extensive notes in yours. I could only get the American edition. It's got a different title, but I think you'll find the footnotes are much more complete and illuminating. Please accept it. Now, let's take a quick stroll before I go back to the office, and you can tell me about the purpose of your visit to Rome."

◆

Tom returned to his office to check on his diary, then thought he'd go and have a sandwich and a beer in the squash bar at his club. As he was climbing the steps, he decided that he fancied a proper meal in the main dining room. He thought again; his overdraft was depressingly large. He'd almost made up his mind to resign from his club. The subscription was now over four hundred pounds a year. Reckoning on two hundred working days a year, on average, that meant he was paying more than two pounds a day before he even ate a sandwich. He could eat at the subsidized staff canteen for less than the daily membership rate at the club! What a way to live! He hated the staff canteen. *Damn the money*, he thought. He ordered the roast in the main dining room. He would resign his membership another day.

◆

Three months later he found himself in Rome, as part of a hush-hush, or informal, British working-party which had gone there to meet a delegation of Albanians.

The British side found the Albanians surprisingly well-briefed, and extremely flexible. Fikri Kupi, the leader of the Albanian side, stood particularly firm on several rather sensitive points, but the British had set out to be reasonably accommodating, in the light of events elsewhere in Eastern and Central Europe and the general lowering of tension and threat. The British Minister was particularly impressed by the contribution that Tom made to the negotiations, and by the excellent rapport that he quickly established with his opposite numbers.

The Minister noted it well, and decided to have a word with the Director of Personnel on his return. Once diplomatic relations were restored, and once the little matters of compensation and of the Albanian gold were settled, perhaps Tom would make an excellent Deputy Head of Mission, even a Counsellor or Ambassador, eventually.

The only problem was, there were not likely to be any resources for the foreseeable future. All the money had been earmarked for Poland, Hungary and Czechoslovakia. Perhaps Tom could be made Vice-Consul, resident in Tirana but reporting to the Ambassador in Belgrade or Rome?

The more he thought about it, the more the Minister realised that the most that could be contemplated was the accreditation to Tirana of the British Ambassador of a larger neighbouring country, probably Italy. He or she could keep a watching eye on developments, at least. If that didn't work, they could always ask the German Embassy to look after British interests for a year or two.

When the Minister explained his thinking on the aeroplane

back to Heathrow, Tom was not amused. He could see himself with his shabby suit, sitting in a small commercial office block in Tirana, without status, without a car or driver, without a proper entertainment allowance even.

He'd be better off in London, mortgage or no mortgage. He could still afford a package-holiday to Corfu, a lot more fun than renting a Spartan room in a crumbling worker's holiday apartment block on the sea-coast at Saranda, looking enviously across the straits at Corfu.

Perhaps he would go and claim the real reward, after all. He deserved it, he felt sure, for all the research he'd done and for the help he'd given. If he didn't get some compensation, there would be a real miscarriage of justice!

◆

Tom couldn't afford to postpone it any longer. He used the club's crested notepaper to express his regret that he wished to resign, "in order to join another *more clubbable club* which offered female members full equal rights with the men".

From then on, the office canteen became his club. It proved to be a friendlier place than he'd imagined. They weren't a bad lot, the junior grades and the secretaries. At least they didn't behave like pushy yuppies or over-ambitious know-alls. Nevertheless, Tom began to feel less and less comfortable with his FCO colleagues, whatever their grades. Did they suspect him? He hadn't done anything wrong, he had convinced himself of that. He started avoiding people; he'd buy a sandwich and take it to St James' Park. When he did go to the canteen, if a colleague brought his tray to the table where he was sitting, he would eat quickly and make the excuse that he had to get back to his desk to take an important phone-call. His behaviour didn't go unnoticed.

◆

The reward was duly delivered, by a driver in an unmarked van, to Tom's home address in North London. Tom thought at first it must be one of the builders, who were still working on the repairs to his house.

In the event, Tom didn't even have to claim a reward. He hadn't been near Betterton Street again, nor had he heard any more from his old friend Fikri Kupi.

He knew it must be something substantial, as it was a very large and heavy package, the size of a small trunk. He wouldn't need to worry about a posting to some sunny Mediterranean country. From now on he would be free to retire to an island of his choice. What would he do? Would he go to Spain, or would he build a villa on the north-east coast of Corfu, where he could have a good view of the Albanian mountains without all the hassle of having to live in Tirana, performing boring diplomatic or consular functions? Not for him the laying of wreaths on Remembrance Sunday, the hosting of the Queen's Birthday Party receptions, the diplomatic round. Early retirement! What sort of yacht would he buy? He felt sure that Fikri would arrange for him to have a free berth in an Albanian port, as they didn't have proper marinas. Fikri would fix it so that Tom could go hunting whenever he might fancy it. He could just imagine what pleasure he would have inviting visiting VIPs to join him on a shooting expedition on the mainland opposite. Perhaps they could do some amateur excavations at Ancient Butrint, if the mood took them.

He'd be very choosy whom he invited to accompany him, none of those arrogant yuppies from the Office. They knew where they could stuff their Know-How Fund. Tom would be *Mister Know-How* in Albania, a special consultant to the Foreign Ministry. Hadn't an Englishman once been offered the Albanian throne? If Albania followed the other Eastern Bloc countries and had its own revolution, he could see great possibilities.

He'd join a new London club, of course; the Savile, perhaps. That was supposed to be very exclusive. He wouldn't need to worry about the length of the waiting-list. He'd buy his way in.

His thoughts turned back to the large, heavy package. He started opening it, with growing excitement.

He should have guessed.

It was the complete works and memoirs of the late Albanian leader, Comrade Enver Hoxha. About twenty volumes were in English; they had all been finely bound in full leather, with gilt edges, the title stamped on each cover in gold letters. Another thirty titles were in Albanian or other languages he couldn't read.

But wait, there was another parcel. Not a book. Banknotes? *The real reward!* Ten thousand pounds? Surely more like a hundred thousand. Was not that the sort of figure one could anticipate for such invaluable services rendered?

There was certainly a lot of money; it fell all over the sitting-room floor, as his trembling hands untied the string.

Thousands upon thousands of *leks*, a mountain of Albanian currency! Enough to make a man a millionaire in Tirana, perhaps, but Tom soon realised that it was all in small denomination notes, and not a lot of use to a minor Foreign Office functionary who was probably about to be interviewed by a friendly British gentleman wearing the proverbial raincoat, who would be looking forward to delivering the news of Tom's final reward.

Exiles' Island

I

For countless generations, the Grammenos family had lived for much of the year high up in the mountain village of Lakones on the island of Corfu, far from the threat of pirates' raids. Their home was a simple, small stone building, approached by a winding cobbled path.

Kyria Evanthia, the matriarch of the family, was a fifty-year-old widow, always dressed in black. She looked a lot older than her years. She had three children. Her nineteen-year-old daughter, Sophia, was beautiful but fiery-spirited, well-built and proud. She had become engaged to Dimitris, who was away doing his two years of military service. They planned to get married after Dimitris completed his national service, and when Sophia's family had saved enough money for a reasonable dowry.

The family was very poor. The two women often worked in some small olive groves they had inherited down by the sea, tending the gnarled ancient trees, which looked as if they had been planted in Venetian times. They had a habitable stone hut and a shed in one of the olive groves, close to the sea, where they could keep their tools, and where Sophia's two brothers, who were fishermen, kept their nets and tackle. The stone hut was equipped with iron bed-frames, rough mattresses, a stove (with a rusty gas canister) on which they could cook, and other basic essentials. They also owned a barn next to their house in Lakones, where they kept a few animals.

Dimitris wrote regular letters to Sophia, who sometimes read them to her mother. They revealed him as an intelligent and independent-minded man with a fierce interest in political matters. Sophia's two brothers, Angelos and Spyros, owned a small rowing boat, long, weighted fishing nets and a mule, on which they rode up the mountain to the village, whenever they had earned enough money from selling their catch to the tavernas in Paleokastritsa. They rarely caught enough to bother taking it to the open-air market in Corfu Town. They usually made just enough to live on, even if they often ate only bread and olives, but they were also trying to save towards their sister's dowry. Spyros was a handsome, strong young man of twenty-two; Angelos was only just fifteen.

Spyros had made the acquaintance of Virginia, a rich American divorcée of about forty-five. One of her husbands had been a Greek businessman, and he had insisted that she should learn to speak Greek. They'd divided their time between Athens and California. She lived alone in a luxurious modern villa overlooking the sea, not far from the family's olive grove with the hut. Virginia would often buy fish from Spyros and Angelos; every day at times.

Up in Lakones, the family had become quite friendly with a young English writer called Ben, who was renting a house in the village. When Ben, who was twenty-four, wasn't trying to write or play his guitar, he would give free English lessons to the village children. He'd studied Ancient Greek at university, and he'd made excellent progress with his Modern Greek. Sophia hadn't been able to study English at a *phrontisterio* or at school, so she also became one of his pupils. They had private lessons. Sophia was curious about Ben, and tended to flirt with him, just a little, when she went to his house for language lessons.

II

Spyros and Angelos were pulling in the last of their nets as it was getting light. They took out the fish that they'd caught, put them in a basket, then laid the nets again, ready for the next day. They rowed slowly ashore and dragged the boat up on the beach. A woman was walking back down the jetty, where she been watching and waiting for them. She had her purse in her hand, and was smiling enthusiastically.

"Good morning, Kyria Virginia, you're up early again."

"*Kali mera, Spyro, kali mera, Angele!* Did you have any luck today? Did you catch anything nice, I've got some friends coming for lunch."

Spyros showed her his basket of fish, and picked out the best of the sea-bass, the grey and red mullet. He weighed them on his simple pair of scales.

"Thirty drachma to you, Kyria Virginia."

Virginia paid him, took the fish, and started walking up the steps to her magnificent villa. She turned to smile at Spyros: "Don't forget to bring me some more tomorrow, Spyro."

The two young men gathered their things together and walked over to their mule, tied to a tethering ring outside their stone hut. It was still too early in the day for the cicadas to be singing. They both got on the mule, and began the slow ride up to the village, talking as they rode.

"We won't take the rest of the catch to the tavernas today. We should get another hundred drachma for the fish up in the village. If we do so well every day, Angele, we'll soon have enough money for our sister's dowry, and perhaps we'll be able to buy a second-hand outboard engine for the boat."

They rode up the winding road, waving to other villagers who were on their way to work. They passed peasant women who were carrying great bundles on their backs, and some with earthenware vessels on their heads. Finally they reached their village. The local priest greeted them with a blessing. They climbed off the mule, and led it down the cobbled path to the house; they tethered the tired animal in the barn, along with the hens and sheep. In the distance they could hear the sound of the goats' bells tinkling.

They went into their house. One large room served as the kitchen, living room and as one of the bedrooms. Icons, faded old family photographs and kitchen utensils were hanging on the walls.

Sophia and their mother, Evanthia, were overjoyed to see them.

"You'll soon have a big enough dowry to marry a prince,

Sister dear. Saint Spyridon is favouring us this year, always a good catch, never an empty net so far," said Spyros.

"Don't brag so much, Spyro, maybe your luck will change, the fish will get wise to you, and you'll catch nothing but seaweed and pebbles. And then I'll have to marry the village *vlaka*. Let's not talk of it. I had a letter from Dimitris today, I can't imagine how he got it past the censors. He's been posted to Konitsa, and he's not very happy. He's tired of eating nothing but beans. They made him stand to attention for ten hours in the pouring rain because he complained about the food. He's always protesting against something. You know they're only issued with one uniform, that's the Army for you. Poor Dimitris was soaked through to the bones, but he had nothing to change into; now he's got a high fever. You'd think they'd treat our soldiers with a little more care and respect, after so many gave their lives for the sake of the country during the last war. Look, he's sent a photograph of himself in his uniform. He looks so thin! I wish Dimitris could come home on leave now. He's got another six months to serve. I don't know how I can wait that long."

"You'll wait, daughter," Evanthia said, "but don't expect Dimitris to marry you if you continue talking with that young foreigner, that *Inglezos* who's come to live in our village, heaven knows why."

"But he's giving me English lessons, mother, and I don't have to pay. He says he's a writer, but he's willing to give lessons to all the village children if they want to learn. Now that more tourists are visiting the island, it's important for us to be able to speak to them. If I can learn English, I can get a good job in Paleokastritsa, and I shan't have to gather olives for the rest of my life."

"As your elder brother," said Spyros, "I'm responsible for you, and for your dowry. My honour is at stake as well as yours. I forbid you to talk with him again. Even if you do nothing, the villagers will gossip and suspect the worst. Dimitris would soon get to hear of it."

Sophia, unable to control her anger, replied, "If *that's* how you feel . . . if you care more about your honour and what other people think . . ."

"Do you want to earn your own dowry?" Spyros retorted.

"That's blackmail!" cried Sophia. "Very well, I won't talk to the Englishman when I walk past his window — but since when were Greeks so ingracious to strangers? You have no *philotimo*, Spyro, and Saint Spyridon will make you suffer for it."

Sophia stormed out of the house, her pride offended. As she left, she picked up a bundle of clothes to wash near the village well. She passed the Englishman's window. Ben smiled as he saw her, and stopped writing on his typewriter.

"Good morning, Sophia, *kali mera*, how are you? When are you coming for your next lesson?" asked Ben.

Sophia didn't answer, but held her head high and walked straight past without acknowledging him. Ben frowned, got up and followed her to the well, where she had started washing the clothes with some other women.

"What's got into you, Sophia, didn't you hear me greet you just now?" asked Ben, perplexed.

Sophia blushed, but continued her work, without answering. Ben looked disgruntled, and turned to walk back to his house. A few minutes later, feeling frustrated, he started playing his guitar. The women laughed at Sophia, who was obviously listening to his playing. Annoyed, she gathered her washing together and stalked off, back towards her house. As she passed Ben's window, he handed her a note, which Sophia quickly thrust inside her blouse.

III

Three days later, Spyros and Angelos were out fishing in the bay. They hauled in their nets, disentangling and folding them as they did so. The nets were almost all onboard but so far they were empty. They couldn't believe their eyes.

"No fish, no money," Spyros lamented. "Three whole days without a single fish, Angele, we can't even buy bread for our supper."

They continued to pull in and fold the nets. Spyros turned his head, with an expression of yearning, towards Virginia's villa which overlooked the bay.

"I should like to live in such a house. Alas! Only in the afterlife!" As he said this, he caught sight of the flashing of binoculars from the window.

"Angele, I'm sure that woman is a witch, if she isn't a spy. She has the power of the evil eye. She's always watching the ships and the boats. It is she who is driving all the fish from our nets. Maybe she wants to catch one of us instead. How else could she, a woman, buy such a palace, unless she had sold her soul to the devil . . . maybe to Enver Hoxha, or even worse, to Chairman Mao?"

Spyros started to pray: "Saint Spyridon, hear me, every year I kiss your silver cask in church. You have always helped poor sailors and those in peril on the sea. Now perform a miracle for us. Let our net be full with the final pull!"

He crossed himself, and they both pulled again. There was just one silver fish wriggling in the net. "One fish only! We shall not eat tonight, Angele. We must sell it to that witch; put it in a bucket of water to keep it alive and fresh."

Up in her villa, Virginia was standing before an artist's easel, a paintbrush in one hand, a pair of binoculars in the other. She was watching Spyros intently through her binoculars as he pulled in the end of the long net. She admired his balance and poise, the way his muscles tensed as he dragged in the net, and she put the finishing touches to her portrait of him on his little boat, a romanticised full-length portrait, without any sign of his brother in the picture; a painting that represented Spyros as a Greek god. She covered the finished painting with a sheet, and ran down to the beach and onto the jetty to meet him.

Spyros stowed away his oars, and tied the little boat to the jetty, rather than taking it to the shore. Virginia ran up to him, a little out of breath.

"*Yassou*, Spyro! I hope you had better luck today than you've had for the last two days. Did you get anything?"

"Just this one fish." He lifted it out of the bucket of sea-water to show her. "The others see my nets and laugh. They tangle them then swim away. I think we've been jinxed."

"Never mind," said Virginia, "Come up to my house, please, Spyro, I have something I want to show you."

"Me, come inside your home, Kyria Virginia? I cannot. I must explain to you, there is a great difference between a foreign lady and a poor fisherman."

"Don't be silly, there is no difference. Angelos will look after your boat for you, you needn't worry, we shan't be long."

"Well, alright. I'll bring the bucket with the fish. It's still alive. It's for you."

Obediently, if reluctantly, he followed her up the steps to her beautiful villa, and they went inside. Spyros put the bucket down at the corner of the living-room floor.

"Sit down, Spyro; first, what would you like to drink?"

"A little ouzo, *sas parakalo*."

"Please don't address me in the plural, Spyro, we're friends. I'm afraid I've run out of ouzo, I only have whisky or vodka."

"Vodka is a drink for communists, is it not? Whisky is for capitalists. I will drink my first whisky."

While Virginia went to pour the drinks, Spyros' eyes wandered in amazement around the vast living room, taking in the designer furniture, the paintings, the modern American equipment. He sat on the edge of the chair, afraid of so much wealth and luxury, nervously playing with his *komboloi*, his plastic, imitation-amber worry-beads.

Virginia came back with the drinks.

"Relax, Spyro, make yourself at home. Tell me, do you know any Greek dances. I've always wanted to learn the *chassapiko*. I think I saw you and Angelos dancing for some tourists at one of the Paleokastritsa tavernas last year. It was very impressive. Will you teach me how to dance the *chassapiko* or the *sirtaki*?" Virginia didn't really know one Greek dance from another, even though she'd seen the film *Zorba the Greek* at least three times

"You know they're not local dances of the Ionian islands, don't you? Nor is the *zebekiko*. That's the one which a man dances on his own."

"I still like watching the *chassapiko*. Will you teach me the dance, one day? In fact, there's no time like the present; what about now?"

"I dance with you? What if someone should come?"

"I have no-one, I'm expecting no-one. I divorced my third husband two years ago. I am so lonely. I have no-one to talk to. At first I was glad to be alone. My psychiatrist advised it. That's why I came to Greece, to this island, to paint, and to forget all my previous life. It doesn't matter. Come on, dance with me!"

Spyros sniffed the large double whisky suspiciously then knocked it back in one gulp.

He jumped up from his chair.

"I am a man. If I must dance, I will dance alone, that's the only way I can express my feelings of despair and disappointment when we catch no fish."

He searched through Virginia's collection of Greek records, and found something he recognised, on a local LP record of a bouzouki band playing instrumental dance music.

"Play this one."

Virginia put the record on the turntable, and selected the track that Spyros wanted her to play.

Spyros knew what the tourists wanted. He put the glass on his head, spread wide his arms, snapped his fingers and started improvising movements in time to the heavy rhythm of the music. Virginia watched him, fixated and fascinated by his whirling, swaying movements and his self-control which he seemed to be on the verge of losing in his manic self-absorption. At times it looked as if he would collapse as he circled round and round, his gaze concentrated on some invisible point, then swooping down to slap the floor, before leaning backwards without falling over, at the last moment regaining his balance. Virginia couldn't resist trying to imitate his movements, which were hardly dance steps. She danced clumsily, with little feeling for the music. She moved closer, knelt down on one knee and started clapping and making a hissing sound in a flirtatious come-on of seductive encouragement, as she remembered seeing someone do in an Athens night-club. She seemed to be offering herself, coming on, then withdrawing. At first Spyros was indifferent, then confused; he grew tense, deeply affected by the whisky and by the suggestive signals of her body. He took the glass from his head, and with a decisive gesture as the record ended, he smashed it on the ground, pulled her up towards him, clutching her tightly with considerable force. In doing this, he tripped and knocked over the bucket with the fish inside. It lay there with its tail flapping frantically on the floor, its gills opening and closing in desperation, until it was still and flapped no more.

They didn't spend more than twenty minutes in the bedroom. Spyros looked around and suddenly felt claustrophobic. He couldn't stand the smell of her expensive perfumes, the touch of silken sheets, the soft mattress on the huge double-bed, his appearance in the mirror, the decadent luxury of the surroundings. He leapt out of bed and pulled on his clothes

"I must go now. My boat may have come adrift; Angelos is waiting for me . . . Saint Spyridon forgive me."

"Wait, Spyro, wait, I have something to show you . . ."

"I have seen everything. You have shown me enough already. I don't want to see more. Let me go. I am a Greek, a man with pride and self-respect, I shouldn't have come here. I may be poor but you cannot buy me, or bribe me with your wealth. Why did you come here from America? You foreigners, with your money and your yachts, you buy our land and build your houses. This one here is big enough for ten Greek families, and yet you live in it all alone and talk about your loneliness. You try to dance like us, but your legs are made of wood. This house of yours with its four bathrooms and its four toilets, tell me, why does one woman need so many? Do you eat so much food that you need four toilets? I see you do. And where does all your food finish up, and the money which bought it? In the sea, polluting our water, poisoning our fish!"

"No, no, Spyro, don't talk like that. You're wrong, so wrong. I have something for you, a present, let me show you."

Virginia pulled on a dressing-gown, took him by the arm and led him to the living-room, walked to the easel and removed the sheet from the painting that she had made of him.

"There, I am not trying to buy you. I am an artist, I have been painting you."

Spyros stopped, looked hard at the painting, recognized his likeness, as depicted pulling in the nets on his boat. His face muscles tensed, his eyes looked wild with rage; he looked round for something with which he could destroy the painting. He saw the dead fish, grabbed it by its tail and started slapping, smashing and crushing it against the picture with intensely violent hatred.

Virginia tried to stop him. He turned on her.

"So you are the devil's agent! That is why there are no fish. You took my manhood from me, tried to possess me by painting me, to gain power over me! *Matiasma!* Evil eye! You shall no longer. I am free again! I don't need your dollars and your silken sheets. Take a Turk to your bed. He will like your sweet perfumes and powdered arm-pits!"

Spyros ran from the house, down to his boat. His little brother had fallen asleep on the sand. Spyros woke him, then they jumped aboard the boat. Together they rowed out to sea, without speaking, before returning for the half-forgotten mule.

IV

Kyria Evanthia, their mother, was with their sister Sophia, busy preparing a meal up in their village house in Lakones. Spyros and Angelos burst in, looking angry.

"Here is a letter for you, Sophia," said Angelos. "A stranger passed it to us on the way up to the village, saying it was from Dimitris, and that he was a friend of his in Konitsa. We would have been here much earlier if it weren't for that American woman. Spyros went to her house, to take her a fish; he was gone so long that I fell asleep by the boat. Spyros won't tell me what happened. He keeps saying that it's because of her that we catch no more fish."

"It's your own fault if you don't work, and spend your time in the company of foreigners," said Kyria Evanthia. "Sophia, read us your letter."

Sophia, who had been holding the letter tightly in her hand, opened the envelope. She read it through in silence, looking worried, but when she'd finished reading, she broke down.

"Oh God! It can't be true!"

"What is it?" shouted Spyros. "Here, let me read it." He took the letter and started reading it out loud.

"My dearest Sophia, I don't know if you will ever receive this letter; a trusted friend of mine, a former teacher, will take it to you if he can. He helped me write it. That is, I found a way to tell him what I wanted to say and he promised to write it out and deliver it, which is why you won't recognise my handwriting. There is strict censorship of all mail. Something terrible has happened. I was arrested by the Military Police and court-martialled by the Army authorities. They're going to send me to a prison island as a political prisoner. They've accused me of being a Communist and a traitor. Ever since the army took control of the government, I've been under suspicion. They have a file on everyone, and they know how strongly I believe in democracy, though I've never been a Communist sympathiser. Last week we got word that the King was planning a counter-coup, in an attempt to restore democracy to the country, and to overthrow the fascist military dictatorship that we have now. Yesterday, I heard that the King had broadcast a message for Greeks to unite and to take up arms against the fascists. Many of our officers were with him. For a few hours it looked like civil war, but nobody was organised, and some people were afraid. Nothing happened, not a single bullet was fired. It was an abortive attempt, as soon as the King saw how things were going, he fled, and now he is in exile abroad. There's no hope. I don't know when I shall see you again, or what will happen to me. All I ask is that you destroy this letter, or you will put yourselves in grave danger. I only hope that you will wait for me, my love. *S'agapo*, Dimitris."

"The fool!" shouted Spyros. "He's ruined his own life, and Sophia's, all because of some half-baked political beliefs and stupid protests. What's wrong with the Military Government, they're better than the last lot, they're at least running the country efficiently and bringing some order to the chaos that existed before." He took a match and quickly set light to the letter. Sophia became hysterical and tried to stop him, but before she could snatch it from his hand, it burnt up quickly and was gone. She wept and cursed him for what he had done.

"If there's one thing I can't stand, it's a weeping woman. Come on, Angele, let's go to the *kapheneio*, to see if we can find out any more news."

V

Ben had clambered up to the top of the acropolis of Angelokastro, the ruined Byzantine castle and fortifications beyond the village of Krini. He was sitting alone on a rock overlooking the sea. He heard a noise and turned round to see Sophia coming up behind him, her eyes red from crying.

"I got your note asking to meet me here. Why did you choose such an out-of-the-way and difficult spot to meet me? I wasn't going to come, but I have to talk to someone, my brother can't understand anything."

"I often climb up here for the peace and quiet. Nobody can overhear what we're saying. But what's wrong, why have you been crying?"

"Dimitris has been arrested for his political beliefs. I may never see him again. They've taken him away to some island. I'm so frightened, I think I was born for bad luck. Last year my father died, now this. When will it end?"

Ben tried to comfort her by putting his arm around her.

"Don't worry, I'm sure they will release Dimitris soon, when they realise how powerless he is. You have nothing to fear."

"But I've heard that they torture people on that island, until they sign a paper declaring that they are in favour of the new government. Dimitris will never do that, I'm sure; he's stubborn and so committed to his beliefs."

"I'll do anything I can to help. Try to calm down. Look, I've brought a bottle of *retsina* with me, would you like a drink to help your nerves? It'll help to take your mind off your worries."

Ben gave her the bottle, from which Sophia took several sips. He still had his arm around her.

"Isn't this a beautiful spot? I often come here to think and to look at the magnificent views. Let's go for a walk around the old castle."

They got up and walked around the top. They both drank from the retsina bottle, and soon began to laugh and to enjoy themselves. They stopped to look at a strange shape in the stone.

"Look at this hollow in the rock," said Ben. "It's in the shape of a man's body. I wonder what it was used for. Perhaps it was a natural stone coffin or sarcophogus?"

"I think I know what it was," said Sophia. "In the middle ages they used to bind prisoners into that hollow, and leave them there to be burnt by the sun."

"That's one way to get a tan," quipped Ben. "They must have been small men in those days; I could never fit in there. Why don't you try?"

Sophia, temporarily putting out of her mind the tortures that Dimitris might suffer on his prison-island, lay down and stretched out in the hollow space. Ben laughed, then took her by complete surprise, by lying down beside her.

"What are you trying to do? *Stop it!*" she shouted, in genuine alarm, even though the *retsina* might have somewhat weakened her ability to resist unwelcome advances. Although she'd always liked Ben as a friend, neighbour and personable language teacher, her mind was suddenly unsure of his intentions, which soon enough became quite clear. She might have enjoyed a little coy flirtation in the past, but this was quite another matter. It was not at all what she wanted.

He was already lying down; he rolled over, pinned her arms to the rock and started kissing her, against her will. He might have tried to force his way upon her, but he became conscious of another noise, another presence. He sprang up and looked around. A priest was standing outside the door of the little church dedicated to the Archangel Michael, staring at them coldly.

"*Panayia mou!* My Holy Virgin!" exclaimed Sophia, "It's our village priest from Lakones. I'm lost. I'm sure he'll misunderstand. He's bound to tell my mother or my brother. Quickly, let's go before he says anything."

They ran away down the rough path. The priest just stood there watching them and crossing himself. He only came up to the church of the Archangel Michael once a year, but he had recognised both Ben and Sophia.

VI

Virginia was in her kitchen, cooking a luxurious meal on her modern infra-red cooker. She called through to Ben, who was sitting in the living-room, flicking through her old American magazines.

"I'm glad you could come to dinner, Ben, it's so nice to have young company."

Virginia set the food on the large dining-table, and they sat down.

"Who is Sophia, Ben, do I know her?"

"You know Spyros, the man from whom you buy your fish. She's his sister."

"Oh, yes, of course. Tell me, Ben, what brought you to this exiles' island?"

"It's a long story. I'm not really sure of the reasons myself. I couldn't bear to live in London any longer, it was destroying me, I couldn't write, it was slowly driving me mad, not just the dirt, the noise, the tube journeys. I suppose I had a rather romantic image of a Greek island, sun, sea, grapes, wine, music, dancing, freedom, that sort of thing. A pagan paradise. In reality, what I should have known, the Greeks have been deserted by the real Dionysian spirit; they like to have their fun, but it's all superficial. They're basically just the same as the rest of the aspiring European and American middle-classes, they're preoccupied with the accumulation of property and material possessions. All they want is a house like you've got here. You can't romanticise poverty and peasants. The political situation in itself is enough to disillusion anybody.

"I came in search of freedom, but here you can't find the truth in the newspapers, they're all censored. The Greeks can't even speak their minds in little village *kapheneia* any longer, there's always someone ready to pin something on a neighbour they don't like, to settle old scores, or a plain-clothes policeman eager to report on people and to have them transported to a prison-island in the Aegean — to have them tortured, if what they say is true. Have you seen some of the parades in Corfu Town, all the schoolchildren marching past proudly with the soldiers and the policemen? They're made to celebrate the Military Coup, too. *No to Fascism in 1940, No to Communism Now.* They're forbidden to say *Yes to Democracy,* which is what most of them want, and which is their ancient heritage, after all. Sophia told me that Angelos was ill on the day of one parade; the police called and accused his mother of deliberately keeping him away from the parade when the rest of the school kids from Lakones were taken by bus to town. They suspect every mother and mother's son of having Communist sympathies. How can you lie at peace under the sun, when all this is going on?"

"I don't trouble my mind with politics; I've got enough problems of my own. My last husband used to torture me in his own way, mentally rather than physically. I came here to forget, to be alone. But I've discovered that I'm not cut out to be an exile. I've got an idea, Ben, why don't I hold a party here next week. To show I'm just as democratic as the rest of them, I'll invite some of the peasant families to come, and the fishermen. I'll invite Spyros and Sophia first, that'll be doing both of us a favour. I'm sure Sophia will come, if her brother escorts her. What do you think? Will you help me organise it?"

"I think your motives are wrong, but I agree that a party is a great idea. Let's create again the Greece that used to be, we'll get them all dancing as if Dionysus and Pan were back in town."

When they'd finished the meal, Ben thanked Virginia, excused himself and left.

VII

Spyros, clutching a long, white candle he'd bought outside the church of Saint Spyridon in Corfu Town, was riding his mule on the narrow, bending road towards the Monastery of the Panayia of Paleokastritsa. If he ever got married, he had it mind to organise the service in the monastery's beautiful church. On the way down from Lakones, he passed a shepherd with his flock. But his mind was too set on some hidden purpose to allow him to greet anyone. When he approached the top of the hill where the monastery was located, with views almost as dramatic as those from the acropolis of Angelokastro, he dismounted from his mule, tethered it to a tree and walked the last hundred metres or so. He entered the Church, which was dedicated to the Virgin Mary, crossed himself and drew near to the icon of the Virgin, which he kissed. He kissed several other holy icons, then lit his long candle and placed it before the icon of the Panayia, and began to pray out loud.

"Holy Mother, and Saint Spyridon who blessed this candle, give me some sign that what I am about to do is right and just in the eyes of the Lord. It was our priest from Lakones who told me of my sister's sin with the Englishman, of her infidelity and damage to our family's honour. It is your commandment that a brother must protect his sister's honour, and that, if it is violated, he must avenge it. Give me courage to carry out just revenge, and give your blessing to what I have to do."

He kissed the icon again, bowed towards the iconostasis, crossed himself and, as he opened the door of the church to leave, he saw the candle flame flicker in the draught. He took this as an answer. He stood outside in the monastery garden for some moments, admiring the view of one of his favourite corners of the island and the blue sea stretching away before him.

VIII

Not far away, as the crow flies, Ben was about to dive into the sea from a rock in a craggy, grotto-like bay near Paleokastritsa, well-hidden from the road. Sophia was already in the water, swimming like a fish or mermaid. Ben dived in, they splashed about together, then Sophia climbed up some slippery steps to lie on a flat rock. After a few minutes Ben joined her.

"I think that this might be the spot where Odysseus came ashore, and first saw Nausicaa."

"I don't think so, Ben. Where's the stream in which Nausicaa and her maidens were washing their clothes? I was always led to believe that the bay of Ermones was the real location. You don't believe those old stories do you?"

"Why not? I can believe anything. Writers like myths and good stories, even tall stories. You will come to Virginia's party, won't you Sophia?"

"If you want me too, and if my brother lets me, I will. But we must behave as if we were strangers. I'm really afraid that my brother may have found out from the priest that he saw us together up at Angelokastro; not that anything sinful happened. We mustn't dance together."

Sophia gave Ben a quick kiss, and started on the long, steep climb towards Lakones, hoping that somebody would stop to give her a lift. Ben waited for a while, planning to take a taxi from Paleokastritsa.

IX

The party at Virginia's grand villa was in full swing. Loud music was playing on the record-player, Greek *chassapiko* and *sirtaki* music (but no Theodorakis songs, because his music was banned), Beatles' songs, American rock music. Everyone was dancing and drinking happily. Feeling brave, Ben asked Sophia to dance. Reluctantly she accepted. As they were dancing, Spyros came up stealthily behind Ben and snapped open his razor-sharp fish-gutting knife.

Sophia saw it and screamed "Watch out!" pulling Ben to one side as Spyros tried to slash at him with the knife. Ben swung round and grabbed Spyros' arm. They fought and wrestled for possession of the knife, crashing into the furniture and the record-player, which at that point had started to play the same *zebekiko* that Spyros had danced in front of an adoring Virginia.

As the stylus jumped across the grooves of the record, another guest grabbed the handle of knife, and two men held Spyros down. He spat in the direction of Ben, shouting "This is not the end! I'll get you some way. You'll pay, *Ingleze*, for what you've done to my sister *and* for what the British did in Cyprus! Greeks never forgive or forget!"

X

The next day, Spyros' family gathered in their house in Lakones and waited for Kyria Evanthia to have her say. In times of crisis, they deferred to the matriarch of the family. Angelos wasn't present; the others had decided that at his young age he didn't need to be a part of the discussion, and they didn't want him to be implicated as a witness.

"You're mad, Spyro. If you had killed him you would have spent the rest of your life in gaol. A whole family of convicts! You may still go to prison. How could we live without you? Calm down, and listen to my plan. What is the point of spilling blood, when you can take the Englishman to court. The judge will make him pay a fortune in compensation for Sophia's loss of honour. The money we will be awarded will make a perfect dowry for her, if Dimitris ever returns. If he doesn't, we can always send her to the town, to find a husband there who hasn't heard any gossip about this local trouble."

"You're right, Mother," said Spyros, "but we must act quickly. I have heard that the Englishman is already packing up and preparing to leave the island. Maybe he plans to catch tomorrow's ferry to Brindisi. He must be very afraid of me; he knows that he was in the wrong!"

At that moment, Angelos burst in.

"Another smuggled letter from Dimitris!"

Sophia, who had remained silent, jumped up and snatched it from him, tore it open and read it.

"He's coming home! He's been released, but he says he's very weak. They tortured him until he broke down and signed the confession. He hopes I will still marry him when I see him again, but he is not the same as he was."

"I hope *he* will still marry *you*," said her mother.

"He says he no longer cares about a dowry. He is so glad to be free again that it no longer matters! So much for your plan to take the Englishman to court."

Sophia ran out of the house, to tell Ben the news. His windows and shutters were closed and the house was locked. Ben had already left.

XI

All the villagers were gathered in the square. They were dressed up smartly, dancing and shuffling round and round in a circle, with Sophia still wearing her wedding dress. In the middle of the circle were four musicians, playing guitar, violin, mandolin and accordion. They were singing *kantades*, four male voices in perfect harmony; the dance was a traditional Corfiot one.

As the circle turned, Dimitris came in view, happily leading the circle of dancers, holding a handkerchief for the next in line, but he himself wasn't making any of the leader's usual little leaps and turns. Sophia tried hard not to look too closely at her husband's face. It was covered with bruises and small, ugly scars from cigarette burns, the result of the tortures he had suffered on the prison-island. He was limping badly, as the result of the lesions caused by the terrible *phalanga* beatings to the soles of his feet.

He turned to look at Sophia, and she forced a smile.

The village priest stayed to watch as the dancing continued. The exile had returned. Spyros was the next to lead the dance, to relieve his limping brother-in-law.

Virginia watched, at a distance.

Beyond the mountains

I

The house was three hundred years old, perhaps older with its grey stone walls. The irregular, roughly-dressed roof-slabs, all quarried by hand, were too thick to be called tiles. The roof-beams sagged under the tremendous weight, but the roof-slabs merged into the stone and the limestone schist-stacks which jutted up from the mountainside, much as Simon hoped to merge and blend into the local environment. Whatever disguise he adopted, Simon Roberts would never be mistaken for anything other than a tall, fair-haired and blue-eyed Englishman in his late thirties. In spite of his appearance, he was more or less accepted by the local inhabitants, mostly elderly widows dressed in black, whose children had long since moved away to the concrete cities and to apartments with modern conveniences, piped water, flush toilets and proper drains, with smoothly plastered walls which did not harbour spiders, scorpions, lizards or snakes.

In spite of the inconveniences, Simon had recognised at once that this was the perfect safe house and base-camp for his assigned mission. A remote village in the mountains of Epirus, it had the advantage of being situated not more than thirty miles from the Greek-Albanian border. It was perched directly above a wild and spectacular gorge. During World War II the villagers had used the gorge as a hiding-place from the Germans; in the more distant past it had provided a refuge and a way to escape from the *klepht*s, Ali Pasha's soldiers and the Ottoman Turks.

Nowadays few people ever ventured near it, apart from the occasional goat-herd, cowherd, or perhaps the odd hunter; it was known to be the home of the few remaining wild bears, as well as wild boar. Even if one didn't meet a bear, there was the very real danger of slipping on scree, of breaking an ankle or leg with little chance of help or rescue.

"You speak pretty good Greek, don't you, Simon?" his Controller had asked one rainy morning, after Simon had completed a mission to Semtin in Czechoslovakia, with great distinction.

"I read Byzantine and Modern Greek at Oxford, Sir. Is there any chance of a stint out there? I could do with a sight of the sea after two years in Central Europe."

"You won't be doing much swimming where we're going to send you; although you might need to keep in practice, just in case you have to escape by swimming across the Corfu Channel."

"Albania!"

"Albania, eventually. Nothing terribly dramatic. We're not going to repeat old mistakes. We're not dropping émigrés in with a view to changing the system or starting a counter-revolution. This isn't going to be an old-style Cold War mission. It's a lot more subtle. You'll do very little for the first eighteen months or so, be little more than a sleeper, an eccentric Englishman with a taste for Byronic landscape who decides to buy a holiday house in one of the Zagori villages in the mountains of Epirus, not more than thirty kilometres from Ioannina. You'll have to buy a place, of course. You'll be recruiting some agents in the area. You'll have to build up your bona fides. Get to know who's who. Find out what their politics are. Drink *tsipouro* with them in the village square or coffee-shop; eat pitta and wild mushrooms. See who you can trust. Go on some day-trips to the border area. Behave like a mountain-loving tourist, not a reincarnation of a World War Two officer parachuted in by the Allied Military Mission. You're not going to emulate Woodhouse or Hammond. Understood?"

"Understood."

"And you'll remember how we failed disastrously in 1949 and 1950, when Operation Valuable was betrayed by Philby. By that time we'd joined forces with the Americans, who'd been planning their own operations, BGFIEND and OBOPUS. The CIA boys didn't really trust us, and we didn't have much faith in their aims and gung-ho methods. We were aiming to subvert and destabilise the Communist regime; they were determined to overthrow it. Quite apart from Philby, the operation was leaky from the start."

"I know only too well how many of the agents we'd trained on Malta and infiltrated from Corfu were killed soon after they landed. The comms were pretty primitive and inadequate and Hoxha's men were lying in wait for them."

"Some of the techniques may turn out to be similar, in the last analysis, but we want you to bide your time. You can't afford to be betrayed or diverted. We're well aware of your weakness for women. It came out in your vetting. Stick to getting to know the lay of the land. The time for action will come when we give the word. We're getting pretty fed up with the regime in Albania. We're none too happy with Papandreou's policies in Greece. You'll get your final orders and a deeper briefing after your Stage Two indoctrination. That won't be for another year. You've got to establish yourself over there first. Give the locals enough time to realise that you're not a spy, because that's what they'll probably think. Oh, and by the way, you might find it'll come in handy if you mug up some basic Albanian. Study the maps, analyse the demographic statistics and where the Greek-speaking villages are, or where there's still a Greek-speaking minority. There'll be lots of homework. But there'll be plenty of rewards. How does that sound to you?"

"No objections. I'm always flexible. But I want some facts. What's the budget? I know the Firm is strapped for cash. The secret vote's getting smaller every year. I'll need money for the house, for furniture and repairs, then for the agents. You won't be sending me any parachute drops of gold sovereigns, I suppose. Oh, and I'll need a good car this time, not another clapped-out Škoda. Four-wheel drive and the usual refinements."

"Your car will be nothing special. Second-hand Ford Escort, if you're lucky. The allocation has been agreed. High-level approval. But resources are limited, as usual, Simon. We're not the Eastern Bloc. £30,000 and not a penny over."

"That's ridiculous. How am I supposed to buy a house, run a

car and recruit agents for that?"

"We reckon you can find a habitable house for under £10,000. You won't need much to live on. There's very little to buy up in those villages. You'll get by with bread, local dairy produce, tins of sardines and pickled octopus. Our chaps were a lot worse off during the German Occupation."

"Maybe, but the locals are a good deal more suspicious nowadays, and a lot less cooperative, I should imagine. There's no great common enemy to be resisted."

"They see things differently in North-West Greece. They're not Athenians. They still care about the fate of their kinfolk and relatives unable to escape from Albania. That's what they claim, anyway. They still consider Southern Albania to be Greek territory. It's Northern Epirus to them. Many are romantic Royalists. They hate Papandreou for having opened up relations with the Albanian regime, and for declaring that Greece no longer has any claims on Albanian territory. Papandreou keeps telling them the real enemy is Turkey. 'Our Northern Neighbours pose no threat,' he says, 'they are our peace-loving socialist brothers. The threat is entirely from the East, not from the North.' The Epirots don't like the Turks, it's true, but nor do they like the Albanian Muslims, or the Bulgarians, for that matter."

"There are some Albanian-speakers still living in Greece, aren't there? Do we have any reliable estimate of the numbers?"

"It's difficult to assess. A lot of them have learnt to use Greek in order to assimilate or survive. But it's not prohibited to speak Albanian. The first wave of Albanians moved down in the fourteenth century. They kept pouring in under the Ottomans and Ali Pasha. Even the Suliots were originally Albanian."

"I've heard broadcasts in Greek from Radio Tirana. They like to stir it up."

"I'm sure you have. The Communists use some of their most trusted Greek-speakers to broadcast propaganda programmes into Greece. Don't forget those poor benighted Greeks have been subjected to forty years of atheistic and Stalinist brainwashing. We don't know how many would want to leave now even if they could. And then there were a large number of unswerving hard-liners who retreated over the Albanian border after the Communists lost the Greek Civil War in 1949. Some of them moved on to Yugoslavia or Czechoslovakia, but quite a few stayed behind. They liked their water-melons too much to travel too far North."

"What do the Greeks in Greece think of Albania on the whole?"

"The Greeks always resented the creation of the State of Albania — it was only created in 1913, you know, and the Greeks were deprived of much of Northern Epirus, even though they'd occupied it during the Balkan Wars. Venizelos claimed it, and Lloyd George had supported Venizelos when he occupied the area. But the Americans didn't go along with the idea of partition as Albania was such a new state. The Treaty of Lausanne in 1923 saw the end of Greek hopes. Northern Epirus went to the Albanians. In the Second World War the Greeks were frustrated once again. They drove back the Italian invaders, and succeeded in occupying Koritsa and Aryirokastro (Korçë and Gjirokastër to the Albanians). They didn't capture Valona, because the Italians recovered sufficiently to hold a line; but the Greeks expected to win back the bulk of Northern Epirus with the coming of peace. But you can read up on this when you study the files."

"Surely the Greeks began to get on rather more friendly terms with the Albanians in the fifties? Didn't both countries agree to clear the Corfu straits of mines?"

"That's true. But remember that Albania had proposed the establishment of diplomatic relations in 1955. They refused the Greeks' main condition, which was to keep open the question of Northern Epirus. The Greeks held the vain hope that the question would be settled in its favour at a future peace conference. Well, Simon, you know some of the general background. Any questions? You're aware that there's no longer a technical state of war. Once the Greeks gave up their territorial claims, diplomatic relations were normalised. But that's not the case with us. We're still at loggerheads with the Albanians over compensation for the sinking of two of our ships in the Corfu Channel. And they want their gold back. Fat chance. We still hold it in the Bank of England. Here, take these files to your office. Study them carefully in the secure room, and return them to me in person by six o'clock this evening. Sign them out first. Otherwise Registry will have you for a major breach of security."

"There is just one other question, Sir. You didn't mention our agent inside Albania. A young woman, I believe. Is she British? Am I to meet up with her at any point?"

"I knew you were going to ask that. Well, you'll just have to wait until your indoctrination, I'm afraid. All I can tell you is that she is the daughter of one of the people parachuted into Albania in 1949. One of the few who wasn't caught and shot after facing a show-trial, as a result of Philby's betrayal of the operation. She was born in 1960. She's half-Greek. That's all I know. You'll be given her call-sign, codename and frequency. You'll be amused by the codename I've dreamed up for you."

Simon took the files to the windowless and bugless secure room, a room within a room, and read with growing interest the contents of the top secret MI6 files marked *Operation Inside-Out.* "At least I won't have to live like a Mount Athos hermit-monk for the whole duration of my assignment," he thought to himself, with just a faint hint of a smile.

II

The Ford Escort may have looked second-hand; the body-work certainly showed signs of wear-and-tear, but the engine was something quite unexpected. The car soared. It flew. It was a rally-driver's dream. It was a pity that the roads in Greece were so bad. Simon had two choices, either to drive down through Yugoslavia or through Italy. He knew both routes well. He couldn't face the hold-ups at the main Yugoslavian motorway exit toll-gates, or at the Greek border, at Evzoni. He didn't enjoy the ferry-crossing from Brindisi either, so he decided to take the ferry from Ancona to Igoumenitsa. It was a slow crossing, but the food was reasonably good, and he would have time to work on his Greek and Albanian.

Igoumenitsa had little to commend it. A Greek passenger told Simon that when the National Bank of Greece first introduced plate glass windows in its Igoumenitsa branch, donkeys would bang their heads against the panes, trying to get at the greenery in the pot-plants inside. His Greek was good enough to understand that joke, at least.

As soon as he'd driven off the ferry, he filled up with petrol, and set off on the ninety kilometre journey across the mountains to Ioannina. Although the journey only took an hour and a half, Simon always found it tedious, especially when stuck behind a lorry or bus on the winding mountain roads. This time he could afford to take some risks, as the Escort's powerful acceleration was superb. "I wouldn't swop this for a Porsche," he said under his breath, as he swept past three cars on a steep uphill bend. The driver of the last car, a black Mercedes, gesticulated angrily at him, shouting out the word *Malaka!* while giving him the Greek gesture of contempt, the palm of his hand and five outstretched fingers. Simon returned the compliment. He was getting back into local habits.

Ten minutes later he pulled up, to give a lift to a hitch-hiker. He expected that she was with a boyfriend, who was probably cowering in a ditch nearby, hiding two huge rucksacks, hoping that her good looks would win them both a ride to Ioannina.

She got into the car with a smile and a polite *Efcharisto poli.* He was pleased to find that no boyfriend came leaping out from the roadside ditch. She only had a tiny rucksack, which she tossed into the back seat.

"Where are you going?" asked Simon.

"To Ioannina, I'm a student at the University there."

"You're Greek?" asked Simon.

"What else?"

Simon paused.

"What's your name?"

"Maria. And yours?"

"Simon. Simon Roberts."

"Are you on holiday?"

"Yes and no. I want to explore Epirus a bit. I'm getting bored with lying on the beach. I want to research the traditional music, and I thought I might do some walking in the mountains, explore the Zagori villages and the Vikos Gorge. Maybe climb up to Drakolimni, the Dragon-Lake. Do you know the area?"

"As a matter of fact, I do. My room-mate comes from one of the Zagori villages. I've been with her to visit her grandmother many times. We usually go for three or four days in August, to take part in the *paniyiri*."

"That's a kind of village festival, isn't it, with lots of dancing and music in the main square? Is that the best place to hear the sound of the *klarino*, and some traditional *miroloyia*?"

"That's right. It's the only time in the year when everybody tries to get back to their villages. They come from Athens, Salonica, Germany, even America and Australia if they can make it. It's a three-day reunion party. But I really prefer the Spring or Autumn when the villages are deserted. The wild flowers are so beautiful in Spring, and in the autumn the leaves turn the most amazing colours. Even the winter is beautiful, although it gets very cold and often snows. It's very romantic if you get the log fire burning in the winter bedroom. The beds are usually like low platforms, built in the Turkish style all around the hearth and fireplace. They can be very cosy if they're covered with a thick *phlokati*, a sheepskin rug."

"I'd love to find a place like that."

"I'm sure you could rent rooms for a few weeks."

"I mean I'd love to buy an old stone village house. It's always been my dream."

"Are you serious? Most of them are falling down. Very few

people bother to maintain them nowadays. People don't want to live that sort of life any longer. They don't want to pull buckets of water from the cistern. They want their creature comforts."

"What about you, Maria?" Simon turned to look at her. She had lovely dark eyes. She gave him a beautiful smile. He had to swerve to avoid a goat which had strayed from the herd.

"I like my flat in Ioannina. It's got central-heating. I don't like wasting too much time doing house-work. I like to keep warm in the winter."

"It's early Summer now, Maria. If you like your comforts so much, why are you hitch-hiking? Why don't you travel by bus or taxi?"

"Greek children are over-protected when they're young. If you don't experiment a bit and break out when you're a student, you never will. Besides, I like hitch-hiking. I sometimes meet interesting people. I can improve my languages at the same time."

"How is it that you speak such perfect English?"

"I grew up in Corfu and we lived next door to an English family. I spent all my free time playing with English children."

"Do you speak other languages too?"

"I speak Albanian quite well. My father came from Aryirokastro, he's a *Voreio-Ipirotis*, a Northern Epirot; my mother comes from Corfu. My father escaped to Corfu in 1952. He was one of the very few who made it from Ayi Saranda."

"I'm very impressed. Do you think your room-mate or her family would be able to give me any advice about houses up in the Zagori villages? I want to find something really quiet, completely isolated. I don't want any noise."

"You're asking something, in Greece. But why do you want to hide yourself in a mountain village?"

"I like walking, and I want to try my hand at writing and landscape painting for a change. I've lived too long in London, working in an airless office. I want a complete break. But I don't want to live in one of the touristy islands. There are too many temptations and distractions."

Maria looked at him, an amused expression on her face: "I'll tell you what. If you find what you're looking for, I'll come and visit you occasionally, to stop you going completely crazy. If you go to live in one of those villages, all you'll have for company is a few old goatherds and some half-demented widows. I don't want you to throw yourself into the Vikos Gorge out of desperation. Or would I be a distraction?"

"Not a *distraction*. No. I would welcome some company."

His thoughts were interrupted by loud hooting from behind. It was a Mercedes with a Greek number plate. It was the same one. He recognised the aggressive driver.

The Mercedes pulled up alongside Simon's car and the driver waved his fist at Simon. He was a very overweight fellow, red in the face and sweating profusely:

"*Vlaka! Malaka!* Stupid *Ingleze!*"

The Mercedes cut in sharply, almost driving Simon's Escort off the road. To the right there was a horrendous sheer drop. Maria clung to his arm, spontaneously; she was trembling and deeply frightened. Simon braked hard and managed to stay on the road. The Mercedes roared away, with the driver still making angry and obscene gestures. Simon pulled in to the side of the road; there was a lay-by with space for just one car.

"Sorry about that. The man didn't like being overtaken by a Ford Escort."

"Are you alright?" He suppressed the instinct to put his arm protectively around Maria's shoulder. She was still trembling.

"It's alright. I'm ok. Really I am. It's just that I had a good friend who died in a car accident in the Pindus Mountains. Have you got a cigarette?"

Simon didn't smoke, but he did carry a package of 200 cigarettes in the car as a hangover from his days in eastern Europe, where they came in useful as a tip in a wide variety of situations. He broke them open, gave her a cigarette and lit it. She inhaled and began to relax.

They had parked opposite a large rocky outcrop, which was

covered in bright blue graffiti. He'd noticed the daubings on the rocks and mountainside all the way up the curving road from Igoumenitsa, but he hadn't paid much attention to the writing. Now his eyes picked out the letters, and he took in the slogans:

"Long Live Northern Epirus!" "Freedom to Our Brothers in Northern Epirus." There were other slogans and names of politicians which had been painted over. Simon could make out the names of two political parties, PASOK (Papandreou's ruling party), and EPEN, with the name of Papadopoulos still visible: Papadopoulos of the Colonels' junta, Papadopoulos who was still in prison. There were traces of green and blue paint everywhere, but it was mostly blue; there was no red, there were no slogans in support of the KKE, or Greek Communist Party, such as could be found covering University buildings in big cities.

"I hate graffiti," said Simon, "it's a form of pollution. It destroys the beauty of the landscape. What would Edward Lear have done if he'd had to set his easel in front of such a disgusting mess? Lord Byron would never have written the Second Canto of Childe Harold if he'd come riding up these defaced mountain passes. Can you imagine it? "Down with Ali Pasha!" "Lord Byron for King!", "Turks Go Home", "Death to the Ottoman Empire".

"You should never make fun of the Greeks; you've got no right to be so cynical. At least they care about politics. Give some thought to the Greeks in Northern Epirus. Don't forget that my own father nearly lost his life escaping from the Albanians."

"I'm so sorry, I forgot. You may be right. But what good do such graffiti do?"

"Perhaps they help to remind people, when the Government has conveniently chosen to forget. Anyway, we should get going, or we'll never get to Ioannina."

Simon set off in silence. He was subdued and thoughtful for the rest of the journey. Maria smoked another cigarette and put a cassette into his player. Instead of music, what she heard was a course in colloquial Albanian. She said nothing as she ejected it and switched on the radio instead. The harsh sound of the *klarino,* the Epirot folk clarinet made conversation impossible, but he pretended to enjoy the oriental-sounding improvisations.

"That's what you'll hear at your *paniyiria*", she said, "but keep your hands on the wheel — and your eyes on the road!"

They reached Ioannina half an hour later than he had expected. He decided to book in at the Xenia Hotel, and she agreed to have a quick drink with him before catching the bus to her apartment.

"I'll give you my address and telephone number," she said as she sipped her iced ouzo. "If you're serious about looking for an old house in the mountains, I may be able to help."

"I am serious. I'm going to start looking tomorrow, but I don't really know where to begin."

"Look, I'm free for a week. I'd be glad to show you round the area. Shall I call here tomorrow at nine, and then at least I can show you the way to the most interesting villages, and perhaps my room-mate can come along too? If not, we'll just make enquiries at the local coffee-shops or in the main squares."

"I'd be most grateful. Yes, please do come. Then I can practise my Greek. I studied it at university, but I never became very fluent."

"I'm sure it's very good. Or perhaps your Albanian's better?"

Maria suddenly got up, took her tiny rucksack, flashed him a warm smile, and left the hotel. She might well prove to be a distraction, he thought.

III

Maria was as good as her word. She was waiting in the lobby of the Xenia Hotel at five minutes to nine, accompanied by another girl of about the same age. Aliki was very different in appearance from Maria, as she had auburn hair and grey-blue eyes.

"This is my room-mate, Aliki. She's agreed to come along with us today."

"I'm pleased to meet you, Aliki. It's very kind of you to help. Which village do you come from?"

"My grandmother comes from Monodendri. Perhaps we should go there first, even though it attracts more tourists than the other villages, because of the Monastery of Ayia Paraskevi, which is situated right at the edge of the gorge. It's a very dramatic sight. Anyway, we'll be able to get a meal of sorts in Monodendri. They're certain to have wild mushrooms. Have you ever tried the local speciality? It's a kind of *pita* or giant cheese pie."

"I've had something similar. Is it made with white feta cheese?"

"Yes, it's a special flour-and-feta flatbread pie, doughy in the middle, with edges like crispy batter."

"Well, that will be something to look forward to. How long does it take to get to Monodendri?"

"About half an hour, maybe less in your car. I hear it's surprisingly fast."

"It goes, if I want it to. But we took over two hours from Igoumenitsa yesterday."

"Yes, I know. Maria told me. But you still managed to upset our local police chief, I hear, by overtaking him on a mountain bend."

"I didn't know he was the Chief of Police! He must have been off-duty. He wasn't driving a police-car. Why on earth didn't you tell me, Maria?"

"I didn't want to alarm you. Perhaps he took your number. But he probably took you as a passing tourist. Aliki's father is his second cousin, so I shouldn't worry about it."

"I see that everyone's related in this part of the world," Simon said to Aliki with a laugh. "Does he speak English as well as you two?"

"I don't think he likes the British as much as some people in these parts."

"Why not"?

"It's a long story. It all goes back to the Second World War and then the Civil War. I wouldn't want to bore you with it."

"Please do tell me. I'm interested in such matters. Greek history is fascinating."

"We'll talk about it on the way to Monodendri, if you insist".

The two girls lead the way to the car. Maria was wearing a pair of faded blue jeans and a loose T-Shirt. She had on a pair of silver ear-rings which had a distinctive pattern of the Ioannina silversmiths. They went well with her long black hair.

Aliki's English was not as good as Maria's, but Simon was impressed by her fluency, as much as by her curly auburn hair and sun-tanned shoulders. Remembering his Controller's warning, he tried not to notice her striking good looks.

Sensing Simon's restrained approval of Aliki, Maria turned and said, "I bet you're surprised to find two English-speaking Greek girls out of the blue like this?"

"It's the luck of the gods. Did Aliki also spend her childhood playing with English children, by any chance?"

"No, I didn't! I acquired my English through hard work and hours of study. I've been taking three lessons a week at various *phrontisteria* for the last ten years, and I got Grade A in the Cambridge Certificate of Proficiency exam."

"Congratulations," said Simon as he opened the car-doors for the two girls. He started the car, and they took the Konitsa road out of Ioannina. He noticed more blue graffiti on the walls and sides of buildings: "Freedom for Northern Epirus".

"My father comes from Zitsa, my mother from Monodendri. My father was always proud of the fact that Lord Byron had visited Zitsa in October 1809. There's even a plaque on the monastery wall there. That's how I became interested in English Literature. My father also knew some Englishmen during the German Occupation. In fact he worked quite closely with two of your officers. He was very fond of them. He hid one of them in our house for six months when the Englishman fell sick."

"His cousin, the police chief, doesn't seem to be quite such an Anglophile."

"He belongs to a different party. And some say that he collaborated with the Germans during the Occupation. He's never forgiven the British over Cyprus. Even my own father felt betrayed and bitter about that. But his wartime friendships were very strong. He brought us up to respect the English language and culture. We can't forget what Byron did for us, can we?"

They had arrived at the turning point off the Konitsa highway, nineteen kilometres from Ioannina. There was a signpost pointing to the right, straight up the mountainside, which said "Monodendri" and "Vikos Canyon".

"What's the difference between a canyon and a gorge?" Simon wondered.

"The road is really quite good", said Maria. "That's one good thing that the Colonels did, whatever their motives. Mind you, the villages still don't have piped water. That's one of the reasons nobody wants to live up here."

The car climbed the ascent effortlessly; the gradient was more gradual than it appeared at first, and they soon reached a thousand metres above sea level, where the air felt cooler and thinner. The views across the mountain ranges and down to the valley and plain below were stunning.

"Good country for a guerrilla war," remarked Simon.

"God forbid," replied Aliki, "we've had enough of that, of fighting against the Turks, against the Italians, against the Germans, and finally against ourselves. And in a few years we'll be waging war against the tourists and the developers, no doubt. God forbid if they ever discover oil!"

"That's unlikely, up here. But you have had some unpleasant incidents in Athens — bombs thrown into hotels, onto cruiseships, that sort of thing. At least you haven't started burning down holiday cottages, like the Welsh nationalists."

"No, the Greeks would never do that, although they do resent it when whole villages are taken over by the Germans or British. The Greeks are more likely to burn down large areas of protected forest in order to clear the way for new buildings."

"I want to find a village where I'll be the only foreigner for miles around", said Simon. "Is there any chance of finding a really isolated hideaway for me?"

"No problem. Choose any pile of stones you see. There are more than forty Zagori villages. Some of them have been virtually depopulated; it's sad to see so many abandoned houses. But here we are at Monodendri. Let's start here."

It was a beautifully preserved stone village, nestling against the mountainside. Simon fell in love with the architecture of the houses, the heavy grey uneven slabstones strewn across the roofs, the drystone walls of roughly-squared stones, the expertly-laid *kalderimia*, or cobbled pathways running between the well-protected courtyard gates of the safely enclosed houses; it was an artist's dream and a hermit's heaven.

"Do you want to eat some *pita* now, or shall we ask if there are any empty houses for sale?"

"We shouldn't rush into it," said Simon, in reply to Aliki. "My resources are rather limited. I don't want them to think that I'm a rich tourist."

"Don't worry, you don't look it! Let's go and look at my grandmother's house first. You'll get some idea of what the houses are like inside."

They turned down one of the cobbled pathways, designed for the villagers' animals as much as for human beings. They came to a large entrance gate, with two big wooden doors. Aliki took an iron rod which was suspended from the door and used it to release a wooden catch at the top of the doors. One swung open, sounding a bell as it did so. The courtyard was paved with beautiful old paving-stones which had developed a shiny patina almost like polished marble, but rough in texture. There was a charming old cistern under an arched and shaded corridor. There were tubs and pots of herbs and flowers everywhere, as well as a plum tree (or was it a damson tree?) and a vine climbing up the stone walls of the house. Aliki closed the gate behind them.

It was a world of its own, completely surrounded by high walls. No wonder the Turks left them alone. Aliki's grandmother was not at home, it seemed. They went into the house, and sat down in the main living room. Simon looked up to see an exquisitely carved and painted wooden ceiling, with centuries-old traditional folk-art motifs. It was sagging in several places, as rain must have dripped through the stone-roof on many occasions.

"It came down once when an Italian bomb landed outside the front door. That was in 1941. The Italians flew in from Albania. They'd detected troop movements in the area. Several buildings were completely destroyed, including the school. Forty children were killed. My grandmother could tell you all about it, if you're interested."

"It shows you that you can't be completely safe, even in an idyllic and isolated mountain village like this. But this is just the sort of house I'm looking for. Where can we find one?"

"There's a village on the opposite side of the gorge, facing Vitsa. It's called Dilopho. You couldn't find anywhere more isolated. It hasn't even got an asphalt road."

"Sounds perfect. Shall we go there now? Do you know anyone there?"

"My cousin runs the local coffee-shop there. We could ask for his advice."

They decided to sit in the village square, under the giant plane tree. They ordered *tsipouro* and a litre of local red wine and an unusual rocket salad with pine nuts, wild bulbs and mushrooms. They found Aliki's grandmother chatting to another old lady dressed in black. She was very friendly to Simon, and expressed the hope that he would choose their village for his home. Dilopho to her was on the other side of the earth. Before the roads were made, it was necessary to walk down to Vitsa, take the cobbled path and steps to the bottom of the gorge, to cross the old Turkish-style arched Bridge of Misiou, then climb the path to Dilopho on the other side of the gorge. It was the best part of a morning's journey, although she had done it often enough in her youth, to take part in the Dilopho *paniyiri*. During World War II, the courageous women of Zagori had carried food and ammunition across the mountains to the fighting men. Now, by car, the journey took only twenty minutes.

"Are there any Albanian speakers in these villages?" Simon asked Aliki quite casually when Maria had gone to find a rubbish bin.

"There are Sarakatsani goatherds and a few Vlach shepherds who probably still speak some Albanian. Borders never really mattered to them. Why do you want to know?"

"Just out of interest. I studied languages at Oxford, and I might write a short monograph on the linguistic geography of Epirus, to bring the work of scholars like Hammond, Campbell and Wace and Thompson up to date. Some of the Zagori villages seem to have Slavonic-sounding names, like Tsepelovo, Kapesovo, Dovra; even the name Zagori sounds like a Slavic word meaning 'beyond the mountains'."

"It's a puzzle. But there have been Greek settlements in this area since the ninth-century before Christ. Archaeologists have excavated them. You can see for yourself in a minute, we're going to pass the site of Ancient Vitsa. They used the same stone and building techniques. You can go and see all the finds in the Museum of Ioannina."

"But there must have been Albanians and Serbs in these parts from the Middle Ages on?" Simon had drunk two glasses of *tsipouro* and three glasses of the delicious red wine; he was becoming loquacious and indiscrete.

"You should be careful what you say, Simon, the Greeks are very sensitive about such theories. You'll make yourself very unpopular if you go round asking questions like that. It's much more likely that Greeks inhabited the whole of Northern Epirus and Macedonia, including what the Yugoslavs have the nerve to call the Republic of Macedonia. Don't forget that Alexander the Great was a Greek and he hellenized half the world."

"I recently read that his mother, Olympias, might have been Albanian!" Simon was being deliberately provocative now.

"What nonsense!"

"I only asked out of academic curiosity. Please don't get me wrong. I'm very sympathetic to the old Greek claims about

247

Northern Epirus. Later on I might like to meet some people who can tell me more about the history of the area. Perhaps you know people who've still got relatives over the border. If I find a house and get to know this part of the country, I might write a travel guide to Epirus, and I'll needs lots of historical and geographical background. It would need a great deal of research."

"You seem to have a lot of projects, Simon. You're going to be kept very busy with your writing and research. You'd better count on leaving some time aside to learn the art of the stonemason. These houses need a lot of maintenance."

Simon looked around. There were a number of ruined houses with caved-in roofs and bulging stone walls. "Stomachs", the Greeks called these disturbing bulges. He got the point.

IV

They drove slowly up the dusty, stony track to Dilopho. Simon remarked enthusiastically about the impressive tall stone mansions, some almost fortified towers, but the village square lacked the charm of the *plateia* in Monodendri. They got out, greeted the villagers in the square, and walked through the village to the church. To the side of the well-restored church was an arched arcade, and above the door of the church were some interesting stone carvings. Aliki wanted to show them the view across the gorge to Vitsa. They strolled across some open meadows to a high point about half a mile beyond the edge of the village, where a centuries-old disused circular stone threshing floor surrounded by a low wall invited them to sit down and admire the wild, spectacular scenery. "Byron would have loved it here!" said Simon. "He must have seen similar views when he went to Zitsa."

They sat in silence and gazed at the entrance at the entrance of the dramatic Vikos Gorge.

"I wish I'd brought my sketch-pad with me."

He felt elated. The air was absolutely fresh and clear, the sky without a cloud, and there was no noise at all, except the distant sound of the tinkling goats' bells, like some magical symphony drifting across space and time from the mountains of Ancient Greece. Surely nothing had changed. The same pastoral way of life, the same bucolic atmosphere, a Theocritan idyll!

Simon loved the threshing floor. What a lovely word, *Aloni*! The ancient Greek theatre must surely have started life in such a space, in such a place. They weren't so very far away from the oracle and theatre of Dodona, after all. Some scholars believed that the original Ancient Greeks had inhabited that area. Before they had even dreamed of creating the circular orchestra of a theatre, the threshing floor must have served another purpose, as a place where people danced for Dionysus and worshipped the bountiful Demeter.

There was indeed something truly magical about this threshing floor overlooking the entrance to the gorge; something almost arousing and Dionysian.

The two girls were sitting either side of Simon on the low wall of the threshing-floor. Without him being aware of how it happened, they had both let their heads drop against his shoulders. The red wine or the home-made *tsipouro* had gone to their heads too. They were sharing the entrancing atmosphere and scenery with him. The symphony of bells seemed to have been composed for them alone. There must have been a hundred bells, tuned to many different pitches. They were ringing in Simon's head, and he began to feel a strange excitement, a sense of recognition that this was the spot where he belonged. The gaze of all three of them was drawn irresistibly towards the opening of the gorge. It seemed to exert a powerful magnetic force. Simon inclined his head to look at Maria; she was smiling dreamily up at him. That was the moment that he was consumed by an extraordinary phantasy; a feeling that they were *all* being consumed by the same erotic phantasy. Was this the Greece of Sappho, of Pan, of Dionysus? Simon would never know.

After what seemed like an hour, a loud, insistent bell

penetrated Simon's consciousness. It was tolling in the village. The church-bell? A service? A funeral? Had the priest been watching them on the threshing-floor? Surely they had only fallen asleep?

Simon jumped to his feet. "Wake up! People are coming!" he shouted in a hoarse voice. He could see some signs of activity near the church.

"My God, it's the Priest!" In the distance he could see the black-robed figure of the portly village-priest, who appeared to be taking a stroll in their direction. The tall black hat, the long white beard, the flowing black robe: all of these elements combined to give Simon the impression that the repressive forces of Orthodox Byzantium were marching towards them to extinguish the pagan excesses and influences of the old Greek gods. Simon was not deeply troubled about what might or might not have just occurred. He felt no sense of sin or guilt, but he did find it hard to believe how easily he had allowed himself to forget, if only in his subconscious mind or in a drug-like dream state, the Firm's rules of engagement and the absolute ban on fraternisation with the locals, even phantasised "fraternisation". Was there a more appropriate word, something like "sororisation"? What had come over them, over him? Was it the wine or the *tsipouro* or some secret aphrodisiac ingredient in the *pita*? He had read about the Vikos Doctors, renowned herbal practitioners of old, who collected wild plants in the gorge and who would travel widely, curing all sorts of ailments. What exotic herbs could have been in that secret recipe of the Monodendri *pita*? Perhaps it was the ingredients of the salad, the rocket or the wild bulbs and mushrooms?

While these thoughts flashed through his mind, he realised that he had been mistaken about the priest, who simply took a few deep breaths and turned back towards the church. He had seen nothing. There was no funeral, no service. Perhaps the bell-ringer was practising, to show the Priest he was not idle.

They'd been partly hidden by the trees, in any case, and the church was almost half a mile away. Simon felt ashamed and rather foolish. He didn't really know why. The two girls had recovered and collected themselves. They behaved normally, as if nothing had happened. Maybe nothing had happened

"We're good friends," said Maria.

"We are," said Aliki, "aren't we?"

A scorpion scuttled into a crevice between two stones in the threshing-floor wall.

"Lucky we weren't bitten by that scorpion," laughed Maria.

"Perhaps we were," observed Aliki, in a more thoughtful mood. "I wouldn't have felt the pain."

"I think you might have screamed," said Simon. "I'm a Scorpio myself."

"Just as well we didn't. We would have had the whole village watching," laughed Maria, ignoring his other remark.

"That's certainly the last time I try that wine at lunchtime," said Simon.

"Really?" laughed Aliki, "I thought perhaps we might come here again and have a proper picnic. Isn't that what the English like?"

"Don't you like this spot?" asked Maria.

"I'm overwhelmed by it," replied Simon, in all seriousness, "It's a long time since I've enjoyed myself so much."

"We have a saying — 'There's a time and a place'."

"We also learnt, 'There's no time like the present'!"

"I was going to offer you English conversation classes in exchange for all your help. I can see there's no need."

"Let us be the judge of that," said Maria.

Not far from the threshing-floor was an abandoned old house. Perhaps it had been used to stable animals since the last humans had moved out, but it was in a remarkably good condition. The walls looked solid, the roof was still intact. It even had a cistern. Simon went up to the cistern, opened the wooden lid and slowly let the bucket down. The rope fell naturally into the deep grooves which were worn into the stone slabs which faced the inner lip of the well-shaft. He pulled up a bucket of ice-cold water. It looked clean. He tasted it. It was deliciously cold and refreshing.

"Here, try some," he said to the girls. He poured water into the palms of their hands,

They splashed it all over their faces and drank deeply.

"That should cool us off," joked Aliki. "Tomorrow we'll take you to the springs of the Voidomatis River, if you want. You can see the water bubbling up from the ground in front of you. It's the cleanest river in Europe. If we climb down the path below the village of Vitsiko, we can even swim. There's something like a little beach on the riverbank, and there's a deep pool of crystal blue water. Nobody ever goes there. Certainly not a priest. There is a little chapel there, so perhaps there is a service once a year. You won't even need to bring a bathing costume. The water is so cold it is very invigorating. The less you carry the better, it's a steep climb back up to the top. You can drink the water straight from the river."

Simon's sense of duty got the better of him. "Thanks for the offer. It's very tempting. But we mustn't let ourselves be distracted from our main purpose. I'm not writing my guide-book yet."

"Englishmen!" retorted Maria.

"Look," said Simon, "this house appears to be deserted, but it's still connected to the mains electricity supply. And it's got water — at least, it's got a cistern to collect the rainwater in the winter. That's good enough for me. All I need is a roof over my head and complete peace and quiet for my writing and painting."

"You'd certainly get that here," commented Maria. "Aren't you being a bit too romantic? You've no idea how cold these villages can be in winter. You could even be cut off for a few days if there's a heavy snowstorm. You'd need to have a large supply of firewood. If you're serious, perhaps Aliki's cousin knows who it belongs to. Maybe they'd be willing to sell. No Greek would be so mad as to live in such a remote spot."

They drank some more water and walked slowly back towards the village square. The village priest was standing by the front of the church. They greeted him, and he returned the greeting in a civil way. The bell-ringer came out of the church at that moment, and stood in the porch. It was Aliki's cousin.

"Come and have a drink in the square, Cousin, what good luck to find you here. Let me introduce an English friend, Simon. You've already met my flat-mate, Maria."

Aliki's cousin was called Alekos. Apart from ringing the church bells, he owned the village coffee-shop. He had half a dozen tables to one side of the village square, under the shadiest part of the plane tree. But he had very few customers, and he didn't bother about looking after his business. That is why very few strangers or tourists ever came to Dilopho. They couldn't get anything substantial to eat. Alekos brought a glass of *tsipouro* for Simon, and some soft drinks for the girls. They might have preferred *tsipouro* too, Simon reflected. They clinked glasses.

"*Stin iyia mas! Kalos orizete!* To our health! Welcome to Dilopho!" Alekos grinned as he knocked down the *tsipouro* in one gulp. He poured himself another glass from the bottle on the table.

"What brings you to Dilopho, Cousin Aliki? I thought you only ever came this way to visit your grandma in Monodendri."

"That's true, Aleko. But our English friend is a writer and painter, and he wants to find an old deserted house which he can use in the summers, maybe all year round, as a place to work in undisturbed. He really likes the view there beyond the village, by the threshing-floor. You don't happen who owns the old stable-house near the threshing-floor, do you?"

"But of course I do, my little soul. It's mine. It was left to me by my uncle. As I'm the only inheritor, I'd gladly sell it if your friend wants to buy it. It's no use to me. It's too far from the village. I let my friend Vasso use it for his animals for a couple of years, but even he is not interested now. If nobody wants it, it'll simply fall down."

"I could be interested if the price is reasonable, and if I can find some workmen to do it up," said Simon.

"Reasonable? What's reasonable? You can have it for six

hundred thousand drachmas, with my blessing. And if you want the threshing-floor, that can be arranged as well."

"Six hundred thousand drachmas. That's about six thousand pounds, at today's rate of exchange. We would have to do the paperwork properly, if we come to an agreement. I shall have to get a proper contract of sale and receipt."

"If you insist. Your handshake's good enough for me. We can go to Ioannina tomorrow if you like, and see the *symvoulographos*, the contract-maker. But let's drink on it now."

"Simon, are you sure this is what you want?" asked Maria. "There are over forty villages in the Zagori. Wouldn't you like to see some more houses first, maybe in Vitsa, Koukouli or Kapesovo? Or even further afield in Papingo? You don't have to make a rush decision, this house won't run away."

Alekos was already refilling Simon's glass with *tsipouro*. They clinked again, knocking back the burning spirit. The deal was as good as done.

Simon had his safe-house. The Firm would be delighted he'd got it so cheaply. He'd have to do a lot of work to make it habitable, but he'd have more money than he expected to spare for the recruitment of his agents. Maybe he'd already found two agents, he thought, perhaps he wouldn't have quite so far to look as he'd imagined. He would have to follow his instincts here, he wouldn't have the security of putting them through any systematic positive vetting process. The idea was absurd in this environment. He could see clearly that Maria and Aliki had all the makings of useful agents. They were risk-takers, fluent in both languages and open for new experiences.

He had time enough. In the meantime he had found his house, with access to the threshing-floor as well as to the Vikos Gorge, and invitations to Ioannina, and to explore the source of the River Voidomatis.

He refilled his glass and asked Alekos to bring two glasses for the girls. When he'd poured them both a drink, he proposed a toast: "To the Source of the River, to the Eye of the Bull!" He raised his glass to each of the girls in turn. Their eyes met and lingered in the intensely penetrating way that Simon had learnt from the Swedes, when they want to say a very personally meaningful *skål*.

V

The legal arrangements proved to be straightforward. Simon didn't have to pay any tax, since he was bringing in foreign currency, and since the house was deemed to be little more than a ruin without any real or objective value. Alekos introduced him to Christos, the local builder, a wiry Epirot of indeterminate age, who seemed to make his living repairing the roofs and walls of most of the houses in the Zagori villages. He even agreed to clean the place and to paint the woodwork. Simon decided to work alongside him, as his assistant. He might learn something, not only about building and stonework, but also about the village, the inhabitants and indeed the whole area.

For the next two months Simon slept in a tent next to the threshing-floor, and the villagers soon came to accept him and to trust him. He became firm friends with Christos and Alekos, who seemed to know everyone and everybody. They knew exactly where people came from, their politics and their family histories. They were quite happy to talk, either in the village square, over a glass of *tsipouro* or *retsina*, or whilst working on the building. The girls came up from time to time, either together or alone. They would turn up out of the blue on the bus from Ioannina, bringing fruit and vegetables, fresh bread or milk. They had postponed the expedition to the river's source, and seemed almost to have forgotten about the "incident" on the threshing-floor. The subject came up on the night of the village festival, the *paniyiri*, when Simon was invited to join in the traditional circle dance, to the music of folk-clarinet, *laouto*, violin and tambourine. The tunes were long drawn-out, rhythmic but endlessly repetitive to his still unaccustomed ears. Simon was dancing in a big circle with about fifty other villagers, many of whom had come back to their native village for the holiday. On his right was Aliki, on his left Maria. They were all holding hands as they danced, and the two girls were laughing at his clumsy attempts to learn the steps of the comparatively simple folk-dance. They seemed to find him amusing, the handsome, eccentric Englishman with his two left feet.

"After all this exercise, we should go for a swim tomorrow. Do you want to come, Simon? We could either walk through the gorge to the source of the Voidomatis, which would take about five hours, or we could drive to the village of Vitsiko, and go down the path which takes half an hour or so."

Simon had in fact already explored the Vikos Gorge on a number of occasions. He was getting to know every cave and crevice, every source of water. That knowledge could save his life one day; but he decided not to tell the girls about his explorations. They didn't need to know.

"Let's go by car to Vitsiko, and walk from there."

"If you're not feeling up to it," said Aliki, we could take the road to Aristi, on the way to Mikro Papingo. There's a very nice spot for a swim there too, but it's a bit public, and it's not as romantic as the spot we have in mind. We'd have to wear bathing costumes if we went there. If you're really feeling fit on another occasion, we could walk to Mikro Papingo and then climb up to the Dragon Lake, Drakolimni, up on Mount Gamila. But there's an old legend that the dragon who's said to live in the lake doesn't take kindly to foreigners who invade his territory. It's quite a hard trek."

"I that case, I vote for Vitsiko."

They didn't go to bed until four in the morning, when the last stragglers at the *paniyiri* were still dancing. Finally the main klarino-player put his instrument in its case, and the *souvlaki*-cook raked out his charcoal embers. Simon offered to drive the girls to Monodendri, but they decided to take up Aleko's offer to sleep in his spare room. Simon's house was still not ready, and in any case they would not have wanted to give the villagers any more scope for speculation.

The next morning they set off by car for Vitsiko. It wasn't much of a village, although its position was magnificent; Simon was pleased that he had settled on Dilopho. The view of the gorge, much deeper here than at Dilopho, was something to be admired, however, and they paused at the top before beginning the steep descent. The gorge was beginning to exercise its strange magic once again, and they stood in silence, perhaps recalling the threshing-floor, perhaps savouring the sense of anticipation of the cool swim they were soon to enjoy.

"I really enjoy these trips with you two," said Simon. "Now the house is nearly ready, I'd like to start exploring further afield. There's so much to see in North-West Greece. I'd really like to go to Molivdoskepasto, on the Albanian border, for instance. I hear there's a wonderful old Byzantine Church up there. And then I want to see Lake Prespa. They say there's some interesting wild-life in that area. Let's visit them before your University term starts in the autumn. We could go to Corfu too, if you like. I know some lovely quiet spots in the North of the island.

"All in good time," said Maria. "Aren't you getting a bit carried away? You've got your work to do, and you'll probably get fed up with our company soon. You haven't explored more than a few of the Zagori Villages yet. And frankly I prefer Paxos to Corfu. We could get a *kaïki* from Parga."

"If Simon wants to go to Corfu, let's do what he wants, Maria. I expect he wants to have his car with him, and it's much easier to catch the car-ferry to Corfu."

"Well, we could take the car from Mourtos to Paxos."

"The reason I want to go to Corfu this time is to see some friends on business. We can go to Paxos next summer."

They started walking down the rough stone path which wound down the mountainside. After walking for ten minutes they had a wonderful view of the river shimmering at the bottom of the gorge, bluer than the bluest water in the Mediterranean. Perhaps the water bubbling up from the ground had traces of copper sulphate, thought Simon.

"I'd like to dive from here," said Simon.

"I'd only do that if the Turks were about to take me, like the women of Zalongo who threw themselves and their babies off the rocks rather than be taken alive by the Turks. You must know the story, and the folksong," said Aliki.

"Be glad you're only being pursued by an English gentleman," joked Simon.

"Aren't gentlemen a bit of a bore?" asked Maria, catching hold of his arm as she stumbled on a loose stone.

They proceeded down the difficult path, with Maria in front and Aliki behind. Soon enough they arrived at the bottom, where they followed a path that led down to the river.

"The source is just five minutes' walk from here. We can go there afterwards," suggested Aliki. "Let's swim here first. I'm really feeling hot."

Simon was feeling hot himself. Aliki pulled her cotton dress up over her head without further ado, and stood there at the edge of the blue pool. Simon expected her to jump straight in, but she approached the water very tentatively.

Maria had gone behind a rock to take off her jeans and blouse. When she stepped out from behind it, the two girls stood side by side at the edge of the pool. Maria put her toes into the water, but withdrew as if she had been stung by a scorpion.

"It's *so co-o-o-old*", she squealed.

The two girls waded in up to their waists, looking like two nereids or naked water-nymphs.

Simon was ready to strip off his clothes and to leap in to join them, but he hesitated; even if no priest was likely to come down to the chapel, a goatherd might spot them, or some foolhardy foreign hiker might emerge from the gorge at the wrong moment.

"Come on in! Don't be shy, Simon! You don't have to be Ali Pasha to get a taste of the harem."

"Didn't he drown a lot of women in the Lake of Ioannina?

Anyway, I can see a goatherd with his flock standing up there on that sheer slope. He must be watching us".

"Don't worry about him. He's old Aristakis. We all call him the Lord of the Gorge."

"That's funny, said Simon. "He looks like a man in a clever disguise — and I think I saw the flash of some binoculars."

Simon felt sure that the way that the old shepherd was standing resembled exactly the stance and posture of his Controller back in London.

The spitting image!

Was he becoming paranoid? Had the attractions of the Zagori diverted him from his mission? Had there been a leak or a serious breach of security?

"Maybe he's just come to give me my Stage Two indoctrination or to tell me my secret codename," thought Simon, trying to guess what it might be.

Standing there at the bottom of the Vikos Gorge, so close to the source and springs of the river, the word *honeytrap* kept bubbling up in his mind.

The film director manqué

It was the spring of 1968. Richard walked down Wardour Street and Frith Street, past the offices of the big film distributors, looking for a small sign which would point him to the office and editing-suite of the Independent Film-Makers Cooperative.

He passed show-windows with lurid posters promoting new feature films — the type of film productions with which, just a few years earlier, Richard would have been excited to have become involved, as an apprentice or in any capacity. Above all else, he wanted to learn the craft. He knew all the film companies in Soho, he'd knocked on every door in the past, looking for a job, any job, as an assistant editor, an assistant cameraman or as a clapper boy. It was always the same story, "Come back when you've got a union ticket" — and the ACTT Union always told him, "You can't get a ticket until you've got a job." It was a vicious circle, but Richard had not despaired. He knew it was an overcrowded industry, and that with so much unemployment the union had to protect its members. Richard didn't approve of closed-shop unions, as he felt he had a right to express himself through the medium of film, just as he had with a pen and paper. Everyone should have the right of access, he believed. He had started off with visions of becoming a New Wave director who would express his personal philosophy of life in critically acclaimed feature films, but he had come to realize that, if he really believed in the medium, he could say what he wanted to say on a smaller scale, and that this way he could also maintain his independence.

He took work where he could find it; he found odd-jobs as a manual labourer, a gardener, a fruit-picker, a kitchen-porter, a lorry-loader. He did these things to save enough money to buy the basic film equipment he needed; slowly but surely he acquired the essential items, some new, some second-hand: a 16mm film camera, a light-meter, a tripod, a sun-gun and other lights, a top quality tape-recorder and microphone.

He also acquired experience and a deeper understanding of the conditions of the workers in the factories and fields where he laboured only temporarily, but where his workmates and colleagues might be labouring as prisoners for life. For Richard, the dehumanizing routine was bearable because he could move on when he pleased. The others may have been somewhat satisfied with their end-of-week pay packets, but how many hours of soul-destroying overtime and piecework did they have to put in to make a living wage? What sort of satisfaction was there for a man or woman whose only respite from the treadmill was a five-minute smoke-break, snatched under the pretence of going to the lavatory? What sort of relaxation was that, dragging nervously at a cigarette, while perched on a lavatory seat or crouching down on the filthy floor of the washroom?

Richard's education and family background had not prepared him for these conditions, but the odd jobs he'd been taking made him confront economic and social realities within a matter of a few months.

When he went home one weekend, his father asked "Why don't you get a proper job? Isn't it about time you did something useful?"

"Yes, Dad. It all depends what you mean by useful. Before you learn to film, you have to learn to see."

"You've done enough learning, my lad! I hope you can see that!"

"I shall be learning all my life."

"Well, I can't support you all your life. You're welcome to stay here as long as you like, you know that, but you must look around for a sensible job."

"I intend to, but give me some more time. I've got to find a job that pays better. I must save enough to buy some more film equipment. I'm going to make films, there's nothing else on earth I want to do."

"I wish your luck, son. I want you to be happy, you know that.

THE FILM DIRECTOR MANQUÉ

From what I've been reading in the papers, there's a lot of competition. Half the technicians are out of work as it is. You'll need a lucky break, lad."

"I can't wait around for someone to give me a lucky break. I've got to make my own break."

"That's the spirit! Never work for anyone, be your own boss, like me. No-one can tell you what to do. I'm a self-made man, and I'm bloody glad. You can work the hours you want . . ."

"Yes, Dad, but you work harder than anyone else I know. Mum only sees you at weekends. You drive yourself too hard. It's a kind of self-exploitation. You don't want to die an early death."

"Don't talk nonsense; I enjoy my work, that's the secret. If you're happy in what you're doing, you never need to take a holiday. I haven't taken one in twenty years. Be independent, that's the best advice that I can give you. There'll be ups and downs; sometimes you may be close to starving, at other times you may be stinking rich. But at all times you'll be a free man, the master of your own fate. I didn't think you had it in you, Richard. I thought all you pampered kids with a university education weren't prepared to go it alone. I thought all you wanted was a cushy number in the Civil Service or with some big corporation . . ."

"You must be joking!" snapped Richard, "can you honestly see me as a Civil Servant?"

"Not as you look at the moment, but given a couple of years . . ."

"Just you wait and see! We're not so different, deep down. We've got that same stubborn streak, you and I. If I ever work for anyone, it will be as a means to an end, either to gain experience, or simply to save money. But I'll always know my aims and destination, and that knowledge will keep me free."

"You may think that now, but the real test will come when you're married and start having children. That's the hardest time, when you've got those responsibilities. You begin to feel your way of life is unfair to them. You become susceptible to the talk of life insurance, widows' pensions and security. It's love that makes you susceptible, not weakness. I didn't take on many commitments, but now I regret it. At the time I couldn't afford it, and as I was self-employed, there was nobody to advise me. If I die, your mother won't be looked after as well as she deserves to be. Thank God, at least you and your brother are grown up and able to look after yourselves."

"Maybe I won't get married."

"That's no answer to the problem."

"How can I be married when I'm doing my sort of work? I plan to travel abroad for months on end. At least you get home every weekend. I'd never see my wife."

"Couldn't she travel with you?"

"I suppose she could, we'll have to wait and see."

◆

Richard soon found the small premises of the Independent Film-Makers' Cooperative. The office wasn't much more than a film cutting-room next to another untidy room intended for meetings. He'd come to talk about his ideas for an underground film, as he called it, but he needed to have access to an editing machine, and perhaps to find some like-minded film-makers who might be able to join a small crew when needed.

He introduced himself to Alan and Liz, and explained why he had come.

"I'm planning to go to Czechoslovakia, have you heard about the Prague Spring?"

"Yes, of course, the country's opening up to the outside world, isn't it?"

"Yes, Dubček is starting to make some important reforms. They call it 'Socialism with a Human Face'. I want to go there this summer, to film what's going on. I have some contacts in Prague, distant relatives of Czechs who managed to escape in 1948, or soon after. Their stories and experiences have always interested me. At the moment young Czechs and Slovaks are starting to come to England again, to study English or to work as au-pairs. I don't know how long they will have this opportunity. There may be a sudden clamp-down. They say the Russians aren't happy with the reforms. It's twenty years since the Communist Coup of 1948. I may need a second camera operator as well as a sound recordist. We'll be shooting hand-held so we won't take tripods. We may have to go there two or three times."

Alan and Liz listened to Richard's excited pitch. Both of them made it clear that they would be interested in participating in the project. They both loved Czech cinema, especially the films of Miloš Forman and Jiři Menzel, and Alan had been in occasional contact with FAMU, the famous film-school, the fifth established anywhere in the world. It was part of the Academy of Performing Arts. He thought it possible that they might be able to get some extra assistance, or even borrow some equipment, from the Czech film-students, depending on the attitude of the school's Communist Party watchdogs to Richard's project, and whether it fell broadly in line with their own ideas about agitprop.

"My film is an independent production. It won't be scripted, it'll be more of a *cinéma vérité* documentary with elements of Free Cinema and *Kino-Eye*. Forget about agitprop, that's not my style. As far as the Czechoslovak authorities are concerned, the line will be that I'm making a documentary hymn in praise of the city of Prague, Golden Prague and its architecture, a kind of visual poem, with a soundtrack quoting from Nezval and Seifert, and with extracts from the music of Dvořák and Smetana."

"Fair enough. We're both keen to get involved. We'd been thinking of doing something about conditions inside the Colonels' Greece, and about the torture of political prisoners, but this seems to be even more pressing, an important and highly topical investigative film report, and potentially consciousness-raising."

"I've got to earn some more money before we go, but put the dates in your diary, for about four weeks in August. I'll keep you informed. In the meantime, we all need to do some research, and maybe try to learn some Czech! If this is a success, I've got great ambitions to make a feature film in Prague, hopefully with the support of the Barrandov Studio. I've been working on a script outline about the lives and deaths of the Protestant Sir Philip Sidney and his Catholic friend from their Oxford days, Edmund Campion, who became a Jesuit.

"I focus on the secret part of Sir Philip Sydney's mission to Rudolf II's Prague in the 1570's. He is sent as the Emissary of Queen Elizabeth to offer condolences on the death of Maximilian. His real motive for going is to learn the techniques of the alchemists, how to transmute base metal into gold, as Queen Elizabeth needs money for her navy. He's told to bring back samples of the alchemists' magic powders. Whilst he's there he has an undercover meeting with his former Oxford friend, the Jesuit Edmund Campion, who's working there as a Professor of Rhetoric at the Jesuit College, and whom he later betrays. The working title is *The Hero and the Martyr*. One of the themes is friendship and betrayal. It will have some bloody scenes towards the end, especially when Campion is tortured, hanged, drawn and quartered in London, as a Catholic traitor. Then Sir Philip Sidney himself is wounded at the Battle of Zutphen, and dies in the Netherlands. There are apparently some great, authentic film locations in Prague, like Vladislav Hall, but please keep this project under wraps. Somebody might steal the idea. If you like, I can send you my film treatment, as it stands. It will need a big budget, which is why I'd like to pitch it the Barrandov Studio bosses. Anyway, even if they don't like the idea, it could give us some convincing cover."

"You are thinking big! It sounds like a very ambitious project, but perhaps rather unrealistic for a would-be independent underground film-maker? Make sure you don't let this detract from the main purpose of going to Prague. Are you sure you're not more interested in the feature-film idea? Even though the storyline deals with a secret mission and conflicting ideologies, it's the *contemporary* political developments that interest us. We're twentieth-century film-makers with a mission. That has to be the priority. We want to express our solidarity with the Czech and Slovak people, to support the end of censorship, their freedom to speak and write, to travel . . ."

◆

Richard went to meet Major Dick for a chat about his dramatic 1948 escape from Czechoslovakia. Major Dick was a former Czech army officer who'd fought with the British, serving on the Western Front, and who was employed after the War by the Embassy as an adviser and Liaison Officer with the British-born Wives' Club, as well as Czech Language teacher (and confidant) to the Ambassador. He'd been arrested on a trumped-up spying charge, and the false allegation that he'd hidden a cache of arms, but the Ambassador managed to secure his release from prison at the end of 1947. Dick attended a lecture by Graham Greene in Prague on the eve of the Communist coup, but went into hiding on the morning after the putsch, on 26 February 1948. The story had been put out that he had committed suicide. Because of his wartime experience, he was unjustly suspected by the Communists of being a spy or agent of the British.

Graham Greene's lecture had been deliberately and unwisely provocative; the Major was the first to slip out. Although Dick had left a "farewell letter", the Ambassador managed to communicate to Dick's wife that he was alive and in safe hands. Before long he would be in the boot of the Ambassador's car to be smuggled out of the country; soon after his escape his wife followed to join him in England. Dick lived in London into his mid 90's, and he had many fascinating stories to tell Richard, not only about that period, but also about recent developments. He wrote very lucid and detailed letters to Richard.

Richard decided to have a crash-course of private lessons in Czech, and he soon discovered that his teacher had also escaped, but by a different method.

She had been part of a group which had hijacked an aeroplane in 1952 and flown, with the help of a complicit pilot, to the West and to freedom.

Between them, they told him more about the beginning of the Prague Spring, how the government was trying to "lift the lid" a little, to ease some of the tension.

By July, Richard felt ready to go. He had prepared all he needed, he'd made friends with some younger Czechs in London; the country seemed to be as open and welcoming as it would ever be. He flew out in advance of Alan and Liz, who would follow by car at the end of the month. Richard planned to get to know the city, to make some contacts, to visit the film-school, and to scout for the best filming locations.

Richard, Alan and Liz met up in Prague at the beginning of August.

In the third week of August, the Russian-led Warsaw Pact forces occupied Prague with tanks and soldiers. The tanks took over the centre of the city. People were bewildered, then defiant. There was a spirit of solidarity and resistance.

Having two hand-held film cameras meant that they could cover much of the action on the streets: people climbing on tanks, accusing their "Friends and Brothers" of an illegal occupation and of attempting to crush their democratic reforms. They got good footage of tanks being set on fire, telling shots of Czechs destroying street signs so that the occupiers couldn't locate key buildings, such as the studios of Czech Radio. There were other news crews trying to get similar material, but they were in a hurry to rush the footage back to their TV stations. Liz, Alan and Richard had another type of film in mind. They planned to edit it back in London. After twenty-four days the tanks withdrew. On the 27th of August, Dubček made a broadcast, appealing for calm and an end of provocations. He was truly a broken man. At the end of August, the three film-makers decided to return to London, but they vowed they would be back. The story wasn't over, their sense of commitment to the country was only just beginning.

They thought it might be safer if they all travelled back by road together. They sensed that they were being followed all the way through Plzeň to the Czech-German border at Rozvadov. It was a grim journey, and the people they passed looked deeply depressed and demoralized. When they got to the border post, they were stopped and ordered to get out of the car. They feared that their cameras and all their exposed film stock would be seized and confiscated, but they were lucky. The border-guards were looking to see if they were hiding anyone, perhaps trying to help a dissident or anti-Communist escape.

"What have you been filming?" the border-guard demanded to know.

"A tourist and cultural documentary about the beauties of Prague — here's a letter of invitation from the official tourist agency, Čedok, and another letter from the Ministry of Culture. I'd hoped to have a meeting at the Barrandov Studio about a bigger film project, a co-production, but recent events prevented that. I hope it will be possible next time I'm here."

It was fortunate that Richard had done his preparation.

By an extraordinary coincidence, he would be back again in Prague in January 1969, when he happened to witness the most tragic event he'd ever seen, the self-immolation of Jan Palach. The young student set himself on fire in Wenceslas Square on 16 January 1969. It wasn't possible for Richard to intervene

There could have been no better way to end his film; still, he was glad he hadn't filmed it. Haunted by this appalling scene, it would be almost two decades before he returned to Prague.

◆

Although he had eventually obtained his ACTT Film Union director's ticket (near the time that the union ceased to be a closed shop), he never managed to make his period feature film, *The Hero and the Martyr*, on the lives and deaths of Sidney and Campion. He kept his precious treatment on file, in case he could ever get to see the bosses at the Barrandov Studios. He never did. He passed me a copy, and gave me permission to publish it, in the hope that an interested producer might read it and take out an option on it.

I've omitted to mention that Richard was happily married with three talented children. I have had to leave out lots of things in this short narrative.

In spite of some difficulties and disappointments, Richard felt that his father, who'd suffered a massive heart-attack and sadly died before his time, and before two of his three grandchildren had been born, would have been proud of the fact that his son *had* done something useful with his life, while keeping his integrity and professional independence.

Still, there were times when Richard had his doubts. He'd had a busy career. His films had been in demand from TV stations around the world. He'd made a good living; good enough. He wanted to believe that he had succeeded in raising people's consciousness of oppression, injustice and famine, and in encouraging resistance to tyranny. He'd won prestigious prizes at film-festivals and been honoured with retrospective screenings in the liberated countries where he'd filmed. His work had been discussed in film journals and in academic studies. Extracts from his films were always being recycled in other people's documentaries. Sometimes he felt that he should have become a conflict photographer in war zones, but still photography hadn't attracted him so much as moving film. He'd always been committed to social change, rather than the exposure of the horrors of war.

◆

In the digital world of the computer, videos and the internet that came to dominate global communication, Richard was never really at ease. He found it hard to adapt to the new technologies. He kept his 16mm film camera on a tripod in his living room. When he had nothing better to do, Richard would count the number of times people had clicked and viewed his old films, which were all there on YouTube, freely available to anyone who was interested, but a million viewings of a video was not such a lot, and the comments were relatively few and not always polite.

269

THE HERO AND THE MARTYR

A film treatment of the lives and deaths of
the Protestant hero **Sir Philip Sidney**
and his Catholic friend,
the Jesuit martyr **Edmund Campion**,
protégé of Sir Henry Sidney.

Copyright, Prague, 1988,
Submitted to the European Script Fund 25 January 1989

European Script Fund

Chairman: Sir Richard Attenborough, CBE.
Secretary General: Renée Goddard

21 Stephen Street
London W1P 1P?
Tel: 01-255 1444
Fax: 01-436 7950

This is to acknowledge the receipt of your
enquiry / script on the . 27. Jan. 1989 . . . .

The hero and the martyr

A film treatment of the lives and deaths of the Protestant hero Sir Philip Sidney and his Catholic friend, the Jesuit martyr Edmund Campion, protégé of Sir Henry Sidney.

CHRONOLOGY

1526 Ferdinand I, the first Habsburg, ascended the throne (died 1564).

1540 Society of Jesus founded by Ignatius Loyola. Edmund Campion born (executed 1581).

1554 Philip Sidney born (died 1586).

1555 Ferdinand summoned Peter Canisius, Dutch priest and Jesuit, to Prague.

1558 Elizabeth I ascended the throne of England, aged 25.

1564 Birth of Marlowe and Shakespeare. Maximilian II ascended the Habsburg throne.

1566 Philip Sidney and Campion met for the first time in Oxford. Royal visit of Queen Elizabeth to Oxford.

1570 Campion to Dublin, under the protection of Sir Henry Sidney. Bull of excommunication of Queen Elizabeth issued by Pope Pius V.

1572 Queen Elizabeth's licence to Philip Sidney to travel abroad. Sidney in Paris at the time of the St Bartholomew's Eve Massacre of French Protestant Huguenots. Sidney abroad for nearly three years.

1573 Campion joined the Jesuits, sent to Vienna in August. Philip Sidney visited Austria.

1574 Campion sent back to Prague in September for next six years, as Professor of Rhetoric at the Jesuit St Clement's

College, 1574–79.

1575 Sidney's first visit to Prague, with Hubert Languet.

1577 Maximilian II died. Rudolf II crowned. Sidney arrived in Prague, as envoy of Queen Elizabeth.

1578 Campion ordained priest. Sidney started to write *Arcadia*.

1581 In the House of Commons Sir Walter Mildmay stressed the dangers to England of Catholic machinations. Sidney was on the Committee which recommended more vigorous penalties against Recusants. Campion arrested in Lyford, Berkshire, sent to the Tower of London, examined under torture, and executed at Tyburn on 1 December.

1583 Philip Sidney knighted following a gift to the Queen.

1584 In Parliament Sidney advocated legislation against Jesuits, left England to aid the Netherlands in the struggle against Spain, posted as Governor of Flushing.

1586 Sidney wounded in battle, died in October. Alchemist Kelley, at Třeboň Castle, is said to have performed the first "Great Transmutation" of base metal into gold on 19 December.

1587 Mary Queen of Scots executed.

1588 Spanish Armada defeated. Dyer travelled to Bohemia to visit alchemists Dr John Dee and Edward Kelley.

1590 Dyer's last visit to Bohemia. Spent five months over winter with Kelley learning alchemical mysteries and processes.

1591 Dyer left Prague.

LOCATIONS

ENGLAND

London: Court of Queen Elizabeth, Westminster Hall, Parliament (then in St Stephen's Chapel), Tower of London, Tyburn

Wilton House and Park, Amateur alchemical laboratory

Stonehenge, Salisbury Plain

Oxford: Christ Church College, Lincoln College, Merton College, St John's College, Church of St Mary the Virgin

Lyford Grange, Berkshire

A Catholic household

Shrewsbury School

CZECH REPUBLIC

Prague: the Old Diet, Vladislav Hall, the Hall of the Court Chancellery, the Equestrian steps, Hall of Wenceslas IV, Charles Bridge, production of Campion's play *Saul* in Prague Castle, the Gothic part of the Karolinum (part of the Charles University since 1383, oriel window around 1400), alchemist's workshop in Golden Lane, Klementinum (historic building complex, a Dominican monastery transformed into a Jesuit college in 1556).

Brno: Novitiate

AUSTRIA

Vienna: banks of Danube, Imperial Court

IRELAND

Kilkenny

Dublin: library in a house

THE NETHERLANDS
    Zutphen, battleground
    Flushing
    Arnhem, death-bed

FRANCE
    Paris: Embassy, Royal Palace, Walsingham's Residence

ITALY
    Venice: by canals, a church, an artist's studio
    Rome: Pope's reception Chamber, a chapel
    The Campagna
    Ponte Molle
    Genoa
    Florence
    Padua

PICTORIAL SOURCES FOR DESIGN

View of Prague from Petřín: Wencenslaus Hollar, 1649 (see opposite).

Inauguration of the Emperor Rudolf II in the Order of the Golden Fleece, 1585, Prague (see opposite).

Interior view of Vladislav Hall at Prague Castle during the Annual Fair: Aegidius Sadeler II, 1607 (see p. 285).

Campion on the Rack; The Martyrdom of Edmund Campion, Alexander Briant and Ralph Sherwin: engravings by Giovanni Cavallieri after Niccolò Circignani in *Ecclesiae Anglicanae Trophaea* (see p. 290).

Funeral procession of Sir Philip Sydney, 1587: an engraving by Thomas Lant from a drawing by Theodor de Brij (see p. 293).

View of Prague from Petřín (1649)

Inauguration of Emperor Rudolf II in the Order of the Golden Fleece

MUSIC

William Byrd: Mass for Four Voices (c. 1592)

William Byrd: "Come to me grief forever" (an elegy for the death of Sir Philip Sidney, composed 1586, published 1588)

Anthony Holborne: "The Countess of Pembroke's Paradise" (Pavane 18, from *The Funerals*, 1599)

Anon: "Sir Philip Sidney's Lamentation" (lute solo), dedicated to Philip Sidney (1580s?)

Folk-song: "Chevy Chase"

SETTINGS OF SIDNEY'S SONNETS AND OTHER POEMS

Guillaume Tessier: "In a grove most rich of shade" (Robert Dowland, *A Musical Banquet*, 1610)

William Byrd: "O Lord how vain" (Robert Dow, *Partbooks*, 1581–1588)

Thomas Bates: "The nightingale" (Bates was music instructor to the royal family, 1660)

John Dowland: "My true love hath my heart" ("Lachrimae, or Seven Tears" No. 6, from *Lachrimae Amantis*, 1604)

SOURCES FOR THE BIOGRAPHICAL
AND HISTORICAL BACKGROUND

Addleshawe, Percival, *Sir Philip Sydney* (London: Methuen & Co, 1909).

Bereblock, John, "Commentarii sive ephemerae actiones rerum illustrium Oxonii gestarum in adventu serenissimae principis Elizabethae", in Thomas Hearne (ed.), *Historia et vita Ricardi II* (Oxford: Sheldonian Theatre, 1729), pp. 251–96.

Evans, R. J. W., *Rudolf II and his world* (Oxford: Clarendon Press, 1973).

Sargent, R. M., *At the court of Queen Elizabeth: the life and lyrics of Sir Edward Dyer* (Oxford: Oxford University Press, 1935).

Simpson, Richard, *Edmund Campion* (London: Williams and Norgate, 1867).

Sidney, Philip, *The complete works of Sir Philip Sydney*, 4 vols, ed. by Albert Feuillerat (Cambridge: Cambridge University Press, 1912–1926).

Wallace, M. W., *The life of Sir Philip Sidney* (Cambridge: Cambridge University Press, 1915).

Waugh, Evelyn, *Edmund Campion* (London: Longmans & Co, 1935).

TREATMENT

KILKENNY, IRELAND. Sir Henry Sidney applying a ruthless policy as Governor. In middle of this writing his first letter to his son Philip, aged 12, at Shrewsbury School. Visual description of the cruel poverty, oppression and misery of the Irish. Punishment of rebels. 60 people condemned and executed in Kilkenny. Sir Henry advocates colonists as solution to Irish problem. His letter to his son: very humane and civilised, in contrast to bloodshed caused by his ruthless suppression of revolt. "Son Philip . . . "

CUT TO Philip reading the letter aloud at school.

CUT TO OXFORD, 31 AUGUST 1566. Royal visit of Queen Elizabeth. Sidney (aged 12) visits Oxford from Shrewsbury School, stays at Lincoln College from 25 August 1566. Royal procession, ceremonies, plays and disputations at Christ Church College, Merton College and at the University Church of St Mary the Virgin. Queen's interest in disputation on "The moon is the cause of the ebb and flow of the tide". Edmund Campion (aged 26) is the respondent in the gripping verbal gladiatorial contest (see the accounts by John Bereblock).

> CUTAWAYS to establish Philip Sidney's admiration, even hero-worship of Campion.

Campion is praised for his eloquence by Elizabeth, Leicester and Sir Henry Sidney, who offers his patronage. Philip is introduced. He makes it clear that he will soon be a student at Oxford and plans to challenge Campion in the Disputations.

CUT TO ONE YEAR LATER. Philip Sidney with his friends Edward Dyer and Greville (perhaps Campion and Wooton?) reading and singing their lyrics in Oxford rooms at St John's or Christ Church College. Sidney is more attracted to poetry than to Disputations. Campion expresses the view that the ideal student should have as recreations painting, playing the lute, singing at sight, writing music with facility and correctness, but above all he should be an accomplished debater, dialectician and orator.

CUT TO Sir Henry Sidney with the Earl of Leicester discussing Philip's future education. It will be continued by foreign travel, to make him more useful in the service of the country. The Queen who is seen to admire the handsome young man (now aged 18), grants her licence for him to travel abroad.

CUT TO DUBLIN. Edmund Campion forced to leave Oxford (where he was Proctor) for Dublin because of his theological views, his openly Catholic convictions. He starts work on his *History of Ireland* in the library of Stanihurst's Dublin house (father of an old pupil). We hear an extract, voice-over, as he sits, thinking and writing. Sir Henry Sidney (his protector) visits the house. They talk about Ireland; it emerges that Sir Henry is a tolerant man, ruthless at times but not anti-Catholic: "An English education is their only hope, our rule their only salvation." Campion himself is influenced by such views. He writes: "The Irish are much beholden to God for suffering them to be conquered, whereby many of their enormities were cured, and more might be, would themselves be pliable." One day Sir Henry warns Campion, at work on his book, that he must leave to avoid arrest; Catholics are at risk because of a rumoured invasion of Ireland by mercenaries of Philip of Spain.

CUT TO PARIS. Philip Sidney arrives at the English Embassy and meets Walsingham, the ambassador and a friend of his father. At the Residence, he is introduced to Hubert Languet, who describes the increasingly dangerous situation in Paris. Languet is a French diplomat. Philip offers to escort him home. It is the night of St Bartholemew's Eve (23/24 August 1572): the Massacre of the French Protestants, the Huguenots. Scenes of horror, carnage and mob violence. From the palace windows scores of bodies are thrown — bodies of Protestants brutally stabbed or put to the sword. The two men watch at a safe distance, and witness the French king delighting in the bloodshed; they hide in a dark corner of the street. Suddenly a shout: "Voilà un Huguenot!" The mob starts to chase after Languet. Philip Sidney manages to fight them off and to lead him to the safety of the Embassy.

CUT TO ROME. Campion in prayer: "Suscipe, Domine, universam meam libertatem. Accipe memoriam, intellectum, atque voluntatem omnem . . ." (prayer seeking complete surrender, the discipline of the rule of St Ignatius). Later, the Jesuit General questions the postulant: "Are you willing to renounce the world, all possessions and the hope of temporal goods? Are you ready if necessary to beg your bread from door to door for the love of Jesus Christ? Do you consent to put on the livery of humiliation worn by Him, to suffer as He did for love of Him contempt, calumnies, and insults?" "I do," Campion replies and is received as a Jesuit novice.

CUT TO CAMPION IN BRNO, MORAVIA, MID 1574. Scene of novices doing household chores in the novitiate: "One returning with his load from the farm; another from market; one sweating, sturdy and merry, under a sack of refuse, another toiling along on some other errand." They fight to clean the pots and brush up the dust with a broom. They are very happy in their charitable humility.

CUT TO VIENA, BESIDE THE DANUBE, 1575. Philip Sidney in company of Hubert Languet, who is now his tutor. We hear Languet's advice about the values of travel (using Sidney's words from his letter to his brother) and on the need for Sidney to cultivate important people (like Cecil), to learn to "smooth his path" by pretending to love Cecil's children (William Cecil, Lord Burghley, Elizabeth's principal minister).

CUT TO VENICE. Philip is having his portrait painted by an Italian friend. They go for a walk by a canal; enter a Catholic Church. Philip behaves "when in Rome . . ." and appears to cross himself as if a Catholic. He wears an enigmatic smile. We are aware of English spies in the background.

BRIEF SCENES OF PADUA, FLORENCE, GENOA, THEN BACK TO VIENNA, THE IMPERIAL COURT. Languet suggests to Sidney that they visit Prague and other cities before Sidney returns to England, after being three years away.

CUT TO PRAGUE, THE CHARLES BRIDGE. "Be sure to keep some great man thy friend, but trouble him not for trifles," Languet advises Sidney as they cross the bridge. Campion crosses in the opposite direction. Sidney and Campion do not acknowledge each other. Slight sign of recognition from Campion, who doubts his own eyes and continues telling his Rosary in prayer.

CUT TO WILTON HOUSE, 1578. Sidney starts working on *Arcadia*; singing madrigals with his friends Wotton, Dyer, Greville; walking with his sister, Mary, the Countess of Pembroke (aged 16/17). Visits Salisbury Plain and Stonehenge. Hears rough old man singing "Chevy Chase". He is moved to tears. He tells his sister he has fallen in love with Penelope Devereux, a beauty with black eyes, while staying with her father at Leicester House in London. Penelope and her father will be visiting Wilton on the following day, says Philip, with other guests. Back at Wilton, we see Philip working with his sister in her alchemical laboratory, constructed for her own use. They dress up in long robes, use mysterious apparatus: athanors, retorts, jars, skulls, talismans, divining rods, gazing glasses. Edward Dyer is present, and Dr Dee visits them (he has a long tapering beard). The next morning Penelope Devereux (later Lady Rich, England's most famous Elizabethan beauty and the "Stella" of Sidney's *Astrophel and Stella* sonnets) and her father arrive. Philip senses some rivalry with Edward Dyer, who is also in love with her. But Philip manages to invite her for a ride in the park, away from the others. He recites one of his poems: "O sweet woods, the delight of solitariness" (on evils of flatterers, traitors, slanderers). A courtly love-scene, an English rural idyll, interspersed with graceful country-house life, the composing of bucolic poetry.

CUT TO LONDON, THE COURT. Flatterers, vain courtiers. The Queen clearly treats Sidney as a favourite. She tells him of his mission to Emperor Rudolf II in Prague. We see the ambitious side of Philip Sidney. The Queen tells him she is sending him away for his own good, so he can take his mind off Penelope Devereux. The Queen cannot stand Penelope's mother, and Penelope is no match for him; her father has less to offer than Philip believes, the Queen intimates. She has another task for Philip in Prague, a secret task: to find out about claims that alchemists in Prague can produce gold from base metals. The Queen warns Philip of the increasing power of the Jesuits in Prague, of Rudolf's likely alliance to Spain (by blood and education). The Queen needs the grand secret of transmutation — to help defer her charges for the Navy. Philip is told to bring back samples of the alchemists' magical powders.

CUT TO SIDNEY ON THE WAY TO PRAGUE as Emissary of Elizabeth to offer condolences on death of Maximilian. Has audience with Rudolf II on Easter Monday. Sidney makes anti-Catholic speech. Puts case for Protestant League. (Queen Elizabeth wrote to William, Landgrave of Hesse, on 11 April 1577 about strengthening a defensive alliance and protective Protestant League; this was also supported by Count Palatine Johann Casimir, a Calvinist. Part of Sidney's secret mission to Rudolf II in Prague was to further this cause.) Sidney tries to influence Rudolf against Rome and Spain. He is presented with "a great chain", but no assurances. International company of artists of every profession, men of culture and diplomats at Castle. Already evidence of Rudolf's interest in paintings and the establishment of a Royal Orchestra.

CUT TO ALCHEMISTS IN TŘEBOŇ. Sidney interested in one particular Bohemian alchemist who claims to have great skills. Sidney watches alchemical demonstration of production of grains of gold. Tries to learn secrets of magic powder to take back to Queen Elizabeth: "I saw the Master put of the base metal into the crucible, and after it was set a little upon the fire, and a very small quantity of the medicine put in, and stirred with a stick of wood, it came forth in great proportion perfect gold, to the touch, to the hammer, to the test."

CUT TO PRAGUE. Sidney meets Campion in secret. Campion explains why he has joined the Society of Jesus. He talks of his escape from Ireland with the help of Sidney's father, who had protected him. Sir Henry had sent him warning in 1571. Campion asks after Irish affairs. Sidney tells him bluntly: "Until by time they find the sweetness of due subjection it is impossible that any gentle means should put out the remembrance of their lost liberty . . . they have a revengeful heart to all English as to their only conquerors, and that which is most of all with so ignorant obstinacy in papistry that they do in their souls detest the present government."

CUT TO MORE SECRET MEETINGS IN PRAGUE. Spies of English Council all around. Campion believes he is slowly converting Sidney to Catholicism. Sidney gathering information. Was he on point of conversion? Promises Campion he'll always be a trusty friend. He gives him alms to distribute to the poor. Campion thinks that "if the plant is watered well", Sidney will be converted. It is clear they like and respect each other. Sidney admits that he made many Catholic friends in his European travels; rumours had reached England that he was wavering and succumbing to the attractions of Catholicism as a result of his intimacy with Venetian friends. He remembers Lord Burghley's advice: "Suffer not thy sons to pass the Alps. For they shall learn nothing there but pride, blasphemy and atheism."

CUT TO SIDNEY WATCHING CAMPION PREACHING IN PRAGUE. A memorable experience, with Rudolf in attendance. Sees scene from Campion's magnificent six-hour play *Saul.* It is clear that foreign Catholic advisers in Rudolf's Court are powerful and belligerently anti-Protestant (the majority of Czechs are still Protestant). Jesuit advisers of Rudolf, like Campion, are also hostile to Protestant alchemists. They are, nevertheless, trying to win popular support through use of elaborate drama and pageantry (banners, carpets etc. provided by the Council of the Old Town of Prague).

CUT TO TOURNAMENT IN VLADISLAV HALL. Philip Sidney takes part (see Wallace, p. 265 for a typical tournament).

Interior view of Vladislav Hall at Prague Castle

CUT TO QUEEN ELIZABETH'S COURT. Sidney reports back with his assessment of Rudolf's "Spaniolated" Catholic views. Praises alchemists. Produces trinket for Queen. She is excited, then disappointed that this is all. His hostility to belligerent Jesuits comes out, and his betrayal of his old Oxford friend Campion begins. He breaks his engagement with Penelope

Devereux on account of her father's death and the discovery that her inherited estates are encumbered with debt. The Earl of Essex, her father, left little money; her mother is detested by the Queen. But the affair continues, even later, after Penelope has become Lady Rich.

CUT TO ANOTHER ROOM AT COURT. Dyer sings and plays the lute; lyrics by Sidney. Sidney suddenly smashes the lute and sings a rough version of "Chevy Chase" (honest music of the people, rather than of the court; he is sick of the sycophantic, artificial life, rivalries and betrayals of court-life). In a rage he knocks flying the table of alchemical equipment, crucibles, retorts, and trinkets; he calls the amateur alchemist a "base charlatan" and "mountebank". Almost immediately he apologizes and becomes obsequious again. He is in debt. He hopes for a high post. The Queen refuses but offers to give him some of the possessions confiscated from Catholics. He is torn. The Queen asks him about Campion. Sidney says little in his favour. "I have heard rumours that he has been instructed to return to Rome and thence perhaps to England. He has never abused the friendship of his old protectors to any man's harm; nor been enriched by any man's overthrow. He bears no grudge against me, nor I against him, but he's a subtle Jesuit, and may come to bear the taint of treason."

CUT TO CAMPION IN ROME. Pope Gregory XIII addresses him, in private audience: "You have been chosen for a noble mission. Our harvest is great in England, but more experienced men are needed, you and others of your Order, to preserve the faith of Catholics in England. Since Queen Elizabeth was excommunicated, by Pope Pius's Bull of Deposition, it has repeatedly been asked whether her Catholic subjects need obey her; it has been decided that it is lawful for Catholics to obey her in civil matters while she rules as Queen, but in the event of an invasion, Catholics should not oppose the invader. It is forbidden to you that you should involve yourself in politics or matters of state. You go to your dear Country for the Glory of God and the benefit of souls." Campion replies: "I shall never give them over. I shall either win them heaven, or die upon the pikes. I shall give the best blood in my body for their salvation!" Campion receives the blessing of the Pope.

CUT TO OUTSIDE, ON THE CAMPAGNA. A rich man is being flogged for adultery. A group of prostitutes is turned loose to be massacred by bandits.

CUT TO PONTE MOLLE, the departure of the small group of Crusading Jesuits. Someone calls out "Martyrium!" as they wave farewell.

CUT TO ELIZABETH'S COURT. An Anglican Bishop in a holy rage: "He's an insolent massing priest, a sower of sedition and treasonable plots ... His allegiance is to others than the Queen! ... We shall see him hang for it!" The Bishop reads out Campion's "Brag", of which many copies have been intercepted (heavy sarcasm in voice): " 'I confess that I am (albeit unworthy) a priest of the Catholic Church, vowed these eight years into the Religion of the Society of Jesus. Hereby I have taken upon me a special kind of warfare under the banner of obedience ... My charge is, of free cost to preach the Gospel, to minister the Sacraments, to instruct the simple, to reform sinners, to confute errors, to cry alarm against foul vice and proud ignorance, where-with many of my dear Countrymen are abused ... And touching our Society, be it known to you that we have made a league — all the Jesuits in the world — cheerfully to carry the cross you shall lay upon us, and never to despair your recovery, while we have a man left to enjoy your Tyburn, or to be racked with your torments, or consumed with your prisons. The expense is reckoned, the enterprise is begun, it cannot be withstood. So the faith was planted; so it must be restored.' " After a brief pause the Bishop exclaims, "The faith of the Anti-Christ! Unworthy he is, by his own confession; if he be worthy of so foul a priesthood, what shall he be worthy of? He shall enjoy our rack of torments and our Tyburn for his insolence and treason! We are on his trail, we shall catch this braggart Jesuit, Your Majesty. For many months he has been travelling round the country in different disguises, conspiring secretly, hiding in one traitor's house after another, preparing for the invasion being plotted by the Pope in Rome, by the Catholic League and by Philip of Spain. The Catholics are waiting for the invasion to declare openly that they do not accept your authority over them ... He challenges any adversaries, any Protestants living, to maintain their doctrine in disputation against him. What say you, Sidney, shall we accept the challenge ?" Sidney replies: "My Lord, I cannot in all honesty advise you to accept the challenge. Campion has been Professor of Rhetoric and Spiritual Adviser in Prague these six years; the most memorable thing I witnessed in all my travels abroad was a sermon by Campion at which I assisted with the Emperor in Prague. Her Majesty may remember how well his mind was trained for disputation even when at Oxford, before he became a Catholic or Jesuit. His mind is lucid, he has great dexterity of argument and wit, he is both learned and persuasive." The Queen speaks: "We will interrogate him on our own terms then. But his challenge shall not go unanswered. We shall organize some Conferences, but first I wish to learn from his own lips whether he acknowledges me as Queen." The Queen takes Sidney to one side, to remind him of the offer of property she has made. Sidney replies: "Some of my friends counsel me to stand upon Your Majesty's offer touching the forefeiture of Papists' goods ... My necessity is great ... Truly, I like not their persons and much less their religion, but I think my fortune very hard that my fortune must be built upon other men's punishments."

CUT TO CAMPION ARRIVING AT A CATHOLIC HOUSE-HOLD, accompanied by his servant. He is travelling in disguise, secretly ministering to recusants. The vestments are taken from a secret cupboard. The Mass is said with the fear of being discovered by informers and spies. The hurried leave-taking on horseback.

SUMMARY NOTE TO DIRECTOR ON CAMPION'S ARREST, TORTURE AND EXECUTION. Sidney's failure to stand up for him, even though he is in high favour and could have helped to have Campion's life spared. Sidney does not want to offend; he is aware of the many rumoured Jesuit plots and alleged threats to murder Queen Elizabeth. So his friend, the man his father once protected, dies at Tyburn as a Catholic Martyr.

CUT TO ARREST OF CAMPION AND HIS FRIENDS AT LYFORD GRANGE, BERKSHIRE, where Campion had given Communion and preached in secret the night before. They are betrayed by government spy George Eliott. The house is surrounded and searched; the following day the priests are discovered, hiding in a secret cell or "priest-hole". They are arrested.

CUT TO THE PROCESSION TO THE TOWER. When the procession reaches Colnbrook it becomes a public parade. The prisoners are pinioned on their horses; elbows tied behind them, wrists tied in front, ankles strapped together under horses' bellies. Campion is driven on in front with a paper pinned to his hat, reading "Campion the seditious Jesuit" (see Waugh, pp. 130–66).

CUT TO CAMPION TAKEN (FROM THE TOWER) BEFORE THE QUEEN FOR QUESTIONING. If he would adjure his faith and enter the Protestant ministry all would be forgiven. He is returned to the Tower.

CUT TO LEICESTER AND BURGHLEY SIGNING THE WARRANT TO PUT CAMPION TO THE TORTURE. They want a confession regarding the sum of 30,000 pounds Campion is reputed to have conveyed to the rebels of Ireland. How collected? How transferred? (See Waugh, p. 136.) What are the names of his associates?

CUT TO CROSS-EXAMINATION WITH THE RACK.

CUT TO CAMPION AND OTHERS IN WESTMISTER HALL, facing, on 20 November 1581, a trumped-up charge of conspiracy to murder Queen Elizabeth. When the Lord Chief

Justice demands if there is any cause why he should not pass sentence of death on the prisoners, Campion speaks: "The only thing that we have now to say is, that if our religion do make us traitors, we are worthy to be condemned; but otherwise are, and have been, as good subjects as ever the Queen had ... In condemning us you condemn all your own ancestors — all the ancient priests, bishops and kings —all that was once the glory of England, the island of saints, and the most devoted child of the See of Peter ... God lives; posterity will live; their judgement is not so liable to corruption as that of those who are now going to sentence us to death." Then the Lord Chief Justice: "You must go to the place from whence you came, there to remain until ye shall be drawn through the open City of London upon hurdles to the place of execution, and there be hanged and let down alive, and your privy parts cut off, and your entrails taken out and burnt in your sight; then your head to be cut off and your bodies divided into four parts, to be disposed of at her Majesty's pleasure. And God have mercy on your souls."

Campion on the rack

The execution of Edmund Campion,
Alexander Briant and Ralph Sherwin

CUT TO STREETS OF LONDON ON DAY OF EXECU-TION. Raining and muddy. Horse with a hurdle at tail, to which Campion is bound. He is dragged slowly through the mud and rain, his face spattered with mire and dirt.

CUT TO TYBURN. Noose put over Campion's neck. "I am a Catholic man and a priest. In that faith have I lived and in that faith I intend to die. If you esteem my religion treason, then I am guilty; as for other treason I never committed any, God is my judge." Someone shouts out: "You die for treason, not religion. Confess your treason!" The cart is driven from under him, the crowd sways forward. Campion is left hanging, until, either unconscious or dead, he is cut down for the butcher.

CUT TO SIDNEY IN CONVERSATION WITH LORD DEPUTY, on Irish affairs. Sidney is thinking of going to Ireland, "It is our duty to coerce the Irish into abandoning their religion and into accepting the religion and overlordship of England, with our customs, manners and laws! By and by, My Lord, know you not of an Irish forefeiture? I have a friend who's sore in need . . . If I shall not go to Ireland, then shall I sail with Drake . . ."

CUT TO COURT, NEW YEAR'S DAY 1583. Sidney's annual gift to Elizabeth of a precious object: "A jewel of gold like a castle, garnished with small diamonds on the one side, being a pot to set flowers in." He is knighted soon after. In September he is married to Frances Walsingham. Queen Elizabeth is displeased. We find Sidney writing a love-sonnet to "Stella" (Penelope Devereux, Lady Rich). Even when he is with Lady Sidney, he dreams of Lady Rich.

CUT TO SIDNEY IN PARLIAMENT, advocating legislation against the Jesuits.

FLASHBACK to his "near-conversion" to Catholicism in Prague by Campion.

FLASHBACK to his father's letter to him as a schoolboy, over scenes of violent suppression of the Catholic Irish rebels.

FLASHBACK to his happy days with Venetian (Catholic) friends. Walking by canals, visiting churches, and behaving "when in Rome . . .".

CUT BACK TO PARLIAMENT. Sidney reading out draft of Bill, ordering "Jesuits, Seminary Priests and such-like disobedient subjects on pain of death to leave the country".

CUT TO FLUSHING, THE NETHERLANDS, 1585. Sidney has been posted to the Netherlands instead of sailing with Drake. He is Governor in Flushing.

CUT TO THE BATTLE OF ZUTPHEN. The fog lifts suddenly. Englishmen and Spaniards see each other almost within striking distance, the disparity in their numbers is revealed. The English have far fewer men. Sir Philip fights bravely where the battle rages most fiercely. In the second charge his horse is killed under him, but he secures another. In the third charge he rides right through the Spanish lines. As he turns to retreat a musket-ball from the trenches strikes him above the left knee, shattering the bone (See Wallace, pp. 377–8).

CUT TO ARNHEM: Lady Sidney at his bedside as he slowly weakens and as he makes his will, dying of blood-poisoning caused by the wound, still calling out for Penelope Devereux, and for forgiveness from Edmund Campion.

FADE TO SIDNEY'S FUNERAL, based on a contemporary illustration (see opposite). Elegiac tributes to Sidney (e.g. by Dyer, Shelley's "A spirit without spot") as voice-over during the final scenes of the funeral (alternatively a verse from William Byrd's musical elegy "Come to me grief forever"), and perhaps extracts from Sidney's own poems such as

> Since nature's works be good, and death doth serve
> As nature's work , why should we fear to die?
> Fear is more pain than is the pain it fears . . .

or

> Leave me, O Love, which reachest but to dust;
> And thou, my mind, aspire to higher things;
> Grow rich in that which never taketh rust;
> Whatever fades but fading pleasure brings . . .

The funeral procession of Sir Philip Sidney. The four cloaked and hooded figures carrying the banners are, from left to right, Henry Sidney, Edmund Parkenham, Edmund Walsingham and William Sidney. (Henry and William Sidney were the sons of Philip's younger brother Sir Robert Sidney, who, as chief mourner, followed the coffin and is not depicted here.) Holding the four corners of the pall that is draped over the coffin, and similarly cloaked and hooded, are Sidney's four closest friends: at the back (only their heads visible) are Thomas Dudley and Edward Wotton, and in the foreground Fulke Greville and Edward Dyer.

CUT TO MUCH LATER MEMORIALS TO CAMPION. The College in Oxford, the biography of Evelyn Waugh, the Chapel at Tyburn, Campion beginning a new chapter of his *History of Ireland*.

FINAL CREDITS over ceiling portraits of Sidney and Campion.

Prague, 1968. Revised 1988.

LIST OF ILLUSTRATIONS

Where no source is given the images are public-domain or uncredited images from the Internet.

front cover The author filming with an Arriflex 16mm camera in a Nairobi school in 1976/77, for an environmental-science teacher-training film series (Voice of Kenya and Kenya Institute of Education).

back cover The author in front of the Tower of the Winds in Athens (photograph by Nina-Maria Potts).

Lightning Source UK Ltd.
Milton Keynes UK
UKHW010718141119
353517UK00001B/21/P